Praise for th

"Sala is a master at
romantic and suspenseful.... with this amazing story,
Sala proves why she is one of the best writers in the
genre."
—*RT Book Reviews* on *Wild Hearts*

"Skillfully balancing suspense and romance, Sala
gives readers a nonstop breath-holding adventure."
—*Publishers Weekly* on *Going Once*

"Vivid, gripping...this thriller keeps the pages
turning."
—*Library Journal* on *Torn Apart*

"Sala's characters are vivid and engaging."
—*Publishers Weekly* on *Cut Throat*

"Sharon Sala is not only a top romance novelist, she is
an inspiration for people everywhere who wish to live
their dreams."
—John St. Augustine, host, *Power!Talk Radio*
WDBC-AM, Michigan

"Veteran romance writer Sala lives up to her
reputation with this well-crafted thriller."
—*Publishers Weekly* on *Remember Me*

"[A] well-written, fast-paced ride."
—*Publishers Weekly* on *Nine Lives*

"Perfect entertainment for those looking for a
suspense novel with emotional intensity."
—*Publishers Weekly* on *Out of the Dark*

SHARON SALA

DARK HEARTS

MIRA®

ISBN-13: 978-0-7783-1877-4

Recycling programs
for this product may
not exist in your area.

Dark Hearts

For questions and comments about the quality of this book, please contact us at
CustomerService@Harlequin.com.

www.MIRABooks.com

Printed in U.S.A.

It's never too late to make amends for a mistake. You can't change the outcome, but acknowledging what you've done is the first step in helping yourself to heal.

I am dedicating this book to people who have learned how to let go of what they did wrong. I'm sure the list is long, and since being first seems to intimidate a lot of people, I will volunteer to add my name first.

My name is Sharon.

I learned to let go.

DARK HEARTS

One

It was raining in Atlanta—what locals called a toad strangler—with water rushing through the streets and into gutters, taking dirt and garbage with it, flowing down into the sewers like shit being flushed down someone's toilet.

Sam Jakes had an apartment in downtown Atlanta, in a building that catered to high-end renters with expensive tastes. He hadn't chosen it because he loved the high life, but because the security factor was second to none. He also liked it for the anonymity it provided for the people who lived there. No names on the mailboxes, just apartment numbers, and no public listings anywhere on site. He'd made enemies running Ranger Investigations, uncovering other people's secrets and lies. He didn't want them following him home.

Sam hadn't always been a loner. Growing up, he had been as normal and fun loving as any young boy could be. He hunted the mountain behind the family farm outside Mystic, West Virginia, and fished in the rivers. He loved football and pork chops with his mama's cream gravy, and as he grew older he'd learned to love Lainey Pickett most of all. Then two planes flew into the World Trade Center and changed his life. Instead of beginning his freshman year of college, he'd enlisted in the army and gone to war.

After his second tour of duty he'd become a bomb tech, learning to defuse everything the enemy could construct, and then went back to war. Nine months later he came home in pieces, burned over half his body and with PTSD so bad that he didn't turn on the ringer for his cell phone for three months. When he could move without screaming, he changed the ringtone to the opening notes of "Amazing Grace," and when the hospital finally released him, he moved into an apartment without telling anyone where he was. He didn't want his family camped out on his doorstep, bemoaning his condition or treating him like an invalid.

It took close to a year for the burns to completely heal and for him to get mobile enough to go through rehab. It took even more time for him to accept himself. His family came to see him once he let them know where he was, but he wouldn't go home. In his mind, Sam Jakes from Mystic, West Virginia, was dead and buried in the sands of Afghanistan, which meant Lainey Pickett was no longer a part of his life. He quit Lainey without giving her a chance to quit him first.

Ten years and three psychiatrists later, he and PTSD had an unsettled truce, and the burn scars on his body looked like melted plastic. Except for the occasional visits his family made to Atlanta to see him, he communicated with them by phone. He lived for work and very little play, and on this particular day, he was trying to catch up on rest after a six-day stakeout.

Although it had been raining with soggy persistency for more than six hours, Sam was sound asleep inside apartment 4B, stark naked and belly down on the king-size bed with his cell phone in one hand and a handgun in the other.

In his dream, he was making love to Lainey. His fingers were tangled into the mane of red hair fanned out around her face, and he was hard as a rock and so deep inside her he couldn't think. He could hear her short, breathless gasps as he pushed deeper into her, pounding harder until she suddenly arched up beneath him and wrapped her legs around his waist. He felt the climax roll through her and was about to come with her when he began hearing his brother cry out, calling his name. He turned to look for Lainey and she was gone. Then the tone of Trey's voice changed to one of terror.

Help me, Sam, help me!

I'm here, Trey, I'm here! Where are you? What's wrong?

Then Sam began hearing music. Someone was playing "Amazing Grace."

And then he heard his brother scream.

Sam woke abruptly, bathed in sweat and shaking. It took him a few moments to realize he'd been dreaming and his phone was ringing.

He glanced at the time as he rolled over onto his back and answered the phone without checking to see who was calling.

"This is Jakes."

"Sam, it's me."

Sam frowned. Trey had been in his dreams and now he was on the phone? Sam didn't like coincidences. And because his voice was still husky from sleep, the anxiety in his gut made him sound angry.

"What the hell's wrong?" he said.

Trey started to cry, and Sam sat up with a jerk and swung his legs over the side of the bed.

"Talk to me, brother."

"Mom's dead, and Trina is hurt bad."

Sam grunted. It felt as if someone had just walked up behind him and coldcocked him with a baseball bat. His ears were ringing, and he couldn't breathe. An ugly little voice in his subconscious was whispering, *Dead. Dead. Everyone's dead.*

He thought leaving the land of blood and sand would get him away from so many people dying, but death had come into his family. How could that be? The room began to spin as Sam lowered his head to keep from losing it.

"Sam? Sam! Did you hear me?"

Sam wasn't sure he could speak, and when he finally did, his voice cracked with the shock of an overwhelming grief.

"Yes. You said Mom was dead. She can't be dead."

Trey was struggling with his own emotions, but hearing the heartbreak in his big brother's voice hurt on a whole other level. "She is, buddy, she is."

"Oh, my God." Sam was starting to shake. He had to focus. "Was it a wreck?"

Trey knew this was going to send his brother over the edge, but it had to be said.

"No, Sam, she was murdered. We believe she was killed for something that happened when she was a teenager. Come home. I need you. I'll explain it all after you get here."

Sam's voice went from shock to rage.

"Teenager? Are you kidding me!"

"No. We're almost certain it has to do with the night she graduated high school, but beyond that it's just supposition."

"How can you be sure?" Sam asked.

"Do you remember the story of Mom being in that bad wreck the night she graduated?" Trey asked.

Sam frowned. "Slightly. Why?"

"There were four people in that wreck, and three of them lived. In the past two months, two of the survivors have been murdered, and the killer tried to make both deaths look like accidents. Until today, Mom was the only one still living."

Sam's hands were shaking. "Why—"

"We don't know, and now that Mom became the third victim, they're taking me off the case even though one of the murders happened in my jurisdiction. That's why I need you," Trey said.

"I'm on my way," Sam said, and hung up the phone, but he was pissed.

Three victims? Why hadn't he known this was happening? Why hadn't they called him?

He grabbed a suitcase from the back of his walk-in closet and threw it on the bed as reality reared its ugly head. Why would they call him? By his own actions he'd shown them he wanted no part of Mystic. It made him sick to think of Trey knowing Mom was in danger and not knowing how to protect her. Even worse, he couldn't imagine how frightened his mom must have been as her classmates were being killed.

Then he remembered a couple of recent phone calls from her that he hadn't returned. What if that would have made a difference in her living or dying? He wasn't sure how to live with that question.

Suddenly his belly rolled and he headed for the bathroom. He got as far as the sink before the feeling of nausea passed. He splashed some water on his face and then leaned forward, staring at his image in the only mirror in the house. He would never hear his mother's voice again, and that was on him.

He grabbed a towel to dry his face, then went to the bedroom to get dressed. He was sick at heart and feeling so guilty he could hardly focus as he began to pack.

The last thing he packed was an overcoat. At this time of year, there was no way to predict what the weather would be like in the mountains. He grabbed the suitcase, and then stopped to get his brown leather jacket out of the hall closet, settled a Stetson the color of dark chocolate firmly on his head and headed for the door. His handgun and ammunition were in the outer pocket of his suitcase, and his cell phone and charger were in his jacket pocket.

He got on the elevator with a heavy heart and rode it down to the lobby. He made one last stop at the front desk to inform the security guard he would be gone for an indeterminate time, and headed for the covered parking garage.

It was still raining, suitable weather for someone trying to hide tears, as he dumped his things inside his SUV and slid behind the wheel. His belly growled, a reminder that he hadn't eaten in almost twenty-four hours. His head hurt, another reminder that he hadn't had coffee. But it would take more than coffee and food to ease the pain in his heart.

He drove from the parking garage and out into the downpour with his wipers on high. Alone in the car, with nothing but memories for company, he quit fighting against the tears and let them fall.

He had so many memories of his mom that he hadn't thought of in years: her teaching him how to fillet a fish because his dad was never home long enough to do it; crying with him when he didn't make the baseball team the year he turned ten; teaching him how to waltz so he could ask Lainey to the prom; the cookies fresh from the oven that were always on the kitchen table when he and his siblings came home from school. He remembered the winter it was so cold that all their water pipes froze and waking up to see his mom sitting in front of the kitchen sink with a hair dryer on high, trying to thaw the pipes and cursing a blue streak with no apologies. She'd been their rock. What in holy hell had she witnessed in her youth that got her killed? And why now?

He glanced up in the rearview mirror and caught a quick glimpse of the shock in his eyes.

"I swear to God, Mom, I will find out who did this to you and Trina, or die trying," he said, and headed north out of Atlanta. It had been a long time coming, but Sam Jakes was going home.

The killer was drinking from a cold can of Pepsi as he gassed up his car at a quick stop. Someone drove by and honked. He grinned and waved, then set the pop can on top of the car as the pump kicked off. He hung up the hose, grabbed the Pepsi and then slid in behind the wheel. Just as he was about to drive away he began hearing the scream of an ambulance siren, so he stayed put until it passed. When he saw Trey Jakes in the cop car behind it and realized the direction from which it had come, he frowned. Why the ambulance and all the rush? Wouldn't they take the bodies straight to the morgue if—

His heart skipped a beat. Unless there was someone to save?

A man came out of the store on the run.

"Hey, what's going on?" the killer asked.

The man pointed at the ambulance. "That killer struck again. Shot Betsy Jakes and her daughter. They said one of them is still alive. I gotta get home. My wife went to school with them. Ain't no telling where that bastard will strike next."

There was a knot in the killer's belly as he watched the man driving away. All he could think was *What the fuck? They had to be dead.*

He started the car, debating with himself as to whether he should cut and run now, or wait and see how this all played out. He decided on the latter and headed home.

Trey Jakes came to a sliding stop a few feet away from the ER, then got out on the run as the EMTs were unloading his sister.

"Is she still alive?" he yelled.

"Yes, Chief, we still have a pulse."

Trey led the way inside, bypassing onlookers and patients, heading straight for the trauma team awaiting their arrival. The moment his sister's body was wheeled into an empty bay, they exploded into organized chaos.

Her clothes were cut off as they began to assess her condition. People were talking loudly, the doctor was issuing orders and a lab tech was getting blood to cross-match while another wheeled in a portable X-ray machine. Someone was putting an oxygen mask over Trina's face, and somebody else was hooking her up to a heart monitor. And then the doctor turned to look for Trey and spoke.

"Gunshot wound, in and out. No bullet."

Trey heard but didn't react. He was past the initial shock. Relief that he was no longer responsible for keeping her alive swept over him, and numbness followed. When his fiancée, Dallas, came running into the ER in tears, he opened his arms and held her without taking his eyes off the team fighting to keep Trina alive. The moment they hooked her up to the heart monitor he heard three beeps, and then she flatlined.

The sound was horrifying, and Trey's first instinct was to run to her, but Dallas held him back. He could only watch in growing horror as someone scrambled for a defibrillator.

When the doctor slapped the paddles onto her bare chest and yelled, "Clear!" Trey jumped at the same time Trina's body bucked from the shock.

Trey saw nothing but a continuing flatline as the doctor reset the defibrillator. "Clear!" he yelled again.

The slap of paddles against her flesh was lost in the chaos, but Trina's body bucked again as the electrical shock went through her.

Trey was praying to God in silence, begging for mercy, when he heard a beep. Everyone watched as her heartbeat began to register on the monitor, and when it picked up a rhythm, the doctor's voice echoed Trey's relief.

"We've got her!" the doctor said. "Somebody grab the IV. There's no time to stabilize her here. We're heading straight to the OR."

They wheeled her out of the bay and began pushing the gurney up the hall. Trey went with it, running at her side. He grabbed her hand, desperate to give her one last message.

"Trina, it's me, baby! It's Trey. I love you. I need you to fight to stay with me! Can you hear me? Fight to stay with me!"

"Sorry, Chief, but this is as far as you can go," the doctor said, as a pair of double doors swung open.

Trey stopped. His heart was pounding as the doors swung shut behind them, and the quiet that swept through him at that moment made him weak. Whatever happened now was out of his control.

He wondered how long it would take Sam to get to Mystic, then let it go. It wouldn't matter when he arrived. Their mom was gone, and Trina would either live through the surgery or she wouldn't. He took a slow, shaky breath and walked back to Dallas. Life as they'd known it was over. Whatever happened in the next few hours would be written on a whole new page.

Lee Daniels was happy for the first time in days. The fight he'd had with Trina was his fault; thinking she'd been cheating on him had been a knee-jerk reaction to his mother's behavior when he was a child.

Being able to see her and apologize at Paul Jackson's funeral had made a bad week better. Everyone was keyed up over a second murder in their small town, and now, knowing it was connected to Dick Phillips' murder as well, had left everyone uneasy. It was hard to believe, but it appeared there was a serial killer in Mystic targeting a trio of old friends.

He was coming out of the supermarket carrying a bag of groceries in one hand and his car keys in the other when he heard an ambulance siren. Out of habit he paused to say a brief prayer.

"God bless whoever is in need," he mumbled, and then dumped his groceries into the front seat of his car and headed back to his apartment.

He had been home about a half hour and had just put up the last of the groceries when his cell phone rang. He glanced at the caller ID and frowned. The Jakes family hadn't been all that happy with him lately, and he hoped Trey wasn't about to read him the riot act.

"Hey, Trey, what's up?"

Trey didn't mince words.

"Mom's dead. She was murdered on the way home from Paul Jackson's memorial service. The killer thought he took Trina out, too, but she was still breathing when I found her. They just took her into surgery. I thought you should know."

Lee grabbed on to the kitchen counter to keep from going to his knees.

"Oh, my God. Oh, my God. I'm so sorry about Betsy. Did they take Trina here to Webster Memorial?"

"Yes. I'm in the waiting room outside the OR."

"I'm on my way," Lee said, then grabbed his wallet and his car keys, and left on the run.

All the way to the hospital he kept remembering those last moments with Trina and the sadness in her voice. She couldn't die. She was the best thing that had ever happened to him.

Trey hung up the phone and looked at Dallas, but they didn't talk. There was nothing for her to say. His mother's body was on the way to the morgue. There would be an autopsy, and since the murder had taken place in Webster County, the county sheriff, Dewey Osmond, had taken charge of the crime scene, just as he had when her classmate Dick Phillips' body was discovered.

Dallas couldn't quit shaking. This was a nightmare—a horrible, hideous nightmare. Both of their parents dead—murdered—for something that had happened when they were kids. When she reached for Trey, he grabbed her hand. She saw the shock in his eyes, and when she saw the tears, she cried with him.

The news of Betsy Jakes' murder swept through Mystic like wildfire. There were plenty who'd been at the memorial service who hadn't taken Trey Jakes' comments all that seriously until now. He'd asked the members of that ill-fated graduating class to think back. He'd said there were some in Mystic who knew things. He'd asked them for their help. He'd mentioned a ten-thousand-dollar reward. Now every classmate left in Mystic, as well as everyone who'd been in high school then, was thinking back to the night of graduation, going through everything they could remember and every bit of gossip they'd heard.

Lainey Pickett lived almost ten miles outside Mystic, and after being dumped by Sam Jakes years earlier, she had purposefully shut that place and the people out of her life. She did her business and shopped in a neighboring town and coped with life the best that she could. She hadn't been at the memorial service because she knew nothing about any of the murders, which meant she didn't know anything about the announcement Trey Jakes made there, either. She made it a habit not to think about the Jakes men in any manner whatsoever.

She'd spent four of the past ten years getting a PhD in history, and for most of the past six years she'd been teaching online classes for the University of West Virginia. Her life wasn't perfect, but she had taken it for granted until last Christmas, when she'd found the lump in her breast.

A double mastectomy and a round of chemo treatments later, she was now minus boobs but cancer-free and getting ready to begin breast reconstruction. Her once-thick red hair was growing back, and she was alive, and for that she was grateful.

She had just finished her last class of the day and was getting ready to answer some student email when her cell phone began to vibrate. She had forgotten to turn the ringer back on, and when it began to rattle across the counter, she grabbed it before it fell off.

"Hello?"

"Lainey, this is Dallas Phillips."

Lainey froze. She and Dallas had once been close

friends because they were dating the Jakes brothers, but that had all gone by the wayside with her dreams. The urge to hang up was strong, but curiosity won out.

"Well, it's been a while," Lainey said.

Dallas heard the chill in Lainey's voice but didn't take it personally. She knew Sam had left her high and dry, which was why she was calling.

"I know, and the reason I'm calling isn't pretty, but I wanted you to know. From one woman to another, you need to be forewarned that Sam is coming home."

Pain shot through Lainey so fast she could barely focus.

"Well, hell must have finally frozen over," she snapped.

Dallas winced. Lainey was still angry, and she couldn't really blame her. Sam had abandoned all of them.

"No, it's worse. Betsy and Trina were shot on their way home from Paul Jackson's memorial service. Betsy is dead, and Trina's condition is critical."

Lainey gasped. "Dear Lord! What happened? Why?"

Dallas frowned. "Surely you know about the recent murders of my father and Paul Jackson?"

Lainey was shocked. "No! I had no idea, and I'm so sorry. I rarely go to Mystic. I do most of my business in Summerton. What happened?"

"My dad was the first. The killer tried to make it look like a suicide, but they figured out pretty quickly it was a homicide. Then Mack Jackson's dad, Paul, was killed. Same thing. The killer tried to make it look like an accident, but it was determined to be a homicide."

Lainey couldn't believe what she was hearing.

"I am so sorry. I didn't know. I just didn't know, but…why Betsy?"

Dallas quickly explained about the connection to the night of their graduation.

"Now all of them are dead," she added. "Trey has been working day and night trying to run down leads, but to no avail, and now this. That's why Sam is coming home. No one's seen him in ages. I don't know what to expect, but I thought it was only fair that you should know."

Lainey's voice was shaking. "I am so sorry for… for all of you. And, Dallas, thank you."

"You're welcome," Dallas said, then hesitated. "Uh…when I asked Trey if I should call you, he said yes. He's sorry about how Sam treated you…how he treated all his friends and family. The war did something to him. He's not the same Sam anymore."

Lainey's eyes welled, but the tone of her voice was angry.

"Yes, life does that. None of us are the same as we once were. Thank you for calling."

She hung up the phone and burst into tears.

Two

Sam drove I-75 northbound for almost two hours without remembering a single mile of the trip. It wasn't until his gas gauge began to signal a need to refuel that he finally had to stop. His head was throbbing and his belly was growling as he went inside the station. He knew he should eat but wasn't sure if anything would stay down.

The woman behind the register was reading something on her cell phone and didn't bother to look up as he walked in.

"How's it goin'?" she mumbled.

Since he guessed that was her standard greeting, he didn't bother answering.

One quick scan of the fried food inside the deli case was all it took to send him on the hunt for something with a longer shelf life, which turned into sweets. He chose a box of doughnuts and a honey bun, and then got a large coffee to go before going to the register to pay.

"Will that be all?" the clerk asked, still focused on her phone.

Sam reached across the register and laid his hand over the phone.

"Ring me up, please," he said softly.

There was a frown on her face as she looked up. The look in his eyes startled her, and she quickly totaled his purchases.

He paid her with cash, waited for his change and then walked out, drinking the coffee as he went. It was too strong and bitter as hell, but it served the purpose, and slowly his belly began to settle.

He put the food in the SUV and began to refuel. As he did, he glanced at his watch. Almost 5:00 p.m. Even though it would be dark soon he was driving straight through. On a good day, the trip was at least an eight-hour drive, but driving in the mountains in the dark was going to slow him down. Still, it didn't matter. No matter where he was, he wouldn't be sleeping.

Once the gas tank was full, he got back inside and called Trey to check in.

His brother answered on the second ring. "Hey, Sam, where are you?"

"About two hours closer to you than I was when I started. Is there any word on Trina?"

"No. She's been in surgery a little over an hour and a half. I'll call when I know something, I promise."

"Would you do me a favor?" Sam asked.

"Sure," Trey said. "What do you need?"

"Get me a room at Grant's Motel."

"It burned down six years ago," Trey said.

"Well, hell. Is there another one?"

"Yes, but you could stay at the farm."

Sam's voice had a don't-argue tone.

"No, I can't stay at the farm. I wouldn't go home when Mom was still alive, and I'm not going back there now. I'll take the motel, please."

Trey took the cue not to argue.

"I'll give them a call. It's at the north end of Main."

"Thanks. I'll drop off my stuff as soon as I get in, and then see you at the hospital."

"Okay," Trey said, and then added, "Hey, brother."

"Yeah?"

"It will be good to see you again."

Sam sighed. He felt like crying.

"It will be good to see you, too," he said.

He disconnected, opened the box of doughnuts and then started the car. He took a bite out of the first doughnut as he was driving away. It was the first of three he would eat before he ran out of coffee to wash them down.

Rita Porter was pouring herself a drink when her husband, Will, came in the back door. Startled by his sudden appearance, she jumped as if she'd been shot and dropped the glass into the sink. Booze and glass went everywhere.

"Now look what you made me do!" she screeched, and then staggered toward the utility room.

Will wanted to strangle her. He had a very short time in which to declare himself a candidate for the state superintendent's job, and everything in his life was going to hell in a handbasket. He wished Rita to hell, too, and headed for his office, picking up the mail from the front hall table on the way and leaving her to clean up the mess.

But Rita wasn't finished with him. She came back,

and then followed him all the way through the house carrying the broom and dustpan.

"I guess you heard about the Jakeses," she said.

Will turned around, still holding the stack of mail in one hand and a paperweight from his desk in the other.

"Everybody in town is talking about it, so yes, I heard."

Rita kept staring without saying a word.

"What?" Will snapped.

She shrugged. "I was just wondering. You graduated with all three murder victims."

His frown deepened. "Yes, and your point is…?"

"I don't know. Just wondered if you knew anything about what's happening."

A wave of rage shot through him so fast he threw the paperweight straight at her, missing her head by inches.

She shrieked.

"You nearly hit me! What are you trying to do? Kill me? That's it, isn't it? You wish I was dead."

Will glared, so angry he was shaking.

"What I wish is that you weren't a fucking drunk. That's what I wish. Now go clean up that broken glass and whiskey before you pass out. I don't want to have to clean up another one of the messes you make on your drunken binges."

She screamed, then threw the broom and dustpan at him, and ran to their bedroom, stumbling and bawling all the way.

"Damn it all to hell," Will said, and then sighed.

He took off his suit coat, rolled up his sleeves and

took the broom and dustpan with him as he headed for the kitchen.

"Damn bitch. I wish she was dead, all right. I just don't want to be the one accused of doing it."

Greg Standish entered the bank through the back entrance and slipped into his office unnoticed. He wasn't in the mood to talk to anyone right now. In fact, he was thinking of all the ways he could fake his death and disappear. His life and his dreams were pretty much over, and if that wasn't enough, between his wife, Gloria, and his daughter, Carly, he was bordering on bankrupt. Once the directors got wind of his situation he would be out of a job, and then that would be that.

He saw a cop car go flying past and frowned. So the last survivor from that wreck was gone. He heard Trey found his mom. And Trina. He couldn't believe she was still alive after being shot at point-blank range. His eyes narrowed. He'd never given much thought to dying, and now he was wondering if it hurt.

T. J. Silver was in the game room playing "Call of Duty" on his Xbox when his dad walked in.

"Hi, Dad," he muttered, without taking his eyes from the screen.

Marcus stood in the doorway, staring at his son and wondering exactly where he'd gone wrong. T.J. was handsome and intelligent, a college graduate, and had yet to turn a finger at anything resembling work. Marcus had been born into money, but he'd always worked. He'd always wanted his dad to be proud of him. T.J., on the other hand, didn't seem bothered to be living an idle life of wealth.

When Marcus didn't answer him, T.J. realized his dad was pissed about something, and immediately stopped the game and stood up. "I guess you heard about Betsy Jakes," he said.

Marcus's eyes narrowed. "Yes, I heard. I also heard her daughter got shot, too. She's not dead, though."

T.J. shrugged. "They say she's not going to make it, though. Injuries were too serious."

Marcus pointed at the Xbox. "Have you done anything today that could remotely qualify as work?"

T.J.'s eyes widened. This wasn't like his dad. Something had him all hot and bothered.

"Yes, I have, actually. I was in the office here all morning, working on details for your announcement party for the senate seat. Then I went to the Jackson memorial—as did you, because I saw you there, but you didn't bother to acknowledge me. So what's your problem, Dad?"

"My problem is that at your age, you should have more to do than play video games. In my day, my father expected me to toe the line."

T.J.'s eyes narrowed as he responded in a tone that was just shy of disrespectful.

"Well, in my day, my father encouraged…no, *expected* me to make a splash all over my college campus, and after I graduated be sure I was mentioned regularly in the society pages by showing up at all kinds of local benefits and things. I thought he was grooming me for something special, like maybe following in his footsteps once he got into politics. That's what I thought *my* father expected."

Marcus grunted as if he'd just been punched in the gut. Twice he started to respond and then couldn't, because he'd realized T.J. was right. He'd never looked at his behavior in that vein before, but everything T.J. had said was the truth. His son was the product of his own raising, and he had no one to blame but himself. He shook his head and walked away.

T.J. was still a little pissed as he watched his father leave. The old man was obviously amped up about another classmate being murdered. Shit happened.

He checked the time. Cook was probably finishing up dinner, and he wanted to shower and change before he sat down to eat. As he headed upstairs to his room, he was debating with himself about what he wanted to wear. He decided on something sporty but comfortable. It didn't pay to be lax about one's appearance— ever. A person never knew when it would matter to make a good impression.

Sunset was only minutes away as Lainey walked back from the pasture with the feed bucket, leaving Dandy out in the pasture eating. There were no other animals on the property now except her horse. He was a big gray grullo with a feisty attitude, and there was a time in her life when that had fit who she was, but no more. Her body was still weak from the cancer treatments, and she had gotten so thin that her endurance was nil. But she was cancer-free, and every day she woke up was a good day and a chance to get stronger.

When she was almost back at the barn, Dandy nickered.

She turned to look, but he already had his head back down in the feeder. She smiled.

"Good night to you, too, big guy!" she yelled.

Dandy looked up, nickered again and then resumed his meal.

Now that her last chore for the day was over, Lainey was left with nothing to deter her thoughts from going back to Sam.

There was a time when he'd been the reason she drew breath. Then life had interrupted their love affair and she'd had to figure out how to live without him. She'd thought she was doing okay until the phone call from Dallas, and now all she could think about was seeing Sam again, if for no other reason than to tell him to go to hell.

She latched the door to the granary and started toward the house. The sun was gone now. She was going up the back steps when she heard a long, high-pitched scream that made her shudder. After one quick glance back, she leaped up the steps and hurried into the house. There was a panther somewhere on the mountain, and she hoped he stayed there. Dandy was too old to fight off a big cat like that now.

After locking up the house, she washed up and began making herself some supper, trying not to think about Sam coming home with a broken heart. She did *not* want to feel sorry for him. She needed to stay mad and hurt and everything in between. She had to, or she would likely get her heart broken all over again.

Sunset had come and gone. Once Sam reached Knoxville, Tennessee, he took 81 North. The dark pavement in front of his headlights all looked the same, even though he'd already left one state and driven into another.

Two hours had passed since he'd last talked to Trey. He kept thinking Trina should be out of surgery by now, but he'd heard nothing, and Trey had promised to call.

Traffic was heavy. At least a dozen eighteen-wheelers had passed him during those hours, along with the constant barrage of other traffic. Now, though, traffic was beginning to slow down, and he couldn't figure out why until he topped a hill and saw a cadre of flashing lights on the highway below. He tapped the brakes to accommodate the slower pace, and as he did, caught a flash of headlights coming over the hill behind him at a breakneck pace.

He tightened his grip on the steering wheel as the lights popped up in his mirror. There was no way that driver would be able to brake in time to keep from hitting him. He was bracing himself for impact when, at the last moment, the car swerved and went airborne into the center median.

Sam glanced over his shoulder as it went flying past him in the dark. It was rolling in midair when it hit and continued to roll after impact, the headlights bouncing up and down in the darkness. When the car finally stopped, it was upside down.

Sam slammed on the brakes and pulled off onto the shoulder. He left the lights on in his SUV as he grabbed his flashlight and jumped out. Other witnesses to the wreck were also stopping and running toward it.

He darted into the grassy median. The car had rolled a good fifty yards away. The beam of his flashlight was not meant to illuminate this much, and he could barely see where he was going, plus he was beginning to smell gas. It must be spilling out.

A man ran up behind him as they neared the wreck.

"I just called 911," the stranger said. "I saw the whole thing. He was flying when he came over that hill."

Sam stopped at the wreck and got down on his knees before flashing the light throughout the interior. Not only was it empty, but the windshield was gone.

Sam stood abruptly. "It's empty. The driver was thrown out. Spread out and start looking."

By now a half-dozen others had joined them, and most of them had flashlights, too. They quickly spaced themselves out and began backtracking in a wide perimeter away from the wreck.

As they were searching, Sam began to hear more sirens and turned to look. One of the patrol cars was coming back up with his lights flashing.

Sam kept moving slowly, sweeping the grassy median with his flashlight as he walked. The first thing he found was a duffel bag, and then a few yards farther he found a red-and-black tennis shoe. The duffel bag was from a college in Tennessee, and the shoe was a popular one with the younger crowd. His heart sank.

"Over here!" someone yelled.

He turned and ran.

The driver was lying facedown on the missing windshield, and when Sam saw him, for a split second the night and the people around him disappeared and he thought he was hearing the *whup whup whup* from the rotors of a chopper and watching blood running out of his buddy's head and seeping into the sand at his feet. The heat of the desert wind was in his face as the flashing lights from the highway patrol car momentarily blinded him. It was the lights that yanked him out of the flashback.

"He's dead!" the man yelled, waving at the patrolman who was coming their way.

As Sam dropped down on one knee to check the body for a pulse, the man said again, "He's dead. I done checked."

Sam was numb. The driver was in his early twenties, and the man was right. He was dead.

A crowd was gathering around the body, and they were all talking at once, wanting to tell their version of what they'd seen to the highway patrolman.

Sam glanced down at the boy one last time, and then turned around and walked back to his SUV. He tossed the flashlight onto the seat beside him, grabbed a canister of hand wipes and began pulling out the sheets to clean his hands, and then he kept pulling them out and wiping and pulling them out and wiping until he realized he was crying. He took a slow, shaky breath as he threw the canister on the floor, then wadded up the hand wipes and put them in a trash bag.

"Jesus wept," he said softly, and then closed his eyes, but the sight was still burned into his brain, and the moment he spoke the words, he remembered a scene from his childhood and the scolding his mother had given him for what he'd said.

Do not use the Lord's name in vain, Samuel Wade.

I didn't curse, Mama. That's a Bible verse. Daddy said it's the shortest verse in the Bible.

Well, your daddy is right, but so am I. Don't say that again unless you're on your knees saying prayers.

Yes, ma'am. I'm sorry, Mama.

Sam rubbed his eyes with the heels of his hands. He wasn't on his knees, but he needed to be.

"I'm sorry, Mama," he said softly. "Sorry for everything."

He could almost feel her hand on the back of his neck.

It's okay, Sammy. When you know better, you do better.

He put the car in gear and slowly pulled back onto the interstate. For some strange reason, home seemed even farther away.

Trey and Lee were alone in the waiting room. Dallas had gone home because the livestock needed tending. He'd put out a couple of round bales of hay for their cattle early this morning, so they wouldn't have to be tended to for a couple of days, but Dallas's hens had to be fed and watered, and the eggs had to be gathered, no matter what else was wrong with their world.

They were still in the waiting room when Trey's phone rang. He saw it was Dallas and answered quickly.

"Hey, honey. Everything all right?" he asked.

"Yes. I'm getting ready to drive back into town. Is Trina still in surgery?"

"Yes, but don't drive back. I was watching the weather earlier, and there's a heavy thunderstorm predicted for this area. I don't want you out on the roads in that."

"But, Trey, I don't want you there by yourself."

"I'm not alone. Lee's here. I'll let you know the

minute she's out of surgery. Just stay home. At least I'll know one of you is safe."

Dallas heard the weariness in his voice and knew if she pushed the issue and went to the hospital anyway, it would be at his expense, so she finally agreed.

"I'll stay home. Just know how much I love you," she said.

"I love you, too," Trey said. "I'll talk to you later."

He disconnected and then settled back in his chair. Lee was dozing sitting up. They didn't have anything much to say to each other and even less to the people who stared at them as they passed the waiting room.

Five hours after Trina went into surgery, the surgeon came into the waiting room looking for her family.

Trey stood abruptly, while Lee eased up from the sofa where he'd been sitting. They were both afraid to hear the verdict.

"Are you here for Trina Jakes?" the doctor asked.

"Yes," they said in unison.

"I'm Dr. Lowell. I operated on her. She came through the surgery and is in ICU."

Lee dropped back onto the sofa and started to cry. Just the news that she was still alive was what he'd been praying for.

Trey wanted details and got them as the doctor continued.

"Her condition is critical. The bullet missed her heart by centimeters, shattered a couple of ribs and punctured a lung. It took a while to remove all the bone fragments. I pulled a couple out of one kidney and one from her liver. The bullet also nicked part of her spine on exit, but the spinal cord is intact. She lost a lot of blood, and for the time being I've put her into a drug-induced coma."

"Dear Lord," Trey muttered, and then the cop part of him kicked in. "Did she regain consciousness at any time before she was moved to ICU?"

"No, and as serious as her injuries were, that was to be expected."

"When can I see her?" Lee asked.

"Check the visiting times in ICU, and discourage anyone but immediate family," Dr. Lowell said.

Trey had his own comment to make.

"Just so you know, I need a no-visitor hold put on her chart, and there will be a guard stationed outside her room. She's the only living witness to the latest of three murders, and the killer isn't going to want her to wake up."

Dr. Lowell grimaced. "Yes, so I was told. I'll make sure that's taken care of."

"On behalf of our family, we thank you," Trey said.

Lee pulled himself together to add his thanks. "Yes, Dr. Lowell. Thank you for saving her."

Lowell nodded. "It wasn't all me. I had a good team with me in the OR. I'll be checking on her on a regular basis, so I'm sure we'll speak again," he said, and left the waiting room.

Now that Trey knew what he had to work with, he moved into action.

"I need to make some calls and get a guard rotation set up here."

"I'm going to find ICU," Lee said. "I'll text you the visiting times."

Trey nodded. "I'm not leaving the area. I just need a little privacy to make those calls."

Lee went one way and Trey the other as they left the waiting room. Trey sent a text to Dallas on the way down in the elevator, then waited to call Sam until he was in a more private place. He was on his way out to his cruiser when he realized the predicted rain was imminent.

Thunder rolled as he made a run for the car, followed by a shaft of lightning that momentarily lit up the sky a few miles away.

He unlocked the car and slid into the seat. The silence was brief. There was traffic on the police radio, but from what he could hear, Dwight Thomas, their night dispatcher, had everything in hand.

He thought about Sam, and then shifted focus to the need for security on Trina. He didn't have enough officers in Mystic to keep someone on guard day and night. He was trying to remember the security service Mack Jackson had used a few months ago for his fiancée, Lissa, when she was being stalked by the janitor where she worked, and looked to see if he still had Mack's number in his contacts. He did, so he hit the call button, and then wiped a shaky hand across his face as he listened to Mack's phone ring.

Three

Trey's heart was so heavy he could hardly breathe, and yet he had to stay focused. When Mack picked up on the third ring, Trey braced himself to say what had to be said.

"Hello."

Trey cleared his throat. "Mack, this is Trey. I know it's late. I hope I didn't call at a bad time."

"No, not at all," Mack said.

"I was wondering if you could give me a contact number for the security guard you used for Lissa."

"Sure, his name is Cain Embry. I don't have it on me, but I'll find it and text it to you in a few minutes, okay?"

"Yes, I would appreciate it."

"Is something going on? Something related to the murders?" Mack asked.

"Yes," Trey said, and then his voice broke. He had to clear his throat again and start over to get it all said. "Yes, something happened. Mom is dead, and Trina just came out of surgery. We still don't know if she'll make it or not. They were shot on their way home from the memorial service."

Trey heard a gasp and then a groan, followed by a couple of anxious whispers, and guessed Mack was telling Lissa.

"Dear Lord! I don't know what to say except that I'm sorry. I'm so sorry," Mack said.

Trey stared out across the parking lot.

"Yeah, me, too," he said. "I keep thinking about that little speech I made at the church, wondering if I pushed the killer into it."

The shock of what Mack was feeling echoed in his voice.

"Hell no, you didn't push the bastard into anything. For one thing, he already killed twice before. Without a clue as to why this was happening, you've been helpless to stop anything. I'm finally coming to accept that they were all doomed from the start. Did Trina say anything? Do you have a lead?"

"No, she was unconscious when I found her. That's why I need the guards. If she pulls through, she might be able to finger the killer. I can only imagine how freaked out he must be, knowing she's still breathing."

"Is there anything I can do? Do you need help—"

"You're helping by getting me the number. I'll be watching for the text. I've got to call Sam. He's on his way home. He doesn't know Trina made it through surgery yet."

"Believe me, Trey, I know everything you're going through right now. Just know Lissa and I will keep you in our prayers."

"I know you do, and thanks," Trey said and disconnected. While he was waiting for Mack's text, he called Dallas to let her know Trina had made it through surgery, then made the same call to Sam.

Sam's eyes were burning, and his shoulders ached. He'd been driving in rain for over an hour, which was making it twice as difficult to see the highway. When his cell phone finally rang he almost jumped out of his skin. Then he saw it was from Trey and put it on speaker so he could keep both hands on the wheel.

"Please give me some good news."

"Trina made it through the surgery. She's in ICU. I'll give you details when you get here. Right now I'm waiting on a phone number so I can get twenty-four-hour security on her."

"Thank the Lord," Sam muttered. "I can help with security when I get there," he added.

"I know, but I'm selfish enough to want you with me. I have a couple of ideas as to where to take the investigation but I'm waiting on you to get here to implement them. Where are you?" Trey asked.

Sam sighed.

"Somewhere in Tennessee. I'm north of Knoxville, and that's all I know for sure. It's raining pretty hard right now. Difficult to see road signs."

Trey frowned. "Be careful. Stop and sleep over somewhere if you need to."

"Yeah, I watched one young man die tonight. I don't want to be next."

"What? Are you okay?" Trey asked.

"Yes. It was a wreck. I saw it, but I wasn't in it."

"I'm sorry, Sam."

"Yeah, so am I, for a whole lot of reasons. I'll see

you sometime tomorrow. That's all I know for sure. Keep me posted on any change in her condition."

"I will. Be safe. Oh…hey, I just got a text. It'll be the info I've been waiting on. I'll talk to you later," Trey said and hung up.

Sam heard the click in his ear and disconnected, too, thinking to himself how his little brother had grown up while he wasn't looking.

He drove for a few moments more, peering past the frantic swiping of the windshield wipers while the relief of knowing his sister was still alive sank in.

"Thank You, God. Now please help me get home."

The killer couldn't rest. He needed to know if Trina Jakes was still breathing, but he didn't want anyone else to know he was calling. He got out of bed, moving quietly through the house to his study as he called the hospital, then leaned forward, resting his elbows on the desk, as the phone began to ring.

"Webster Memorial Hospital."

"I'm calling to check on Trina Jakes' condition."

There was a pause, and then the operator said, "She's in ICU. I'll ring the nurses' desk."

"Thank you," he said, and waited.

"ICU."

"Hello. I'm checking on the condition of Trina Jakes and the visiting times."

"She's in critical condition and can't have visitors."

"But we go to church with her and we wanted to—"

"No visitors. I'm sorry."

He disconnected with a measure of relief. For now she wasn't talking, but, damn it, she was still alive.

He'd come so close to a perfect sweep, and now this. His first thought was to pack and run, and then it hit him.

"What the hell's wrong with me?" he muttered. "Even if she never wakes up, even if she dies, they'll still be looking for a killer, and I'll be the one who left town right after the shootings."

Right now he had to deal with more immediate issues, so he began to run through scenarios as to how to rectify this mess. He needed to make sure she never woke up, but how to get to her? He would bet his life there were guards on her around the clock. Trey Jakes wasn't a fool. His sister was his star witness— if she lived.

But even if he couldn't get to Trina's room, he could still get to the hospital. It could catch fire. It could blow up. There were all kinds of things that could happen in such a volatile environment. The fact that many more lives would be lost was of no consequence. They would be nothing but collateral damage.

It was beginning to rain as Trey left the parking lot and headed back into the hospital. Lee's text stated ICU visiting hours were from 10:00 a.m. to noon, from 2:00 p.m. to 4:00, and from 6:00 p.m. to 8:00. Tough. Even though it was midnight, he wanted to see his sister's face.

He took the elevator up to the third floor and was on his way to the ICU waiting room when Lee stepped out into the hall.

"I was just coming to look for you," Lee said.

"Why? Did something happen? Is she worse?"

"No, but we aren't going to get to see her until to-morrow."

"No, we're going to see her now, even if I have to throw my weight around to do it," Trey said.

Lee shoved a shaky hand through his hair. There was something he needed to say to Trey before this day got any older.

"Wait a second, okay? Before we go in, I need to apologize to you."

Trey frowned. "Why?"

"For being such an ass...for hurting Trina like I did. It all had to do with shit from my childhood, but that's no excuse, because I'm no longer a child. I apologized to her at the memorial service. We were going to meet tomorrow and talk." Lee's voice was starting to shake. "When I think of how close she came to not having a tomorrow, it makes me sick. I love her, Trey. So much. I'm with her for the long haul and, if she'll have me, for the rest of our lives."

Trey had new respect for Lee. Those words couldn't have been easy to get said.

"I appreciate your honesty, man. Now let's go see our girl. She might not know we're there, but I need to know she's still breathing."

Lee managed a brief smile and walked with Trey to ICU. It was two minutes after midnight when they entered. Lights were on, and nurses were moving in and out of the patients' rooms. Trey paused at the front desk.

"Which room is Trina Jakes in?" he asked.

Clarice Powell, the RN on duty, was about to send the man packing when she looked up.

"Oh, hello, Chief. You know this is past visiting hours."

"Yes, ma'am, I do."

She was sympathetic to all his family had been through, and wasn't about to push the issue.

"Your sister is in 12B."

"Thank you, Clarice, and to give you a heads-up, she's going to have to have guards around the clock and a no-visitors sign on her door. No one except for immediate family. I'll give you a list of names."

"Dr. Lowell told us. We'll take care of her, and we're very sorry for your loss. Your mother was a good friend to everyone who knew her," she said.

"Thank you, Clarice. Oh…just so you know, this is Lee Daniels. He's Trina's significant other, so he'll be in and out as much as the rest of us, okay?"

Clarice eyed Lee closely. "I know you from somewhere."

"I work for Peterson Heat and Air."

"Right! You worked on my central air last May."

"Yes, ma'am," Lee said. "You said 12B?"

"That way," she said, as she pointed to her left.

They started down the aisle, trying not to stare at the patients inside the glass-walled cubicles. The beeping of so many heart monitors accompanied them down the hall. Between the steady stream of nurses moving in and out of rooms and the occasional groan or cry for help from someone sick or dying, it was a depressing place to be.

The last time Trey had been in a place with this many seriously ill patients was the VA hospital right after they'd flown Sam stateside. He wondered about the PTSD that had haunted Sam for so long and if this place would trigger a flashback. He'd witnessed a couple of them during the first year Sam was home, and they'd given him pause. They'd also helped him understand why Sam had chosen to stay away. At that time in his life, he could easily have hurt someone he loved.

But while Trey was lost in thought, Lee was looking for the woman he loved.

"There!" Lee said, and lengthened his stride as he darted into the next bay.

Then he stopped just inside the doorway, too stunned to go farther, as Trey hurried past him. Trina was as pale as the sheet on which she was lying, and hooked up to a half-dozen machines. He didn't know which ones were keeping her alive and which ones were monitoring her vital signs. The room looked like a lab scene from a bad movie. He couldn't think. He forgot to breathe.

Trey, on the other hand, had seen her covered in blood and been sure she was dead. The fact that he could hear her heartbeat made all of this reassuring.

The nurse who had just finished checking Trina's vitals and was adjusting the drip on the IV heard footsteps behind her. She turned and quickly recognized Trey.

"Hello, Chief. Really sorry about your mother."

"Hi, Annie. We're all sorry about Mom. Our gift is that Trina is still alive. How's she doing?" he asked.

"Holding her own," she said.

Lee took a breath and moved closer. Those were the words he needed to hear.

"Annie, this is Lee Daniels. Lee, Annie Dixon. Annie and I grew up together."

"Nice to meet you, ma'am," Lee said.

"Not ma'am, just Annie," the nurse said. "I'm going to get her another blanket. I'll be right back."

Trey moved to one side of the bed while Lee went to the other. Trey reached toward Trina and rubbed the back of his finger against her cheek.

"Hey, Trina. It's me, Trey. Just want you to know that you're safe. You're in ICU. Sam is on his way home. We love you. Just rest and get well."

Lee was struggling for words and fighting back tears as he slid his hand beneath hers so that he could hold it.

"Hi, baby. It's Lee. I just want you to know I love you. Like Trey said, just sleep and heal."

The stillness of her body was frightening. Even though they both knew she was in a drug-induced coma, she looked as close to dead as a person could and still be breathing.

Trey and Lee kept talking to her, but when Annie Dixon came back with the blanket, she ran them out.

"Sorry, guys. Visiting time is over."

"Bye for now, sis. I'll be back," Trey said as he patted Trina's shoulder, and then walked away.

Lee leaned over the bed rail and kissed her forehead.

"Love you, baby," he said softly, and then caught up with Trey, who was writing down the names of the people who were allowed to visit for Clarice.

"Under no circumstance is anyone else to see her. Not even a preacher, okay?"

The nurse's eyes widened. "Surely you don't suspect—"

"Right now I suspect everyone," Trey muttered and pushed the doors wide as he exited.

Lee caught them and slipped out before they shut. "There's no one on guard yet," he said.

Trey stopped short, his shoulders slumping. He should have noticed that, but he was so tired and so stressed he was losing focus. "You're right."

"I can do it," Lee said.

"A security team is on the way. They'll be here within a couple of hours."

"Then, let me do it until they show. Please, Trey. I need to do this for her."

Trey went back into ICU with Lee beside him.

"Clarice, I have a security team on the way, but until they get here, I'm assigning Lee Daniels to the job. He'll sit in a chair just outside her room without bothering her or any of your medical staff in any way. His job will be to follow anyone who goes into her room and observe everything they do until they leave, understand?"

"Yes. Come with me, Mr. Daniels."

Lee glanced back at Trey. "Thank you," he said and hurried to catch up.

Trey left ICU again, but in a different state than when he'd entered. His horror at what had happened was slowly being replaced with rage. Three people had been killed on his watch. Now Trina was in as much danger as the others had been. Even as he was thinking about the guards who would be with her, he realized there was a weak link in his plan to keep her safe. If the killer worked in the hospital, he had just unwittingly dumped her back in the bastard's lap.

The first thing he had to do was get the names of

everyone who'd graduated with his mother, and then find out where they were and what they did for a living so he could eliminate them as suspects. And he knew exactly where to start.

It was raining like hell when he walked out of the hospital, and even though he ran to the cruiser, he was soaked by the time he got in.

He glanced at the time.

Almost twenty minutes after twelve. It was tomorrow. Sam would be here soon, and knowing Sam, the shit was likely to hit the fan.

Lainey couldn't sleep, but it had nothing to do with the storm, even though wind was blowing rain against the windows. Intermittent lightning and thunder rattled the panes. Although it was after midnight she was pacing the floor from room to room, unable to settle down. All the lights were on, and so was the television, because she wanted the noise.

The fact that Sam Jakes was coming back to Mystic had thrown her life out of rhythm. It had taken her years to get over him and get on with her life. At least she'd thought she was over him until Dallas's phone call. All she'd done since the call was relive the past. Earlier she had tried to convince herself that hating him would keep her safe. He'd already broken her heart. But hate was an emotion that didn't go with Sam Jakes.

When he'd first flown back to the States, she had understood the level of pain he was in and why he was unable to take phone calls. But she hadn't understood why he refused to see her. Still, she coped with disappointment by sending notes and cards via his family, even though he never sent a single message back.

She'd waited and waited and tried not to feel excluded from the healing journey he was on, until, finally, she broke. He obviously didn't want to see her, and she wanted to know why, so she left Mystic in secret and drove all the way to the VA hospital without telling anyone she was going.

It was five days before Christmas, and the day was bitter cold. She had wrapped her mother's blue wool scarf around her to block the air from blowing down the neck of her coat and tied a matching blue ribbon into her hair. Her hands were shaking as she entered the hospital, and her voice broke when she asked for the number of his room.

It wasn't until she was approaching his door that it dawned on her she might run into some of his family. Nervous all over again, she hesitated for a few moments outside the door, listening until she was certain he was alone, and then carefully slipped into his room, only to find him sleeping.

She didn't know what she'd expected, but it wasn't what she saw. In that moment she began to understand why he had shut her out. She saw the man lying in that bed and was unable to find any part of the Sam Jakes she knew beneath the bandages. When he began to stir, she'd bolted in a panic and left without anyone knowing she was there.

After she got home she kept telling herself that when he got better she would go again, but she didn't, and then one day she called Betsy for an update and found out that he'd been out of the hospital almost a month and no one knew where he was.

That was when she realized she'd been abandoned. He hadn't given her a chance to prove she could love him no matter how he looked. He'd just made the decision for her. It had taken her years to get over the heartbreak and to realize she hadn't fought for herself when he was rejecting her. Now when she thought of Sam it was with disappointment in the man she'd thought she knew. Her dilemma now was how to feel about seeing him again.

Trey Jakes' first job this morning had taken him straight back to Mystic High. He hadn't been inside the school since the day he graduated, and he was mildly surprised by the updates, even if it did still smell like school.

He headed straight for the superintendent's office and took off his hat as he approached the secretary.

"Ma'am, I need to speak to Mr. Porter, please."

The secretary was startled by the appearance of the police chief and wondered if one of their students had done something wrong. "Just a moment," she said.

Trey waited as she went to let her boss know he was there. Then the outer door to Will Porter's office opened, and he was standing in the doorway.

"Chief Jakes, come in," Will said, and stepped aside as Trey walked in. "Have a seat."

Will was suddenly anxious. He'd finally made a decision to run for state superintendent and had been in the act of filling out the paperwork when Trey Jakes arrived. Now he was wondering why a cop was sitting in his office.

"Now, what can I do for you?" he asked.

"Do you have back copies of the high school yearbooks? Particularly the 1980 yearbook?" Trey asked.

Will's eyes widened.

"I don't think the school does, but I have one at home," Will said. "I would be glad to loan it to you."

"That would be much appreciated," Trey said. "Can I stop by the house and pick it up?"

Will frowned. Even though it was early in the day, God only knew what shape his wife would be in.

"My wife isn't home right now, so why don't I run by the house and pick it up? I'll drop it off at the precinct for you, okay?"

Trey nodded. "Thank you, Mr. Porter. I'll make sure to return it as soon as we've gotten the information we need."

"This has to do with the murders, doesn't it?" Will asked.

"Yes, sir, it does," Trey said.

"Do you think someone from my class is doing this?"

Trey shrugged. "I think it has to do with the school. Whether it has to do with your class or not is another subject."

"I don't know what I think, except that what's happened is a tragedy," Will said.

"That it is," Trey said. "So I won't keep you any longer. Thank you for your help," he added as he stood. "Don't get up, I'll let myself out."

As soon as Trey was gone, Will grabbed his keys and left his office, only pausing for a moment to tell his secretary where he was going, and then hurried home.

It was nearly 11:00 a.m. when Sam Jakes came around the curve in the road and saw the Mystic city-limits sign. He'd done this so many times in his dreams that there was a part of him that thought he was still dreaming, that he wasn't actually there.

Then he passed a man walking down the side of the road with a stringer of fish over his shoulder and not only identified the kind of fish the man had caught but also recognized the face. It was one of the Pryor brothers who lived up on the mountain. This had never been part of the dream. This had to be real.

He drove into town with a knot in his belly, and the farther he went, the bigger it grew. He slowed down as he passed the police precinct but didn't stop and kept driving north until he saw the motel.

He was stiff from the drive and stood for a few moments after he got out, stretching his legs and letting the muscles relax. After he entered he paused at the counter, thinking the woman looked familiar, and then realized this was going to be a continuing thing. Just because he'd left Mystic didn't mean everyone else had, too.

"Welcome to Mystic," she said, and then gasped.

"Sam Jakes! Oh, my word! It's been ages." Then her expression fell. "I'm sorry. I'm so sorry."

"Thank you," Sam said. "I think Trey reserved a room for me." He slid a credit card across the counter.

"Yes, he did, but he didn't say it was for you. You don't remember me, do you? I'm Delia Summers. Your mother was one of my best friends."

Sam eyed her closer, seeing the woman she'd been beneath the extra weight and white hair.

"Yes, now I do. It's good to see you again," he said.

She scanned the credit card, gave it back and then handed him the room key.

"Room 130. It's around back, which will give you a little more privacy."

He was surprised by her thoughtfulness.

"I appreciate it, Mrs. Summers."

"Delia! Please! And give Trey my best. We all have Trina in our prayers."

He left the office and drove around back and easily found the door to his room. He swiped the key card and was pleasantly surprised by the quality of the furnishings as he went in. It had a tan carpet, brown-and-gold bedding and tan-and-gold curtains.

He left his suitcase on the bed and sent Trey a text that he was in town. Now that he was there, he felt the need to hurry and get to Trina. He washed up in haste, and when he saw Trey hadn't returned the text, he began to worry. Being chief of police in your own hometown had to have its own set of challenges.

By the time he got to the hospital he had a knot in his stomach. Hospitals made him antsy anyway, and having his sister in critical condition made it worse. Last night's rain had left puddles in the parking lot, and from the look of the sky it appeared more rain was imminent.

He was walking toward the hospital when his phone signaled a text. It was Trey.

I'm just leaving the high school. I'll be there soon. Lee will fill you in. He's Trina's boyfriend.

Sam frowned as he reached the entrance. Damn it to hell but he hated hospitals. He took a deep breath, walked inside like he owned the place and headed for the information desk.

A uniformed volunteer smiled at him as he approached.

"Ma'am, how do I get to ICU?" he asked.

She pointed down the hall. "Take the elevator up to the third floor, take a right and go all the way to the end of the hall."

"Thank you," Sam said, and headed down the hall. Three women were already waiting at the elevator when he walked up. They turned out of curiosity. While he didn't recognize any of them, they obviously knew who he was.

The elevator opened, and he followed them on, pressed the button for the third floor and then moved all the way to the back of the car.

A thin brunette was the first to speak. She was clutching her purse against her chest like a shield as she turned around.

"You have my sympathies," she said.

An older woman nodded. "And mine," she added, while eyeing him from head to toe.

The third woman was a buxom blonde whose gaze was more intent and less into consolation. "Long time, no see, Sam," she said.

"I'm sorry, you ladies have me at a disadvantage," he said.

"We're Harpers," the blonde one said. "Wilma is our mother, Wilda here is my younger sister and I'm Wynona."

He had a vague memory of skinny kids running wild along the creek.

"You lived across the creek from my parents' farm," Sam said.

Wilma nodded. "We still do. We're so sorry to hear

about your mama. This whole killing business has been horrible. Just horrible. I haven't had one good night's sleep since they found Dick Phillips hanging in his barn."

Sam flinched. Obviously one of the details Trey had yet to fill him in on.

The elevator stopped on two and the women got off.

"It was good to see you again," Wynona said, and then winked.

Sam's phone rang just as the door closed between them. He noticed it was from the office and let it go. He'd already told his secretary to cancel his appointments until further notice. Whatever was happening, it could wait.

He got off the elevator on the third floor and headed down the hall just like the lady had said, following the signs to ICU.

The nurse on duty at the desk looked up.

"What room is Trina Jakes in?" he asked.

"What's your name, please?" she asked.

He frowned. "I'm her brother Sam."

"Could I see some identification, please?" she asked.

His frown deepened as he handed his license to her.

She checked it against a list, then handed it back with an apology.

"I'm sorry, but we're under orders from the chief of police to limit her visitors to immediate family only, and I'm new to Mystic and don't know anyone."

Good call, little brother. "It's okay. I appreciate your diligence."

"She's down that way in 12B. There'll be a guard at her door who will probably ID you, as well."

Sam heard her, but he had begun to hear what was going on in here, as well, and when the skin tightened on the back of his neck, reminding him of all the time he'd spent in ICU, he knew it was going to be a hard visit to make.

He lengthened his stride and saw a man standing guard by a door. Room 12B.

"Sam Jakes. I'm here to see my sister," he said and flipped open his wallet, letting the guard see his private investigator license as well as his ID.

The guard looked closely at both before he gave the okay for Sam to go in.

"Good to meet you, Mr. Jakes. I'm Mike Cantrell with Embry Security. Visiting will end at noon and resume again at 2:00 p.m."

"Thanks," Sam said and entered the room.

As he did, the young, dark-haired man sitting beside her bed suddenly stood.

"I'm guessing you're Lee," Sam said.

The man nodded.

"I'm Sam Jakes. Nice to meet you."

"It's nice to meet you, too, sir," Lee said. "I'm going to step outside and give you some time with Trina. She's in a drug-induced coma, so don't worry about her not responding to anything you say. The doctor said she's holding her own. That's the update."

He eyed Sam curiously as he left the room, and Sam could only imagine what he was thinking—probably something along the lines of *Where the hell did* he *come from?*

Four

Sam's hand was shaking as he reached for Trina's arm. This was a slap-in-the-face wake-up call to point out what he'd been missing. She'd grown up and nearly died before he could get his ass home, and right now he couldn't remember even one good reason why it had taken him so long.

"Hey, little sister. It's me. Sam. I don't know who did this to you yet, but I promise we'll find him. Just get well and know we love you very much."

During the time he'd been in the hospital he'd gotten good at deciphering the readings on the various pieces of medical equipment, and from what he could see Trina appeared to be stable, so she was doing her part. But being back in this hospital made him remember all the times his mother had come to see him. All the nights she'd stayed at his side, the tears she'd shed listening to him scream as the doctors began to debride his burns. His family had been there for him. All this time he'd thought he was protecting them by isolating himself, when it appeared he'd hurt them much more with his absence. He swallowed past the

knot in his throat, determined not to cry, and was so
lost in thought that he didn't hear the footsteps behind him. Then he felt the pat on his back, and his
vision blurred.

He turned, saw the weariness and the grief in his
brother's eyes, and in that moment their mother's
death was finally real. "I am so sorry," he said.

"So am I, Sam," Trey said, and hugged him, taking comfort from the strength in his brother's grip.

"You have hell on your hands, don't you?" Sam
said.

"Yes, and I don't know why," Trey said. "It's noon,
which means they're going to run us out of here for
a couple of hours. I need to swing by the precinct
to pick up Dallas, and then we can go to lunch and
catch up."

Sam looked back at Trina, and then leaned down
and kissed her cheek. "Be strong, little sister."

"We'll be back," Trey added.

They walked out together with a nod to the guard,
and left the hospital.

Dallas was on the computer in Trey's office when
he and Sam walked in.

"Hey," Trey said.

She looked up, then smiled when she realized Sam
had arrived.

"Sam. I am *so* glad you're here," she said, and got
up to give him a hug. "It's been a long time. You look
good," she added.

"Not as good as you," Sam said, and hugged her
back. "I understand congratulations are in order."

She turned the engagement ring on her finger.

"Thanks." Then her eyes welled. "Betsy was so happy Trey and I were together again. She kept talking about weddings and grandchildren and—"

Sam shoved his hands into his pockets. "I'm glad someone made her happy, because it damn sure wasn't me," he said.

Trey frowned. "Don't do that, Sam. She wasn't *unhappy* with you. There's a difference. She accepted your reasoning as sound, figured you knew yourself better than anyone else, and none of us ever heard a complaint about it from her."

It didn't change the fact that Sam felt as if he'd let her down, but it was good to know his mother had understood his fears.

Dallas shoved the hair back from her face as she sat back down. "I've begun working on the list you gave me," she said to Trey.

Trey showed Sam the 1980 yearbook from Mystic High School.

"I borrowed this from Will Porter. He was in the class of 1980, too. We're going through the list of graduates, trying to find out where they all are, so we can start eliminating them as possible suspects."

Sam sat down on the other side of the desk as Trey started pacing. He'd done that ever since he was a kid. When he was thinking something out, he paced.

"My first question is, why do you think the killer's someone from their graduating class?" Sam asked.

"Something we found after Paul Jackson was murdered. When we went through his lockbox in the bank, he left a letter and a bloody tassel in an envelope for his son. The tassel came from a 1980 graduate, but it didn't belong to any of the four who were involved in the wreck."

"Okay, so if no one else is murdered, then we can assume that it does have something to do with that wreck they were in, right?" Sam said. "Otherwise, if more people are targeted, that would remove the wreck aspect."

Trey nodded. "Yes. We believe Trina was shot only because she would have been a witness the killer couldn't afford. Mom thought the murders had to do with something they saw the night they graduated. Once she mentioned dreaming about seeing a body. I asked her if she thought she'd been a witness or an accessory to a killing."

Sam flinched.

"You actually asked Mom if she'd killed someone?" Trey's chin jutted defensively.

"More or less. Yes, she was my mother, but I'm also the chief of police, and I was trying to solve Paul Jackson's murder. She told me she dreamed the four of them saw a body. She thought they were on their way to report it when they wrecked. She gave me a journal she'd been keeping of the dreams. A couple of times she wrote something about the four of them seeing someone die, and then being chased."

"My God," Sam said. "All those years, and that was locked inside her memory."

"Apparently," Trey said, and then glanced at Dallas. "How's it going?"

"Slow. About half the class moved away."

"I want to know where all of them live now," Trey said.

"What about the ones who live here?" Sam asked.

"What about them?" Trey asked.

"You should confront them when they're together. I've found that once you get a bunch of people together, if they have something to hide, one of them will say something that opens a floodgate."

Trey glanced up at the clock. "The paper goes to press at three," he said. "I just might have time to get a request in for tomorrow's issue."

"Tell me what you want said. I'll take it over there myself," Sam offered.

"Wait," Dallas said. "Let me pull up a blank screen and I'll type it for you."

"Tell me when you're ready," Trey said.

She nodded. "Ready."

"Chief Trey Jakes requests the presence of every graduate of the class of 1980 still living in the area at City Hall day after tomorrow at noon. They will be interrogated regarding the night of their high school graduation. Anyone who doesn't appear will be brought into the precinct for questioning at a later date. As a reminder to all, there is a ten-thousand-dollar reward for information leading to the arrest and conviction of the person responsible for the murders of Dick Phillips, Paul Jackson and Betsy Jakes."

Dallas's fingers were flying over the keyboard as she typed. Then she finished and read it back to him. When he okayed it, she printed it out and handed it to Sam.

"The paper is still in the same place," she said.

"I saw it," Sam said, and settled the Stetson a little more firmly on his head as he left the room.

His stride was long, his steps sure as he left the precinct and headed down the street. He could have driven the three blocks, but it felt good to be walking somewhere.

Trey had filled him in on the details of all the murders, even the condition of his mother's body when he'd found her. He was still reeling from the knowledge and imagining his brother's horror.

He paused at a stop sign before he crossed a street, and saw the look of recognition on a driver's face before he honked and waved.

Sam nodded and kept on walking.

A few minutes later he entered the newspaper office and recognized the man behind the desk.

"Afternoon, Mr. Sherman. I have a notice that Chief Jakes needs you to run in tomorrow's paper."

Glen Sherman frowned. "We're about ready to put the paper to bed."

"It's important," Sam said. "It concerns the murders."

Sherman's expression shifted. "Let me see it."

Sam handed it over and watched the changing expressions on the editor's face.

"Tell him I'll run it on the front page. My headline didn't amount to shit anyway."

"Thank you," Sam said.

"You're Sam Jakes, aren't you?" Sherman asked.

Sam nodded.

"I'm real sorry about Betsy. She was a friend. I heard your sister came out of surgery okay. How's she doing?"

"So far, so good," Sam said. "I'll pass the message on to my brother, and thank you for the placement. Maybe it will rattle a few memories."

Sherman grimaced. "Most likely skeletons," he

said. "They're always around if people care to look, and ten thousand dollars makes for a lot of incentive."

Sam was still thinking about that comment as he walked back to the precinct. Rattling skeletons. Maybe he could rattle some nerves tomorrow while they were at it.

That evening Sam was in the lobby of Cutter's Steakhouse waiting on Trey and Dallas to come in from the farm.

Nearly everyone who entered did a double take, recognizing him as the hometown boy who had gone away to war and never come home.

Many of them spoke. A few of them just stared and passed him by. He felt their judgment and knew it was fair. He should have come when Betsy was still alive, not waited until it was time to bury her. There was nothing he could do to change what was, except to help his brother find who killed her.

He'd just received a text from Dallas telling him they were on the way when a family walked in. The man nodded cordially but without recognition before looking at him again.

"Sam Jakes?"

Sam stood and shook the banker's hand. "Evening, Mr. Standish."

"It's been a long time. Our condolences on the loss of your mother. It's a tragedy. A true tragedy," Standish said.

"Yes, sir."

"And how is your sister?" Mrs. Standish asked.

Sam remembered the wife's face but not her name,

and assumed the young girl with them was their daughter. "She's holding her own."

"That's wonderful news. I'll make it a point to visit her soon."

"Thank you for the thought, but Trey has her under guard, with a no-visitation order. I'm sure you understand."

Gloria sputtered a bit, as if shocked that she'd been refused in any way.

"Of course we do," Standish said. "Her survival has put the killer on notice."

Carly Standish had been politely quiet while the adults spoke, but she hadn't missed a thing about Sam Jakes' appearance. She thought he was good-looking for an older guy, except for the scars she could see on the back of his neck.

Sam caught her staring, which made her flush.

"I think our table is ready," Standish said. "Ladies…"

They had no sooner walked away than the door opened again, and Marcus and T. J. Silver walked in.

Marcus Silver was about to walk past Sam when T.J. saw him and stopped.

"Sam Jakes, right?"

Sam nodded.

"Dad. It's Trey's older brother."

Marcus's eyes widened. "I'm sorry, I didn't recognize you."

"No problem," Sam said. "It's been a while since I've been home."

T.J. frowned. "I'm so sorry about what happened to your mother and sister."

"Thank you," Sam said.

"Yes, our sympathies are with all the family," Marcus added.

The door opened again, and this time it was finally Trey and Dallas who arrived.

"Sorry we're late," Trey said, and nodded toward the Silvers. "Marcus, T.J., it appears we all had the same idea tonight."

"Yes, it does. Enjoy your meal," Marcus said, and then headed for the hostess desk with his son.

"Everything okay?" Sam asked.

Trey shook his head. "The digital version of the newspaper is already up, and I've been getting phone calls like crazy. Everyone in town wants to come to the meeting day after tomorrow," Trey said.

"What did you tell them?" Sam asked.

"I told them unless they had specific knowledge and information to share, it was only for the members of that class."

"Good call," Sam said.

"Let's go eat, guys," Dallas said. "Tomorrow is going to be crazy, but tonight we can just be family."

There was a knot in Sam's throat as they were being seated. Dallas's innocent remark about just being family had gone straight to his heart. All these years while he was living on the edge of life, they had been completely immersed in it—joys, heartaches, rejections, accomplishments. Now, thinking about what he'd lost, Lainey Pickett was at the top of the list.

As they ordered their food, talking about what they had yet to face and what they hoped to uncover during the meeting, Sam was wondering what would happen if he tried to fit back in—if he should even try to fit back in—wondering if they would resent him after the way he'd kept them all at arm's length.

Lainey was in bed with her laptop and a beer.

After her conversation with Dallas, her curiosity had been piqued. She was reading through back issues of the Mystic newspaper in an effort to catch up on what had been happening.

She had a whole new level of empathy for Dallas after learning how her father had died, and what she'd been through afterward that had nothing to do with the murder. Attacked by a feral dog, running for her life from criminals in hiding on her property and all the while determined to prove her father had not committed suicide. When Lainey got to the discovery of Paul Jackson's body, she was struck by the cold-blooded way the murder had been committed. The killer would have had to stand and watch Paul being crushed to make sure he was dead.

The bottle of beer was empty by the time she got to the story about Betsy and Trina being ambushed, and for her, it struck closest to home. She'd imagined being part of their family most of her life, picturing Betsy as her mother-in-law and Trina as the sister she'd never had. When she began reading about the shooting and discovered that Trey was the one who'd found them, she burst into tears.

She started out crying for the Jakeses and ended up crying for herself from the shock and grief of being abandoned by the man she loved, to the ensuing years of loneliness and the day she was diagnosed, all the way through to the last day of chemo. She cried until her eyes were swollen and her head was throbbing before she staggered into the bathroom to get something for the pain.

After that she wandered through the house, straightening a picture hanging on the wall, fluffing pillows on the living room sofa, gathering up a glass and bowl she'd left on a side table, loading the dishwasher and then making sure everything was locked up for the night.

Finally the lights were out in the front of the house, except for the night-light in the hall. She wandered back into her bedroom and got back in bed, then picked up the laptop. She started to click out of the paper's site, then decided to see if there were any new articles relating to the crimes.

The headline for the digital issue of tomorrow's paper caught her eye.

GRADUATES OF CLASS OF 1980

The subhead was a shock.

MANDATORY MEETING AT CITY HALL

The hair stood up on the back of her neck as she read the notice posted by Chief Jakes, and then a more inclusive story the editor had added to it. As difficult as it was to grasp, the police were convinced that the three murders were tied to the night the victims all graduated high school, which was why all of the classmates had been summoned.

Lainey's heart skipped a beat. Her mother, Billie, had been a member of that class, but her mother was dead. Would she have known anything? Had she heard any gossip that would shed light on this mystery? And then she remembered her mother's diaries. She'd been obsessive about writing in them on a regular basis when she was younger. Lainey remembered reading from them all the time when she was growing up and then talking to her mother about her life. Oh, how they had laughed. For Lainey, it had the feel of being a child *with* her mother instead of just reading about her at that age. But now that she'd remembered them, and now that she understood the seriousness of the meeting, she couldn't let go of the idea that there might be something in them that would help.

She set the laptop aside again and moved back through the house, turning on lights until she got to the hallway between the utility room and the kitchen, heading for the stairs leading to the attic. They were the old-fashioned kind that pulled down from the ceiling. She grasped the short dangling rope above her head and gave it a yank, then walked backward as the stairs unfolded at her feet. The light switch in the hall turned on the floodlight in the attic above.

She hadn't been up here in over a year, and as she reached the top she could easily see the thin layer of dust covering the floor and most of the boxes. She knew where the diaries were because she'd packed them away herself after her mother's death. In fact, she'd packed them away in chronological order, so she knew exactly where she would find the one she wanted.

The boxes stacked against the north wall were all labeled Diaries, so she began to look for the one from the year 1980. As soon as she found the right box, she scooted it across the floor to the stairs, then backed down one step at a time, balancing the box in front of her as she went.

It was now after midnight, but she knew she would never be able to sleep until she was satisfied there was nothing in those diaries that would matter, so she wiped the dust from the box, removed the lid and dug through until she found the volume that began with Billie's senior year, as well as the ensuing two diaries that had everything else through the night of graduation.

This time, when she went back to her bedroom, she had the diaries in one hand and a cold bottle of Pepsi in the other.

She crawled back into bed, took a drink of the pop, opened the first diary and began to read.

It was the wind blowing a branch against the side of the house that woke Lainey the next morning. She rolled over onto her back, wondering why she was sleeping at the foot of the bed, and then saw the diaries and remembered. She glanced at the time and sat up with a groan.

She headed for the bathroom to shower, and was so anxious about the day ahead and getting all her lesson plans done that for once she paid no attention to her too-thin body or the scars on her chest where her breasts used to be. And when she got out of the shower to dry her hair, it was so short that it didn't take long. Other than the fact that she was beginning to panic about seeing Sam again, the day passed without consequence.

She went to bed and set the alarm, then dreamed all night that she was trying to find Sam. In the dream, everywhere she looked he was already gone. She woke up frustrated and anxious, then headed to the bathroom to get ready for the meeting.

She could already tell the day was going to be cold, because the house was chilly. When she went back to her room to get dressed she turned up the thermostat in the hall. Her clothes didn't fit well anymore, but she managed to cope. She put on a pair of blue jeans and a thick sweater. Her jeans were held up by a belt, and the cable-knit weave of the loose sweater helped hide her flat chest.

It was 11:00 a.m. by the time she headed out the door. It would take about fifteen to twenty minutes to get to Mystic unless traffic delayed her. The meeting began at noon. If she didn't get a chance to catch Trey before he went into City Hall, she would have to wait until it was over. Either way, she would feel better knowing she'd done her part.

The day was cold, the wind sharp enough to bring tears, as people began filing into Mystic City Hall. They walked with their heads down, their shoulders hunched against the weather, but it made them appear as if they all had something to hide.

Trey was already inside. He had his officer Earl Redd guarding the entrance to the meeting, with orders to keep out the curiosity seekers.

Sam and Trey had made a plan, and Sam was in his car, parked at the back of the courthouse until closer to the time for the meeting to start.

Lainey had the diaries in her hand as she ran up the front steps and inside, then quickly explained her reason for being there to Officer Redd, who let her into the courtroom. She slipped into the room and took a seat in the back just as Trey walked up to the front to begin the meeting. He had an updated list from Dallas regarding the people who still lived in the area, and would know if anyone was missing.

As Trey turned to face the group, he glanced out the windows and saw Sam on the sidewalk. His entrance should rattle the group. It was time to get started.

"Thank you for coming. Beginning with you on the end, tell me your name at the time of graduation, so I can check you off the list."

He pointed straight at Marcus Silver, and Marcus promptly replied. Then Gregory Standish, then Will Porter, and on through the crowd until he noticed Lainey Pickett in the back of the room and frowned.

"Lainey?"

"I'm here on behalf of my mother, Billie Conway. She kept diaries. I brought the ones pertaining to her senior year."

Trey's heart skipped. Something must be in them or she wouldn't have come. Before he could say anything else, the doors at the back of the room opened, and everyone turned to look as Sam Jakes came in and strode straight down the aisle toward Trey, glaring at everyone he saw.

Lainey could tell from his expression that he didn't see her, but she saw him, the wide set of his shoulders beneath his coat, the dark brown Stetson on his head, and struggled with the urge to run. Then he reached the front and turned to face the crowd, and she lifted her chin and stared back, waiting for him to see her.

Sam looked out across the room, meeting gaze after gaze, waiting until each person looked away before moving on to the next. Then he saw the woman at the back of the room. Stunned by her presence, he was the first to turn his gaze elsewhere.

Then Trey began to speak, saving him.

"All of you know my brother, Sam. He owns Ranger Investigations in Atlanta, and he's come home to help me find a killer, which is also why you're here. You're going to help us find him, too."

"What makes you think it's a man?" Will Porter asked.

"Because Dick Phillips was over six feet tall and weighed two hundred and five pounds, and there are precious few women anywhere in the world who could lift that much dead weight and hang it from the rafters of a barn."

Will flushed. "Yes, of course. I didn't think," he mumbled.

"Well, I *have* thought," Trey said. "I've done nothing *but* think ever since this nightmare began, and this is what I know. Something happened the night of your high school graduation. I believe Connie and Betsy and their boyfriends Dick and Paul witnessed a crime, and we think it had to do with at least one of your classmates, because police found a bloody tassel in Paul Jackson's pocket the night of the wreck, and it didn't belong to him or anyone else in the car. Theirs were all accounted for. My mother dreamed about seeing a dead body, but she never saw a face. I believe they wrecked because they were trying to get back to Mystic to tell what they saw. I know they were going too fast when the car left the road, and the logical explanation for driving so recklessly was because they were being chased."

"Or the fact that they were drunk," someone muttered.

"Oh, yes, we know that, but that doesn't explain the bloody tassel. It's being tested for DNA, by the way."

People were beginning to shift nervously in their seats, which was exactly what Sam had been waiting for.

"One of you knows something, and your silence has aided a killer in getting away with murder...three times for sure, and maybe a fourth back then. Is that how you want to be remembered? Talk to me, damn it!"

Lainey stood up, holding the diaries against her chest.

"My mother is gone, but her words are not. She kept diaries. I have them, starting from when she was nine all the way through her first year of college."

Sam saw her lips moving, but he couldn't focus on what she was saying for looking at the desolation in her eyes.

"Is there anything in there that you think would help us?" Trey asked.

"A couple of things, I think. I'll leave them with you, of course, as long as I can have them back at some point. The first thing that caught my attention was her writing about gossip flying through the school about cheating on tests. I teach history at the University of West Virginia, so I'm aware that's an ongoing issue, but according to my mother's entries, it pertained to the senior class specifically."

Sam shifted focus. "Was it true? Was someone cheating?"

The room was silent.

"She mentioned names," Lainey said, and just like that the room erupted.

Five

Sam was elated. This was exactly what he'd hoped would happen. Everyone wanted to tell their side of the story before someone else accused them of doing the cheating.

"Hey! Shut the hell up!" he shouted.

Lainey flinched. The power in his voice surprised her and obviously startled the others because the room went quiet.

Trey held up the list Dallas had given him.

"Dallas has been checking the whereabouts of your classmates. There are a few names we still can't verify. I'm going to read them off, and if anyone knows anything, speak up."

"Harold Martin."

Will Porter raised his hand. "He was in Sarasota, Florida. He died about ten years ago."

Trey nodded and marked him off. "Charlotte Marshall," he said.

"She's in Washington, DC. Retired. Lives with her youngest son and family," a lady offered.

Trey marked her off, and one by one, he went through the list until they were down to only two.

"Anthony Castle."

Greg Standish held up a hand. "He's a Catholic priest, and last time I heard was living in Bolivia running an orphanage."

"One more here, and then the rest of them are all sitting in this room. What about Donny Collins?"

The room was silent.

Sam glanced back at where Lainey had been sitting, and his heart sank. He needed to talk to her, but she'd slipped out of the room.

"Anyone? Donny Collins?" Trey asked again.

They were all shaking their heads.

"Last time I saw him he was giving the salutatorian address," a woman said. "Donny was smart."

"So what about the cheating?" Trey asked. "What do you know?"

One by one, they admitted they'd heard about it, but they all had the same story. No one had known who was involved. And then a woman Trey recognized as one of his mother's friends raised her hand to speak.

"I can't believe cheating on a test would ever be a reason to kill someone. I mean...what would be gained if someone told and what would be lost if someone was found out? Just a bad grade, that's all. At least that's what it would have been back then. It sure wasn't something worth dying for."

"That's not always the case to the people involved," Sam said. "You said Donny Collins was salutatorian. Who was valedictorian?"

Marcus Silver raised his hand. "I was."

Sam nodded. "So what did you have to gain by being valedictorian?"

"Nothing," Marcus said.

Then a woman stood up. "That's not true. There was that five-thousand-dollar scholarship."

Sam watched the man's face for a sign of guilt but saw nothing.

"At the risk of bragging about my family's status, my father was well-to-do and you know it. I didn't need the scholarship to go to school. It was already paid for," Marcus said.

Sam glanced at Trey and could tell his brother was satisfied with that answer.

"So Donny was salutatorian. What did he get?" Sam said.

"There wasn't any money for salutatorian," Will Porter said.

Sam stood there with his hands on his hips, staring at the faces of people he'd known all his life, trying to picture one of them being a cold-blooded killer, and couldn't do it.

"Look," Sam said. "Here's the deal. No matter what you think you're hiding by staying silent, the truth is going to come out, and when it does, whoever has been hiding what they know is likely to be charged with aiding and abetting. So when you go home today, ask yourself if keeping a secret is worth losing your freedom."

There was a gasp from the back of the room, and then everyone went silent.

Trey guessed they'd stirred up all the ghosts he could stir today, and he wanted them to leave here as unsettled as they could possibly be.

"Just so you know, I'm pretty disgusted by the lack of compassion you're all showing. Dick Phillips wouldn't have stayed quiet. Paul Jackson would have told. Betsy Jakes was trying to remember. It haunted her sleep until the day she died. They would have done anything they had to do in the name of justice for you. Someone hanged Dick from the rafters of his own barn. He wasn't dead when they strung him up. They broke his neck by yanking down on his legs."

A woman in the front of the room moaned, and then began to cry.

Trey kept pushing them.

"Paul Jackson was working late doing someone a favor. The killer, being the coward he is, used the familiarity of his face to catch Paul off guard. Paul died from a crushed skull. My mother knew she was a target. She didn't want to die, but she also wasn't going to hide." Trey's voice started to shake. "The son of a bitch shot half her face off, and I was the one who found her. My sister is hanging on to life by a thread right now because she was in the wrong place at the wrong time, and one of you knows something you're not telling."

Everyone in the room was visibly moved.

Sam jumped in before Trey lost his composure.

"If anyone knows anything, you better tell it now, because if I find out who did it and learn that any of you knew and kept quiet, I will make it my personal business to see you behind bars." Then he waved his hand. "We're done here."

Not one word was spoken as the old classmates got up and walked out of the meeting, and when they exited City Hall and came face-to-face with half the town watching them exit—waiting for news—they started trying to get away.

People began crowding around them, talking, pushing, trying to get the lowdown.

Glen Sherman was asking everyone who walked past him if they would give him an interview, but no one was talking.

Trey and Sam were the last to exit, and Trey saw Sherman heading straight for him just as his phone rang. He spoke briefly to the caller. "I'm on my way," he said, and then grabbed Sam's arm. "I've got an emergency. I'll talk to you later."

Sam nodded.

Glen Sherman frowned. "Is there anything either one of you would like to say?" he asked.

Sam paused. "I guess there's one thing that was said in the meeting that needs to be repeated."

Sherman pressed a button on his cell phone to record the statement, and then held it close to Sam. "Go ahead," he said.

"We'll find out the truth whether someone helps us or not, and when we do, whoever is keeping secrets to protect the killer is going to wind up in prison for aiding and abetting a murderer."

"Thank you," Glen said, and then he added, "You know, Betsy was real proud of you. She talked about all her kids all the time, but she had a special place in her heart for you, I think."

Sam was shocked, listening in disbelief as Glen continued.

"She always said you were most like Justin, and you know how much she loved your daddy. She said you took on more burdens than you needed to in an effort to protect everyone you loved. Anyway…thanks for the statement." With that, he hurried back toward the newspaper office.

Sam watched him go, trying to find the impetus to move.

Lainey drove home in a daze, barely aware of the tiny snowflakes that were beginning to fall. She'd dropped the diaries in the officer's hands and left City Hall on the run, pushing her way through the crowd outside, ignoring their comments and stares. Right now it hurt to breathe, and tears kept blurring her vision.

He'd finally come home—ten years late, but he was here. Sam. Her Sam. He'd gone away a boy and come home some kind of warrior. He scared her, and at the same time she thought she would die from the pain of wanting him. Damn him to hell and back for quitting her like he did. All these years she'd thought she was over him, and right now she felt as if she'd suffered a beating.

The snow was falling a little heavier by the time she got home. She drove into the garage, and then went inside, upping the thermostat as she went to her room to change. She wanted warmer clothing, and turned on the light in her closet so she could see to find what she wanted from the cedar chest.

She sorted through the folded sweaters and winter slacks until she found the sweatshirt she was look-ing for and began to pull it out. But it was hung up on something, and she stopped before it made a hole in the fabric. The moment she realized it was caught on the corner of a picture frame, her heart sank. She knew which picture it was and remembered all too well packing it away. It was the height of irony that this would happen today of all days.

She pulled it out and stared.

It was a picture of her and Sam taken only days before he'd left for boot camp. They had been on a picnic down at the family pond with Trey and Dallas. She could still hear Dallas's giggles as she kept telling Sam to stand still. As usual, he had ignored what she said and swooped Lainey up into his arms just as the picture was snapped. Lainey's feet were up, her head was falling back against his arm and she was reaching for him with one hand, thinking he was going to drop her. And she was laughing.

Lainey kept staring at her face, remembering the joy. Then she noticed Sam's expression, and it broke her heart. He was looking at her with so much love.

Her heart was pounding now, and it hurt to even breathe.

Damn that war.

Damn Sam Jakes for not trusting her love.

She rolled over on her side, pulling the shirt and the photo against her like a pillow, and cried herself to sleep.

The killer was anxious and trying to hide it. Knowing that the police were slowly putting clues together was nerve-racking, and learning about Billie Conway's diaries had been a shocker. Definitely not something he had expected or prepared for. His only saving grace was that they were focused on one angle while he was coming from another. If he could just silence Trina Jakes, his troubles would be over, and he had an idea for how to make that happen.

* * *

Sam stepped out of the hospital elevator and into the lobby with a heavy heart. It was getting dark, and the snow was falling faster now. It was close to Thanksgiving, but a little early for this kind of weather.

Trina was no better, but she was also no worse.

He'd stood at her bedside watching her breathe until he couldn't take it any longer, and seeing the way Lee was with her made him realize something else. Lee was there regardless of the consequences of her condition. *He* needed to be with *her*. He needed to know in his heart that he was doing all he could to give her strength and courage to fight her way back to them, while *he* had never given Lainey that chance.

When he had returned stateside, he'd been so hurt in mind and body that he had mentally crawled into a shell. He'd lied to himself, believing no one would want anything to do with him. It wasn't so much that he'd feared she would be disgusted by his wounds. It was more about how disgusted he had been with himself. And now here they were, ten years later, and because of him, they were still in limbo.

He walked out into the snow, heading for his car. He hadn't eaten any dinner, but he wasn't hungry, either. All he wanted was a shower and a bed. Maybe he could sleep away some of this heartache.

The drive to the motel was brief. He pulled around back, parking beneath one of the security lights, and when he got out, the snow swirled around him like bugs swarming beneath a streetlight. He ducked his head and made a run for the door. Once inside his room, he shed his hat and coat, kicked off his boots, got his handgun from the suitcase and stretched out on the bed. He laid his phone on his belly and turned on the television, and within minutes he had fallen asleep.

"What's Mama doing?"

Sam frowned at his little brother. "Shh. She'll hear us."

Trey leaned closer to Sam's ear and whispered, "But what's she doing?"

Sam was watching their mama put two boxes up on the top shelf in her closet. He knew she was hiding their Christmas presents. He'd found out a couple of years ago that Mom and Dad were really Santa, but Trey was younger and still believed, so he wasn't going to tell.

They watched her step away from the closet, and when she shut the door it squeaked loudly. The boys jumped at the unexpected noise, and then, fearing they had been found out, they hightailed it back to their room and into bed. They heard her coming down the hall, and when she peeked in on them moments later they were bunched up beneath the covers in their usual places, seemingly dead to the world.

A loud squeak sounded outside Sam's motel room, and he sat up with a jerk and grabbed his gun, ready to shoot whoever was coming in the door. And then he realized the squeak was from the wheels of someone's suitcase being rolled past his room. It was five minutes after 4:00 a.m., and he'd come close to shooting someone.

"Son of a bitch," he muttered, then set the gun aside and shoved his hands through his hair. He heard the heating unit come on and realized the room was chilly, so he got out of bed, turned up the heat a little and looked out to see if it was still snowing, which it wasn't, and then headed for the bathroom.

When he came back, he took off his jeans and shirt and got between the covers. He tried to go back to sleep, but he couldn't get the dream out of his head and tried to remember what she'd hidden. He thought it was new cowboy boots for the both of them but wasn't sure. He hadn't thought of that night in years and chalked it up to coming back to Mystic. That was resurrecting all kinds of memories.

He rolled onto his side and pulled the covers up over his shoulders and closed his eyes. And as he did, he remembered the expression he'd seen on Lainey's face in the courtroom. She hated him. He didn't blame her. But he had to talk to her. Tomorrow. He would do it tomorrow. No, it was already tomorrow. He didn't know where she lived, but that was no problem. He found people for a living. He could surely find her, too.

It was after nine when Sam woke up again. Someone slammed the door in the room next door, and he sat straight up in bed with the gun in his hand.

"Shit," he muttered and laid the gun on the side table as he got out of bed.

The motel bathroom was small, but the lights over the vanity were bright enough to light up Broadway. He stripped, and then paused and stared at himself, turning to the right and then back to the left, eyeing the puckered burn scars on his back and down the backs of his legs. Then he turned to face the mirror and looked again, eyeing the burns across his belly and down the fronts of his legs to just below the knees. He used to be disgusted at the sight. It had taken years for him to appreciate the simple fact of still being alive when so many of his buddies were not.

He showered quickly and shaved just as fast. Thirty minutes later he was dressed and heading out the door. The wind was still sharp, and he held on to the Stetson with one hand as he headed for his SUV. He got a text from Trey as he was starting the engine and quickly put the car in Park.

Trina is the same. Dallas is home sick and I'm transporting a prisoner from here to County. Be back after noon.

Sam texted him back.

Where does Lainey Pickett live?

Where she always did.

Thanks. Safe trip.

Sam sat there looking at the words while a wash of emotion swept over him.

She was right where he'd left her.

Then he sent Trey one last text.

Is she married?

No.

He didn't know he'd been holding his breath until he saw the answer, then he let himself breathe and headed to Charlie's to eat breakfast.

* * *

Lainey woke up around midnight on the floor of her closet with a sweatshirt wadded up under her head and Sam's picture clutched against her chest. She rolled over with a groan, and then squinted against the light shining down in her eyes.

I fell asleep in the closet just from seeing Sam Jakes? What the hell will happen to me if I ever talk to him again?

Disgusted with herself for falling apart, she returned the picture to the cedar chest, kept the sweatshirt and headed for the bathroom.

When she came out, she went through the house locking doors and pulling draperies closed, then turned up the heat before going into the kitchen.

It was too early for coffee and too late for supper, but her belly was grumbling and she was already in trouble with her doctor because she'd gotten too thin. The chemo had made her sick, but that regimen was over. At this moment she was cancer-free. She still had regular checkups, and they would have to keep close watch for the next five years to make sure she didn't have a recurrence, but so be it. She'd gotten through all of this and refused to borrow trouble.

She poured a glass of milk, cut herself a generous slice of poppy-seed cake with cream-cheese frosting that she'd made last week and carried everything to the living room. After turning on the television, she scanned through the channels until she found a show about Marie Antoinette on the History Channel and decided it fit her mood. Off with their heads. Let them eat cake.

Poor Marie.

Poor Lainey, but at least she had cake.

With sweets in her tummy and her mood somewhat calmer, she carried her dishes to the kitchen then turned out lights on the way back to her bedroom. She switched her clothes for a nightgown and crawled into bed.

The moment she closed her eyes she saw Sam's face. She didn't know the man she'd seen in City Hall. He was bigger and gruff and angry. The anger she understood. It was because of Betsy. But he wasn't the hurt and broken man she'd last seen in that hospital bed. She didn't know this man, but he scared her.

She fell asleep with tears on her cheeks and woke up to daylight and a large resounding crash from somewhere outside. She jumped out of bed and raced to the window to look out. One pickup was in a ditch in front of her house, and another one was out in the pasture beside it.

Dressing quickly, she ran into the living room, dropped her phone into her old coat and went out the door, pulling on gloves as she went.

The air was cold and there was an inch of snow on the ground, but the wind from last night was gone.

She recognized the drivers of the vehicles as two of her neighbors. Both were already out of their vehicles as she ran up the drive.

"Are you guys okay?" she yelled.

"I think so," Bud Decker said.

"Yeah, I'm okay," Larry Kinney yelled back.

She eyed them closely. Both men had a penchant for making homemade wine and imbibing without caution.

"What happened?" she asked.

"Slick road," Bud said.

"No room to pass," Larry added.

She eyed the crushed front ends of both vehicles. Obviously they'd hit each other head-on, which meant neither one of them was telling the truth, but none of that was her concern.

"I'll call the sheriff," she said.

Their shoulders slumped.

"Tell him we need a couple of wreckers, too," Bud added.

Larry pointed at his car. "Sorry about your fence."

She didn't answer. She was already dialing 911.

Six

Two hours later the vehicles had been towed and a deputy from the county had taken Bud and Larry to jail for drunk driving, leaving Lainey with a fence to fix on her own. Her old horse, Dandy, was in the pasture somewhere, and she needed to get the fence back up before he had a chance to get out.

She had the fence stretcher on the ground beside her and the post driver in her hand, getting ready to replace another T-post, when she paused to rest. She hadn't begun to address the broken wire on a four-wire fence and was becoming overwhelmed with what she had left to do. Even though she was wearing gloves, her fingers were numb from the cold, and her physical strength was almost gone.

She was at the point of tears when she heard a vehicle coming down the road, and when it began to slow down and then pulled off into her driveway and stopped, she turned to look, expecting it to be a neighbor who'd come to help.

But it wasn't a neighbor.

It was Sam.

She watched him get out, settle his hat firmly on his head and start toward her. The long stride and the way one shoulder tilted down just the tiniest bit were as familiar to her as her own face. The urge to run was huge, but she stayed her ground. This was her turf, and he was the trespasser.

"Lainey."

His voice yanked a knot in her gut.

"You're obviously lost," she said, then turned her back on him and went back to work.

He stepped up beside her, slid one hand over the post driver, took it out of her hands and gently eased her aside. And she let him do it. Partly because she was shaking too hard to hold it, and partly because she wanted the fence fixed badly enough to let the devil do it if he happened to pass her way.

"What happened?" Sam asked as he set the next T-post in place and began to pound it into the ground.

"Bud Decker and Larry Kinney hit each other head-on. Bud went in the ditch. Larry went through my fence."

"Were they drunk?" Sam asked, as he set the last post and pounded it in.

"Yes."

"Some things never change," he said.

"And some things *do*," she snapped, and grabbed hold of the broken ends of the bottom wire and began patching it back together.

Sam picked up another wire and did the same. When they'd repaired all four wires, Lainey held them in place as he clipped them to the T-posts. When he was finished, she began putting her tools into the back of her ATV.

"Thank you for helping. What are you doing here?"
Sam felt her rage. "I want to talk to you."

She was pulling off her gloves as she turned and, for the first time since his arrival, looked him square in the face.

"I am so sorry for what happened to Betsy and Trina," she said, and then slapped him hard across the face. "That's for abandoning me without a fucking word, Sam Jakes."

She turned on one heel, got onto the ATV and drove off toward her barn.

Sam's cheek was stinging from the impact, but it was nothing he didn't deserve. He hadn't come expecting a party. He'd come to make peace, but he couldn't do that standing out here in the cold, so he got back in his SUV and headed for the house.

Lainey was walking up from the barn with her head down when he got there. He could tell she was crying. Seeing the end result of his desertion was even worse than he had imagined.

He knew she wouldn't open the front door for him, so he followed her into the house from the back. The fact that she let him was somewhat of a relief. Since he wasn't sure how she would react, he stopped just inside the door, feeling the warmth of the kitchen and watching as she kicked off her work boots and hung up her old coat.

She walked past him with her chin up and tears on her cheeks. He was waiting for her to give him a sign that she would hear him out when she paused at the kitchen counter, picked up a coffee mug, then spun and threw it at his head.

He ducked as it shattered on the wall behind him.

She had another one in her hand when he took a step backward, holding up his arms in a gesture of surrender.

"Please don't break any more of your dishes. I came to apologize. Hear me out, and then I'll never bother you again, if that's what you want."

"If that's what I want? *Now* you're concerned with what I want? Ten fucking years later you care what I want?"

Her voice broke on the words, but the expression in her eyes never wavered.

Everything he'd planned to say went out the window. Words would not explain him. How he'd been. What he'd become. He took a slow, shaky breath and began taking off his clothes.

Lainey thought nothing of it when he took off his coat, but when he began unbuckling his belt and then pulling at his shirt, she shouted, "Stop! What do you think you're doing?"

"There's nothing I can say that will explain why, but I can show you."

She flashed on the day she'd sneaked into his room at the hospital, remembering the bandages and all of the monitors and machines keeping him alive.

Her voice started to shake. "Don't, Sam. It doesn't change anything. You didn't trust me to love you then. Why would it make any difference now?"

His panic grew as he kept undressing. No one but his doctors and nurses had seen him like this. The more that came off, the more still she became, until she was completely motionless. She didn't flinch when he tossed his shirt on the kitchen table, and when he stepped out of his jeans and she saw the thick, ropy scars of melted flesh that covered his body, she didn't shriek, she didn't cover her eyes in disgust, and in those moments something inside him broke. She was facing his truth and standing firm. He didn't know he was crying until she threw a box of tissues at him across the room.

Stunned by her response, he caught it on reflex.

"Yes, I can see life dumped a load of shit on you," she said, and without looking at him, began taking off her sock cap, then tore off everything she had on, revealing the little cap of red curls on a head that had so recently been bald and a woman's too-thin body with scars where her breasts used to be. Then she held her arms out at her sides as if she was about to be nailed on a cross and looked up—straight at the tears rolling down his face.

"Yes…cry me a river, Sam Jakes. I cried one for you."

She never saw him move.

One moment he was across the room, and the next she was in his arms. He buried his face in the curve of her neck and just kept saying the same thing over and over.

"I'm sorry, I'm sorry, I'm so sorry."

She didn't feel the scars beneath her hands as she wrapped her arms around his neck, but she felt his tears, and she felt his body shaking beneath her grasp.

"I loved you, Sam. It wouldn't have mattered. I loved you. How could you forget that?" she cried.

"But I didn't love myself. Ah, Lainey, you don't understand. I tried so hard to die."

The words shattered her. Ten years of heartache bubbled up and came out in harsh, ugly sobs.

Sam couldn't breathe past her pain. He couldn't quit thinking that he'd done this to her. He'd wounded her heart like the war had wounded him. And he didn't even know her prognosis. Was she healed? Or was she going to die?

Without thinking, he picked her up in his arms and carried her through the house that he knew so well, down the hall and to her bedroom, to the chaos she'd left behind her when she'd been awakened by the wreck. He sat down on the bed, settled her on his lap and cried with her until there were no more tears to cry. When she was still and he could breathe without choking, he began to talk.

"After they let me out of the VA, I had PTSD so bad I nearly killed my first landlord. Mom talked him out of pressing charges. I lost three jobs because of it. I was afraid to be around the people I loved most. I was afraid I might hurt them…hurt *you*. So I figured since I couldn't work for anyone, I should work for myself."

She listened to the nightmare that had been his life with growing horror.

"And now?" she asked.

"I cope. I sleep with a handgun and my cell phone. I haven't been at the powder keg level in five years. I see a psychiatrist who works with veterans. I own a successful private investigation business. But I'm alone, Lainey. Always."

She covered her face with her hands, but she couldn't hide from his truth.

"Don't hate me," he whispered.

She looked up at him then.

"No. I won't hate you ever again," she said.

"Thank you, more than you can know."

Her shoulders slumped. Out of instinct she started to cross her arms over her breasts and then remembered they were missing, but she did it anyway, because she was too naked in his arms.

Sam saw, but instead of looking away he tilted her chin and made her look at him.

"Are you okay? What is your prognosis?"

"I'm cancer-free. I begin reconstructive surgery in a few weeks. I was waiting until the end of the semester so I'd have all of Christmas break to heal."

"You teach?"

She nodded. "World history for the University of West Virginia, online. I teach online courses from home."

"That's wonderful, Lainey."

"I like it," she said.

He threaded his fingers through hers, then noticed how fragile she appeared and was afraid that he might hurt her, so he eased his grasp.

"Your parents?"

"Dad died about a year after you came home. Mom died a couple of years back."

"And you stayed."

She nodded and looked away.

"Why?" he asked. "Didn't you ever want to see the world? See if there was something more than Mystic?"

She was struggling with words. She pushed out of his lap and grabbed a robe from the end of the bed, then turned her back to him to put it on.

"I'll be right back," Sam said, and left the room.

She could hear his footsteps moving through the house, and then a few moments of silence before she heard him coming back. When he walked into the room again he was wearing his shirt and jeans. He sat down on the side of the bed and held out a hand.

"Just talk to me."

She sat down in the rocker across from the bed.

"Why did you stay here?" he asked again.

For a moment she couldn't answer. Wasn't sure how to put what she'd done into words. Finally she leaned forward, looking straight into his eyes.

"You know how you hear about mothers whose children disappear, women whose husbands disappear, and no one ever finds out what happened? And how they refuse to leave their homes for fear that one day their loved ones will come looking for them and they'll be gone?"

Sam was caught in the sadness of her gaze. He felt the words coming and knew they were going to gut him, but he wouldn't look away.

Her fingers were curled around the arms of the rocker, and her face had turned pale. He knew she was struggling. He wanted to hold her again, but she had a "keep away" look on her face.

"Do you remember what you said to me the day you left for boot camp? You said you'd come back to me. You promised me, Sam. I couldn't leave. I was waiting for you to come home."

The ache in his chest was so great he couldn't move.

"You know he died there, don't you, girl?"

Lainey's eyes widened as the meaning of what he'd said began to dawn.

"Your Sam died in a desert in Afghanistan. They sent his body home, and this is all that's left. I don't know what to say to you. I don't know how to make this right."

She leaned forward. "What do you want from me, Sam? Why are you here?"

"I want...no, I *need* you to forgive me. I need you to understand."

She was crying again—a weak, helpless cry without sound. "Understand what?"

"That I could hurt you. I'm broken."

"So what does that make me?" she asked, splaying the palms of her hands across her chest. "I'm in pieces, too, and I don't quit." She sagged against the rocker and closed her eyes. "Go away, Sam. You said your piece, and I heard it. I am not your priest, but you are absolved of your guilt. So go back to Mystic. Help Trey find out who killed your mother, and then go back to wherever you came from. Hide from what's left of your life. Be the cripple. Be the victim. Just leave me alone."

He wanted to be angry at her, but she had done nothing but speak her truth.

"I hear you, and I'm leaving. But we're not done here," he said. "I'll call you tomorrow."

"You don't know my number. Go away," she said and turned her face to the window.

Sam walked out of her bedroom with a knot in his chest. Then he noticed the house still had a landline, and with an ache in his heart, realized he still remembered the number. He picked up the receiver and verified the number on the dial, then left the house. All the way back to Mystic he kept running scenarios of how he could make a relationship work, what kind of safeguards she might need if they gave it a try.

When he saw the city-limit sign he had no memory of how he'd gotten there. The farther he drove, the deeper the pain became. He didn't yet know how to fix this, but he had to make it right. No matter how long it took, or what he had to do to convince her to let him try, he had found out one definite truth. He could never leave Lainey behind again.

Lainey heard the door slam as he left, and there was a moment when she thought she should run screaming from the house, begging him to take her with him. But it wasn't her place to beg. It was his. If he wanted her bad enough, he knew where she lived, and if he did not, when he was gone, so was she. She'd held up her end of the bargain when she'd waited, but she'd fought too hard to survive cancer to bury herself out on a farm all alone.

When he started his car, she got up and watched him as he drove away. She understood the horror of what his family was going through. She got it that Trina's life was hanging in the balance either way. If she survived the shooting and the surgery, they still had to find a way to keep her alive until they could apprehend the killer. And what irony it would be if her own mother's childhood diaries became a focal point in solving such a mystery.

She glanced at the clock and then dropped the robe and went to get dressed. She had classes for two hours straight this afternoon and hoped to God she could remember the lesson plans. Right now she was so rattled she wasn't sure she could spell her own name.

Sam was at the hospital with Trina when Trey entered ICU. He paused at the door to her room to speak to the guard.

"How's it going, Mike?" he asked.

Mike Cantrell stood up. "It's good. No problems here. Everything is straightforward, and other than medical visits no one but you, Dallas, Sam and Lee visits. I'm off in a couple of hours, and Cain Embry will take over."

Trey nodded. "And don't forget, if you see anything that strikes you as even the faintest bit off, don't hesitate to tell me."

"Yes, sir. I understand," Mike said, and then sat back down as Trey went inside.

Trey glanced at Trina, and then raised an eyebrow at Sam to ask how she was.

Sam just shook his head, indicating no change.

"Are you okay to leave?" Trey asked. "I need to run something by you."

"Yes. I've been here ever since I got back from seeing Lainey."

Trey heard something in Sam's voice that he hadn't heard in years. "So how did that go?"

Sam shrugged. "Just about how you'd expect. She slapped my face, threw a coffee mug at me and then cried. I won't go into details, but right now I guess I hate myself more now than I did when I was hurt."

"I'm sorry," Trey said.

"Yeah, so am I," Sam said, then turned and gave Trina a kiss on her forehead. "Rest and get well, little sister. Know that you are safe."

They left together, saving their conversation until they were outside the hospital, when there was no one around to overhear.

"Have you had lunch?" Trey asked as they exited the building.

"No stomach for food," Sam muttered, then kicked at the melting snow. "At least this is going away."

"You need to eat something, and I'm hungry. Meet me at Charlie's Burgers. You can eat pie. I want real food."

As Sam was walking toward the café, the killer was walking out. He paused, hoping the expression on his face was one of concern and not panic.

"How goes it, Sam?"

Sam shrugged. "Okay."

"So how's Trina? Is she still in a coma?"

"She's stable, and yes, they're still keeping her medicated."

"Stable is good," the killer said. "Just know my prayers will be with her."

"Thanks," Sam said and went into the café as the killer walked to his car.

He waved at Trey Jakes, who had just pulled up, and then got into his own car and drove away.

Trey walked inside, saw Sam at a booth and quickly joined him.

The waitress came with menus and coffee. As Sam began to relax with his brother, he decided to eat something after all. By the time the waitress came back, he was ready to order.

As soon as she left, Trey leaned forward and lowered his voice. "I need you to do something for me."

Sam nodded. "Anything."

"I need you to go to Mom's. I know you don't want to, but consider this part of the investigation. Go through the house with a fine-tooth comb. You know what to look for. She was keeping journals about her dreams. She brought me several, but I don't know if what I have is all she wrote. You know?"

"Yes, Mom was big on journals."

"If you find anything even remotely referring to her memory issues, bring it."

"I will, but I'll need a key."

Trey took his key from the ring and handed it over. "Keep mine. Dallas has another. I can make a copy."

"Are there still cats in the barn?" Sam asked.

"Yes, Dallas and I have been feeding them, but there's no livestock on the place anymore."

"I'll check on them and feed them today," Sam said. "Food still in the same place?"

Trey nodded.

Sam threaded the house key onto his key ring, and then reached for his coffee. It was hot and fresh, and it took the chill off his mood. As they sat, he watched Trey fielding texts and then turning the sound down on his handheld so the radio traffic wouldn't disturb the other diners.

"You are a good man, Trey. I don't think I ever thanked you and Trina for taking care of Mom."

Trey's voice broke. "I didn't do a very good job of it. And I'm not doing a very good job of finding her killer, either."

"Don't talk like that. From what I've heard, both the city and the county are at a loss on this case. After all that's happened, you still have next to no clues."

"I know, and it's hard to take," Trey said.

Sam saw the dark circles under his brother's eyes. He was suffering the loss *and* dealing with guilt. Had to be hell.

"Life is hard sometimes, but we do the best we can with what we're given," Sam said.

Trey looked away. Silence hung heavy between them until the waitress returned with their food.

They ate in comfortable silence, speaking now and then as brothers do, without concern for polite conversation, and when they were through, Sam picked up the check as Trey went back to the office.

When Sam exited the café, he glanced up at the sky. It was clear but gray, and still damn cold—a fitting day for the prodigal son to go home.

Lainey was set up and ready for the class to begin, but her head was throbbing. She'd cried harder this morning than she'd cried her whole life. What she couldn't get over was that Sam had cried with her. Despite the hopelessness of their situation, it had been healing to be held, to be loved. The really sad part was that she believed Sam still loved her. He'd known why they were apart when she had not. She wasn't sure how to feel about him. She would always love him, but love had to be shared to grow, and they hadn't shared so much as a conversation in years.

What she wanted was the past ten years of her life back. What she would have done was go back to that hospital again. What she should have done was ignore what Sam wanted. Maybe then he wouldn't have had such a hang-up about himself.

But there was also the PTSD. It wasn't all about the physical scars. He'd said he'd tried to kill his landlord. He'd said he hadn't been able to hold a job. She thought of being in the middle of that kind of chaos and wondered whether she would have been strong enough to cope at that age. It pained her to admit it, but there was a part of her that was coming to accept he'd been right—at least about that. So where did that leave them? Alone and apart. A completely ridiculous, unacceptable answer that was making her sick.

She popped a couple of painkillers, washed them down with water and clicked through to her "classroom." It was time to earn her pay.

For Sam, the drive back out to the farm felt surreal. He'd dreamed of this moment so many times over the years but had never made it happen. Doing it now felt like betrayal. But if he could find something that would help catch the man who'd killed his mother, it would be worth the guilt.

When he came over the hill and looked down the slope to the mailbox on the side of the road, he realized that was where the attack had happened. That was where his mother had died. He could tell by the amount of grass that had been disturbed where the rescue vehicles had parked. A wave of emotion washed through him as he thought about how Trey must have felt when he found Mom and Trina.

"We'll find him, Mama, I promise you," he said, and turned off the blacktop and down the dirt road to their house.

The porch light was on. He guessed Trey had done that. He was just about to get out of the car when his cell rang. It was Trey.

"Hey, Sam, where are you?"

"Just about to go inside."

"Oh, wow…glad I caught you. I forgot to tell you there's a security system in the house now. The four digit key code is Mom's birthday. Do you remember the date?"

"December 13. So the code is twelve-thirteen?"

"Yes."

"Glad you remembered. It would have sucked eggs to set that off."

"Let me know how it goes," Trey added.

"I will."

Sam dropped the phone back in his pocket and unlocked the front door. The keypad was right beside the light switch, and he quickly deactivated the alarm.

Then he stood for a few moments, looking at the house in which he'd grown up. God, how he wished his mom would come running with that smile on her face and her arms wide-open. He could almost hear her voice.

Welcome home, Sammy, welcome home.

He locked the door behind him, and then turned up the thermostat as he shed his coat. He turned on lights as he went through the house, noticing the changes that had been made and checking where everything was before he began a real search. There was new carpet in the bedrooms, and the hardwood floors in the rest of the house had been refinished. Some of the furniture was unfamiliar, but it fit.

When he walked into his mother's room, the scent of her perfume still lingered. It was hard not to be angry that the scent of her perfume was still here but she was not.

He headed for the kitchen—not because he thought he would find any clues there, but because he remembered his mother's penchant for baking when she was bothered and wondered if he might find evidence of her state of mind.

There was a pie in the refrigerator that hadn't been cut and a cookie jar half full of oatmeal cookies. It was as he'd expected. His vision blurred as he put the lid back on the cookie jar, and then walked to the kitchen window to look out at the mountain behind the farm. So many memories…

He turned away.

"Okay, Mama, I'm about to put my investigative skills to the test. If you left messages, I *will* find them, so forgive me for any trespasses along the way. We need to keep Trina alive."

Seven

Sam began searching the kitchen and found nothing written down but a partial grocery list. He moved into the living room, going through his dad's metal desk, through his grandfather's antique secretary, through the tables at both ends of the sofa.

He was digging through the hall closet when he suddenly paused, then pulled out his dad's old rifle. It used to be in his parents' bedroom. She'd moved it closer to the front door, and it was loaded. He thought of her being nervous enough about her own safety to do that, and felt sad all over again as he set the rifle back in the closet and walked away.

When he got to the bedrooms, he searched Trina's first, although he didn't expect to find anything. If his mom was keeping any secrets, this room would have been her last choice.

Trey's old room was across the hall. He dug through the drawers, the closet and then under the bed but found nothing.

When he walked into his mom's bedroom, he started with her dresser, then went from there to the bedside tables. There were a journal and a pen inside the drawer closest to the phone, but the journal was new, with only a couple of pages used. He could almost hear her talking as he read through what she'd written, but none of it was relevant, so he slipped the journal back into the drawer and continued the search, but with no luck.

The only room left other than the utility room was his old bedroom at the far end of the hall, and as he started toward it, he began to feel as if he was entering a time warp. He'd walked this way so many times before that when he opened the door, he almost expected to see his stuff still sitting around the room.

But he was wrong.

His high school things had been packed away. The bedspread was blue. The curtains white. It looked nondescript and appeared to be a guest room now.

He started digging through the drawers without expectations and found nothing. He continued moving through the room, looking through books on the shelf, then inside the closet. He glanced at his old desk and started to pass it by, then out of curiosity opened the front drawer.

Seeing his name in his mother's handwriting on the outside of a small padded envelope gave him a chill. It was a message from the grave. He sat down on the side of the bed, then hesitated before he finally opened the envelope.

A tiny jewelry box fell out, and when he opened it he flashed on a moment from the past: his mother taking him aside before he left for boot camp and showing him this same ring. He could still remember the tears in her eyes when she'd cupped his cheek.

*This was your grandmother's wedding ring,
Sam. It's been handed down to the eldest son
in my mother's family for at least one hundred
and fifty years. I want you to know it's here for
you when you need it.*

Sam put the ring in his pocket and pulled out the
letter next. God, he didn't want to be reading this.

Sam,

*If you're reading this, then I guess the worst
has happened. I have become the killer's last
victim. Trey has been trying so hard to figure
this out. I've tried to remember but my dreams
were all disjointed. Nothing made sense. And
other things were beginning to happen when I
was awake. I had a couple of hallucinations,
and I was beginning to lose track of time. It's a
scary way to feel, and I thought of all my children, you would be the one to best understand
what it's like to live with that kind of fear.*

*I love you so much, but you know that. I wish
I knew how to make you happy. I wish you'd
give Lainey a second chance. She's still on the
family farm. I think she's waiting for you, but I
don't talk to her anymore. She ended our relationship, and I honored that.*

*I already gave Trey my journals before I
wrote this, so I can't remember now if I mentioned one specific dream. I dreamed it again
last night, so I'm going to tell you, just in case.*

I keep seeing a body, and it's down in a hole.

*A very deep hole, like a mine shaft. Tell Trey
about the mine shaft.*

*Give the world a chance. You are a survivor.
You deserve to be happy. And just so all of you
know, I'm fine with this. By the time you're reading this, I am back in my Justin's arms. I missed
him so much, Sam. I am not sorry I am gone.*

*I love you all,
Mom*

He was stunned. His hands were shaking as he
folded the paper and put it back in the envelope. There
was a message in there for all of them. But this wasn't
the time to share.

His heart was pounding as he sent Trey a text.

Call me.

The phone rang within moments.

"What did you find?"

"She wrote me a letter. I found it in the desk in
my old room. Damn, Trey, it almost felt like a suicide note. She was so passive about being in danger.
She also wanted me to ask you about her journals."

"What about them?" Trey asked.

"She couldn't remember if she'd already written about a specific dream, so on the off chance she
hadn't, she put it in the letter."

"What was it about? I've read them all several
times so I should remember."

"Did she mention a dream about seeing a body in

a deep hole, like a mine shaft? She made a specific point about the mine shaft."

"No! Oh, my God! Are you serious?"

"That's what she said. So about that wreck they were in…where was it?"

"Going west…toward the Colquitt Mining site."

"How long has the site been inactive? The wreck happened in 1980. If they were working mines then, someone would have found a body if it was there," Sam said.

"I don't know. I'll have to check, and I need to let Sheriff Osmond know, too, but this is big, Sam. Thank you. Thank you for doing this. I know it wasn't easy."

"Oh, hell, Trey, I don't deserve easy. I'm going down to the barn to feed the cats, and then I'm leaving. I assume I set the alarm with the same code that deactivated it."

"Yes, there's a ninety-second delay, so set it, then just lock the door on your way out and it's good to go."

"Talk to you later," Sam said and disconnected.

He put the letter in his pocket, and then paused on his way out of the room and looked back. There was nothing of him in here anymore, and that was okay. Like he'd told Lainey, the boy who'd grown up in this room was dead. He went back through the house turning out lights, lowering the thermostat, then put his coat and hat back on and set the alarm as he left.

As he circled the house toward the barn, he stopped to look up at the mountain, remembering all the years he'd spent playing on it. It had been a large part of his childhood, but it had been there long before a Jakes ever set foot on this land and would endure long after all of them were gone. Even though the emotions that came from being here were inevitable, he felt a sense of sadness with them—a loss of one thing as he moved on to another, like a torch being passed. On impulse, he took off his hat. It was an odd thing to do, but in his mind it was an honoring of the boy who never made it home.

When he was about halfway to the barn a few cats appeared in the doorway. As he got closer, a couple more appeared, along with a litter of kittens.

He thought about teasing Betsy about becoming an old lady with too many cats, and then a brief moment of heartache reminded him she was gone.

He hastened his steps, anxious to be gone. By the time he got to the barn and found the cat food, they were meowing at his feet.

"Chill out, guys," he said shortly.

After a quick look around to see his mother's setup, he carried the sack over to the aluminum feeding pans near an old granary. The dry cat food rattled as it hit the metal, but it was obviously music to their ears. The meowing ceased.

He could still hear them crunching as he walked away.

Beth Powell was a born-and-bred resident of Mystic, and she had a dilemma, which she was about to fix with food. She was in the kitchen dipping into a bowl of ice cream. She ate sweets when she was nervous. Actually, she ate a little too much regardless of her mood, but right now her future felt dark and scary.

Yesterday she'd learned about the class of 1980 cheating scandal coming to light. She had been told by more than one person about what Chief Jakes had

said. Anyone who knew something and didn't tell
might go to prison for aiding and abetting in a murder. Well, she didn't believe that would happen, and
she wasn't going to get involved. All of that was in the
past, and she had nothing to do with what was happening now, so mum was the word. To punctuate that,
she added one more scoop of ice cream to her bowl.

Trey was in his office waiting for Dewey Osmond
to return his call. The dispatcher had told him the
sheriff was at a dentist appointment but was expected
back at any time.

While he was waiting, he'd pulled up a county
map on his computer and was looking at the locations where all the Colquitt Company mines had been.
According to the internet, the company had ceased
mining on the property west of Mystic in 1978. That
would explain how a body could have been dumped
there and never found.

If the missing graduate, Donny Collins, turned out
to be the body his mother had seen—the one to whom
the bloody tassel found in Paul Jackson's safety deposit
box belonged—then why had no one ever reported
him missing? He needed to do some more research on
the kid. Maybe go back to the school and talk to Will
Porter. He'd graduated with Donny and would know
some personal history. Then he glanced at the time.
School was already out for the day. Maybe he could
catch Will Porter at home. He picked up the phone.

Rita Porter was lying facedown in the hall on her
belly when Will found her. For a fraction of a second
he hoped to God she was dead, but then he saw the

spilled bottle of liquor and guessed she'd passed out. He couldn't leave her like that, so he began trying to wake her. When he couldn't rouse her, he thought to feel for a pulse and was horrified to discover it was irregular and slow.

He leaped to his feet, ran back into the kitchen to get his cell phone and quickly called 911. A few minutes later Rita was on her way to the emergency room and Will was in the car, following the ambulance.

He was just pulling into the parking lot when his cell phone rang. He wasn't going to answer, then saw the call was from the police department and picked up. "Yes? Hello?"

"Mr. Porter, Trey Jakes here. Do you have a minute? I need to ask you a question."

The ambulance was already backing up into the bay to unload their patient, and in that moment Will Porter chose a phone call over being with his wife.

"Yes, how can I help you?"

"Remember how no one at the meeting knew anything about where Donny Collins went after graduation? We're still investigating him so we can eliminate him from our list. What do you remember about his home life?"

"Not much, why?" Will asked.

"I'm still in the elimination process here and don't want to focus on someone who may not have anything to do with this case. No one seems to know where Donny is currently, but if he really went missing back then, why wasn't it reported? See what I mean?"

"Oh. Right. I do see. Well, let me think. I know he was a year older than the rest of us because he got held back in first grade. Don't know why. He was smart enough. Maybe it had to do with social skills. Donny was a small kid in elementary school. He was about average size by the time we graduated."

"What about his family?" Trey asked.

"I can't really remember if— Oh, wait. I remember one thing. He was a foster child. I think he lived with the Harpers. But you know how when kids are eighteen they leave the foster system? Donny would have been close to nineteen when he graduated. Maybe the Harpers could give you some more details."

"Are you referring to the Harpers who live across the creek from my family farm?"

"Yes."

"I'll give them a call. And thanks."

"No problem," Will said. "Glad to help." Then he let out a big sigh, hung up and headed for the hospital. It was time to go pretend he gave a shit what happened to Rita.

Back at the precinct, Trey was searching for a phone number for the Harpers but couldn't find one, and he didn't want to have to drive all the way out there to question them. Then Sam walked in.

"What's going on?" Sam asked.

Trey explained.

"I'll go out and talk to them," Sam said. "I saw them at the hospital when I was visiting Trina."

"That would be great," Trey said. "I'm still waiting to hear back from Sheriff Osmond."

"I'll be in touch," Sam said, and went back to his car.

Glad to have purpose, Sam left Mystic behind, winding along the rural roads and then turning onto the blacktop that led toward the Harper farm, and then, a half mile on, crossing Possum Creek and taking the first turn right over the bridge.

The road was rough and full of ruts, and the weeds and grass on both sides were overgrown. An old swayback mare behind a sagging three-wire fence was nibbling at the sparse grass in the pasture. And as he neared the house, his appearance roused a bluetick hound lying against the wheels of the family car.

The dog didn't get up but began to bay and kept it up until the front door opened and Wilma Harper walked out.

"Shut the hell up, Buddy!" she yelled, and then folded her arms across her breasts as Sam approached the porch. The door opened behind her, and Wynona came out in tight jeans and an even tighter button-up shirt, threw her leg over the porch railing like she was sitting a horse and grinned at him.

"Well, hello, neighbor," Wynona drawled.

He nodded at the two women. "I'm sorry to come without calling, Mrs. Harper, but we couldn't find a phone number for the family."

"I ain't no missus. Never married. Just call me Wilma, and you can't find a number because I don't have a phone. Can't afford it. My girls have cell phones for when we need to call someone. What're you here for anyway?"

"I'm helping my brother investigate the recent murders, and a name came up that we wanted to ask you about," Sam said.

Wilma frowned. "Ain't none of my people having anything to do with all that!" she snapped.

"No, ma'am. That's not what I meant. We were

told your family once took in a foster child named Donny Collins."

Sam saw from the corner of his eye that Wynona rocked back and forth on the railing, and threw back her head like she was riding a man instead, but he refused to look directly at her.

Wilma nodded. "Yeah, that was Mam and Pap's doin'. I was still living at home, but I'd already graduated. Back then they got thirty dollars a month extra to keep him. Helped out in the hard times."

Sam wondered how much of that thirty dollars ever went to Donny Collins' welfare, then let it go.

"So where is he now?"

Wilma threw up her hands. "Oh, Lord, I have no idea. They let him stay in our house out of the goodness of their hearts for six months after he turned eighteen so he could graduate. Pap said it was the godly thing to do."

"So he was living with your family when he graduated?"

Wilma nodded. "Yes, that he was."

"So when did you see him last?" Sam asked.

Wilma frowned as she thought back.

"I guess the last sight we had of him was after he walked across the graduation stage. We carried his suitcase to town for him when we took him to the commencement ceremony. He told us he was going to catch a bus later that night and go to California. I expect he's out there somewhere."

"Do you have his social security number anywhere?"

Wilma frowned.

"Mam and Pap would have had that information,

but they're long dead. I don't think I'd be able to find it anywhere now," she said. "But the child welfare people would know. They came out twice a year to check on him and us. They would have all that."

Sam nodded.

The moment was anticlimactic. He still didn't know what happened to Donny Collins, but if he *had* gone missing, he now knew why no one would have looked for him. He stood there for a moment, trying to imagine a young kid starting out on his own without a backup plan. They were going to have to run a trace on him now to see if he was alive anywhere.

Wynona stopped rocking. "It's real chilly today. Y'all want to come inside and have a cup of coffee? It would warm you right up," she said.

Then she ran the tip of her tongue along the inside of her lower lip and leaned forward just enough for her cleavage to show. It did nothing but aggravate his impatience with fools.

"Thank you for your help, Ms. Harper. Wynona, I appreciate the offer, but I'll have to pass," he said, then touched the brim of his hat in a gesture of courtesy and went back to his car. The dog woofed as he passed but still didn't bother getting up, and then Sam drove away.

He waited to call Trey until he got back on the blacktop.

Trey answered quickly. "Yeah, Sam…what did you find out?"

"The Harpers did foster Donny Collins. They even let him stay six months past his eighteenth birthday, 'out of the goodness of their hearts, so he could graduate,' Wilma said."

"I can only imagine," Trey said. "So where did he go after that?"

"She doesn't know. Assumed he went to California because that was his plan. He took his suitcase to graduation, they watched him walk across the stage and that was the last they saw of him."

"I need to do some more checking," Trey said.

"I asked about a social security number, but she doesn't have it. She said child welfare did regular visitations on him twice a year until he aged out, so should have it on file."

"Good job. That I *can* check," Trey said. "It's getting late. Get some food. Get some rest. If I find out anything more, I'll let you know. Otherwise, see you tomorrow."

"Yeah, okay, but I'm going to see Trina before I go back to the motel."

"The guard at her door has changed. The guy's name is Cain Embry."

"Have you talked to her doctor today?"

"No. He hadn't made rounds when I was there. Maybe you'll catch him."

"If I do, I'll text you with an update."

"Thanks," Trey said and disconnected.

Sam laid his phone in the console, and then focused on the road stretching out before him. It was strange how normal this seemed, driving on this road as if he'd only been away for a little while. A wave of guilt washed over him, followed by such overwhelming sadness that it was all he could do to keep driving. His voice broke as he said, "I'm so sorry, Mama."

He could almost hear her saying, *Don't be silly, Sam. There's nothing to be sorry for.*

He'd seen a lot of the ugly side of life, but never imagined it infiltrating his family like this. And Lainey. He'd never meant to, but he had hurt her badly.

He glanced down at the phone and thought about calling her, but he still felt too raw from this morning. Shit. He'd chosen being alone. She hadn't. He'd started out doing it because it was necessary, and it had become who he was. He'd identified himself as a soldier who had gone to war and come home a monster, both inwardly and outwardly. But that was all based on perception—*his* perception. Seeing Lainey today had made him realize how wrong he'd been— about almost everything. She didn't deserve what had happened to her, but then neither had he, and yet it happened. She'd come through with the mind-set of a survivor, and he'd turned into a victim. He wanted what she had. Guts to face the truth.

And so he drove back into Mystic with something of a plan. Make peace with Lainey. See if there was anything left between them. Find out who killed his mom. But not until after he went to see Trina.

Trey finally got the call back from Sheriff Osmond and was relaying the new information.

"Yes…like I said, Sam found a letter from Mom referring to a dream that wasn't in the journals she gave me. It had to do with seeing a body in a deep hole. She thought it was a mine shaft."

"Isn't there a Colquitt Mining site out by where they had that wreck?" Sheriff Osmond asked.

"You're thinking the same thing I thought," Trey said. "Yes, I checked. It closed in 1978, and the wreck happened in 1980, so if someone did drop a body down the shaft, it's very unlikely it would be found."

"I'll see if I need a search warrant to get on that property."

"Good. Let me know, okay?" Trey added.

"Of course."

"Hey, Trey, one last thing. If we assume a murder was committed, how on earth did four kids become witnesses?" Sheriff Osmond asked.

"I know part of that answer from reading Mom's journals. There was a place off the west highway that was a party spot for teenagers. Whether it was the old mine or not, I couldn't say. That could explain why they were there, but it still doesn't tell us who else they saw. I have one student from the 1980 graduating class who I haven't located. I got some new information today that I need to follow up on. I'll let you know what I find."

"All right, Trey. Thanks for the info."

"No problem," he said and disconnected.

He looked up at the clock. It was almost 7:00 p.m., and he'd been up since five. It was time to go home.

He went to make sure the night dispatcher was okay, and that officers Carl and Lonnie Doyle were on duty.

"Hey, Dwight, how goes it?" he asked as he stepped into the dispatch center.

"It's all good, Chief. The Doyle brothers are on duty. Carl's out on a disturbing-the-peace call, and Lonnie is locking up a drunk."

"I'm out of here, then," Trey said. "Call if you need me."

"Will do, and have a good evening, Chief."

"Here's hoping it's a calm one, as well," Trey said, and then walked out the back door and headed home.

Lainey was in the kitchen making potato soup. There was a pan of corn bread baking in the oven, and she'd already fed and watered Dandy. The house was locked up for the night, and she was taking comfort in the warmth and the fact that the food she was making not only looked good but smelled good, as well.

She was chopping up the last vegetables to put in the soup when her doorbell rang. Frowning, she wiped off her hands and headed through the house, wondering if it was Larry coming to pay her for what he'd done to her fence.

She turned on the porch light, then opened the door and saw Sam on the doorstep with a coffee mug in one hand and a half gallon of ice cream in the other. She sighed.

His expression said it all. Regret, remorse and a great big "please open the door."

She thought about shutting him out but knew it wouldn't help. He would be back doing whatever it was he thought he needed to do, and he wouldn't quit, so she might as well get this over with. She unlocked the storm door and let him in.

"What are you doing here?" she asked as she shut the door behind him.

He handed her the new coffee mug. "For the one you broke." Then he handed her the ice cream. "For auld lang syne?"

"It's strawberry," she said.

"Is that not your favorite anymore?" he asked.

She sighed. "Yes, it's still my favorite."

"But I'm not," Sam said.

She frowned, then went to the kitchen. He followed, watching as she put the ice cream in the freezer and the mug in the cabinet.

"Something smells good," he said.

"Corn bread," she said, and picked up the cutting board, using the paring knife to slide the vegetables into the pot.

"What's that you're making?"

She turned around with the knife still in her hand. "Are you angling for an invitation to supper?"

"Not if you're going to use that on me," he said, pointing at the knife.

She rolled her eyes and laid it aside as she stirred the soup, and then turned down the fire a bit.

"Why are you really here?" she asked.

Sam took off his hat and set it aside.

"I need to know if there's enough of me left in your heart to love again."

The question was a punch to the gut. She was afraid to hope. Afraid to want.

"What's changed between us since this morning? You remember this morning? When you told me you were too broken to be with me?"

"It was what you said about me thinking of myself as a victim. And then I found a letter from my mom."

It was the break in his voice that made her relent.

"A letter to you?"

"Yes. It was in my old room."

Lainey leaned against the counter and folded her arms across her chest. She got the significance of his admission.

"You went home," she said.

"May I sit?" he asked.

She waved her arm toward the kitchen table.

He took off his coat and hung it on the back of a chair, and then sat down. She didn't think he was going to answer her, but he finally did.

"Yes, I went back to the house. It didn't feel like home."

Quick tears blurred the sight of him. "Because Betsy wasn't there," she said.

He nodded. "I waited too long."

It was the total devastation in his voice that broke her. She crossed the room, sat down in his lap and hugged him.

"I'm sorry," she said.

Lainey's heart hurt for him. He was so still. He wasn't crying. He just wrapped his arms around her and laid his head in the curve of her neck.

"You were my home, too, Lainey. Did I wait too long for you?"

Eight

Lainey looked over at the bubbling pot of soup on the stove, then at the familiarity of the house. It was where she'd grown up, but it hadn't felt like home since her mother's death.

She knew the same loneliness she'd heard in his voice.

"I don't know, Sam. What do you want me to say?"

He raised his head, needing to see her face.

"That you are willing to give me another chance."

"I never stopped wanting that or I would have married someone else. I just gave up hope," she said. "So if you want another chance, how do you see us now?"

"On new ground. We have history, but we're both different people."

"That's for sure," she said, and unconsciously splayed a hand across her chest.

He grabbed her hand and held it to his heart.

"Don't do that! Not around me. Not ever again. I don't give a shit about that. I'm just so damn grateful you're alive to be pissed off at me."

"I need to stir the soup," she said and got up.

He watched her moving about the kitchen with the ease of a woman who knows her place in the world. But she still hadn't answered him.

"You want to stay for supper?" she asked.

And just like that, his tension eased.

"I thought you'd never ask."

She smiled, and when she did, Sam saw the girl he remembered. In that moment she was so beautiful it took his breath away.

"Would you like to set the table for me?" she asked.

"Yes, I would," he said.

She pointed out where plates and bowls were, the drawer where the flatware was kept and turned him loose so she could return to the meal in progress.

A few minutes later she took the corn bread from the oven and set it on the back of the stove to stay warm, then she checked the vegetables. They were done to perfection, and the broth they had cooked in was condensed enough that it was time to add the milk and butter.

She added whole milk and a half stick of butter to the pan and stirred until the milk was hot and the butter melted, then she tasted it once, added a little more salt and turned off the heat.

"It's done," she said, and then looked back at the table.

If she'd been alone, she would have carried a plate and bowl to the stove and served herself from there, but since he'd already set the table so nicely, she thought maybe she should carry the soup and corn bread to the table. And while she was thinking it, Sam picked up their plates and bowls and carried them both to the stove. She grinned.

"What?" he asked.

"I almost got all proper and took the food to the table. You reminded me it's just us."

Sam's eyes widened. He set down the plates, pulled her into his arms without a word and just held her.

Lainey hesitated, then wrapped her arms around his waist. It had been a very long time since anyone had held her. That it was Sam made it even better.

"What is this all about?" she asked.

"You said it's just us. There hasn't been an *us* for a very long time. I liked it."

She didn't realize she'd said that. She sighed. In her heart, she'd already welcomed him back.

"I guess you're right," she said.

"It's not too late, is it, Lainey."

He hadn't asked a question. He'd stated a fact, and when she didn't deny it, he was overcome with both joy and relief. It had been a long time coming, but he'd finally made it home.

"No, it's not too late, Sam."

He picked her up in his arms and swung her off her feet. "Thank you, thank you, thank you."

She laughed. "Corn bread's getting cold. Let's eat."

He hated to put her down, but he wasn't going to push anything. He set her back on her feet, then picked up a plate and bowl and held them out to be filled. After she fixed some food for herself, they carried their meals to the table.

As they began to eat, the window behind where Sam was sitting suddenly rattled.

Lainey frowned. "Sounds like the wind is rising. The weatherman said it might rain tonight."

No sooner had she said it than wind-driven rain splattered against the panes.

"Good night for soup," she said.

"It's a good night for lots of things," Sam added, and then took a big bite. "This is so good. Thank you."

"For what?"

"Well, for starters, feeding me and forgiving me."

"I'm happy to oblige. I'm also supposed to be gaining weight, so pass the butter. I know there's a lot in the soup, but this corn bread is begging for some, too."

He pushed the butter dish toward her and watched her slather butter on the corn bread, but the reference to her too-thin body had brought him back to her reality.

They talked about small things as they ate—about how she'd gotten into online teaching and how he'd stumbled into the business of private investigation. It continued to rain all through the meal and while they were cleaning up the kitchen.

It was almost ten o'clock by the time Sam began getting ready to leave.

Lainey leaned against him, tired, but so content at this moment that she felt as if she was living a dream.

"Hey, Sam?"

"Yeah?"

She leaned back in his arms. "Is this real? Are you really here, or am I still dreaming?"

He cupped her face and leaned forward. There was a moment when he paused, his lips only a breath away from hers. When he made contact, it was like lighting a match to dry tinder.

Lainey had been without him too long. She gasped

as his mouth touched her lips, then she wrapped her arms around his neck.

He pulled her closer as he deepened the kiss, and somewhere between her gasp and his moan, his ten-year absence was gone.

In Sam's mind he was already naked and getting ready to settle between her legs when he felt her tense. It was the cold-water dunk he needed to remember he was on a trial basis here. The last thing he wanted was to mess this up again. It was with extreme effort that he backed off from the kiss.

"God, you feel good in my arms. I almost forgot myself there."

Lainey was reeling, trying to come down from where he'd taken her, and he was talking about forgetting. She didn't want him to forget anything—not ever again.

"That's because we're still us," she said.

He brushed a thumb across her swollen lower lip. "Can I come see you again tomorrow?"

She frowned. He was still planning on leaving?

"Would you like to go to Cutter's Steakhouse for dinner tomorrow evening?" he added.

She nodded.

"Can I call or text you whenever I want?" he asked.

"Give me your phone," Lainey said, and when he handed it over, she added herself to his contact list, then got her phone and put him in hers.

"Does this mean we're a thing?" Sam asked.

She was still trying to reconcile his sudden withdrawal. Did it have to do with some hang-up of his, or was it her? He'd already seen her naked. Was he turned off by how she looked? She didn't understand what was going on.

"I guess so," she said.

He paused, then cupped the side of her face.

"I won't lie. I want to make love to you right now so much I hurt, but that's not happening until you feel safe with me, and you won't know that until we've spent more time together, okay?"

"I feel safe with you now," she said and made no apology for saying how she felt, even if it did sound as if she was begging.

"That's because nothing has triggered an episode. I haven't been pushed or felt the need to push back," he said, and then brushed his mouth across her lips.

She sighed and he read that as uncertainty.

"So I guess I'd better be leaving."

"We never did eat that ice cream," she said.

He was at the front door by then, but he looked back and saw the want in her eyes.

"Lainey?"

"What?"

"Love you."

There was a good six feet between them. She hadn't heard that vow in over ten years, and he was getting ready to walk out the door? Oh, hell no!

"Damn it, Sam!"

He blinked. "What? What did I do?"

"I waited for you for ten years. When you came back, you didn't come back for me. You came back because your mother was murdered. We're back together now by accident, and I keep thinking to myself that it still might be too late. So don't you dare walk out on me. You can be all proper and protective and in charge, and whatever the hell else you feel like being, but tomorrow. Right now you need to take me to my bedroom, where we will get naked and make love until the sun comes up."

His eyes widened, and then he locked the door behind him and took off his coat. He tossed his Stetson on the sofa and picked her up in his arms and started toward the back of the house.

The hall was in shadow. Her bedroom was dark. But he could see where he was going by the glow of the security light at the far end of the yard as it slipped through the blinds.

He set her on her feet and within seconds had her naked. Without giving her time to think about what was happening, he backed her up to a wall and slid a hand between her legs.

His name was a sigh upon her lips. She grabbed on to his shoulders to steady herself, and within moments her legs were shaking, her heart was pounding and she felt herself coming undone. It had been too long; she'd been without him for so many years. There was no filter on her senses. No control button to slow anything down. A rush of heat rolled through her, spiraling downward to what he was doing with his hands.

She moaned.

He leaned forward and whispered in her ear, "Come for me, baby."

And she did, in an explosion of sensations so strong she would have gone to her knees if he hadn't held her upright. She was still shaking when he picked her up and carried her to the bed.

She watched from the shadows as he slipped out of his clothes. She saw the size of his erection and shuddered as lust crawled through her belly. She wanted that. She wanted *him*.

He paused and pulled a condom out of his wallet. She watched as he rolled it up his penis, and then he crawled onto the bed and straddled her legs without touching her.

When she reached for him, he stopped her.

"All in good time," he whispered.

She sighed. "Make love to me. I want to feel you inside me. Let me give you pleasure. Let me love you, Sam."

He parted her legs, and then settled between them. "You're so fragile I'm afraid I'm going to hurt you," he whispered.

"I was hurt when you didn't come home. I need this from you. You need this from me. It will heal us, Sam. Make love to me now."

She was warm and wet when he took her, but it was caution that made him pause, allowing her to adjust to his size as he kissed her. Her hands were locked behind his neck, her legs around his waist, pulling him deep, and he began to move.

The wind had settled, but the rain was still falling, peppering the roof and the windows as Sam made love to his girl, stroking her body, making promises to her of how he was going to make her feel. She rocked beneath him in perfect rhythm, a reminder that she was made for his love.

Time ceased. There was nothing but Sam and Lainey and the passion building between them. When he began to feel the contraction and tremors within her, he knew she was racing toward climax. He began stroking harder, pushing deeper, getting his own high from the sound of her satisfaction. As she began to breathe faster, he drove harder. When every muscle in her body tightened and he heard her moan, he let go and rode his own climax all the way to the end in a rocky crash and burn.

Spent and shaking, he rolled onto his back with her still in his arms. Now she was lying on top of him and he was still inside her, unwilling to let go of their connection. Her head was tucked beneath his chin, and he could feel the thunder of her heart against his chest. As he slowly stroked his hand up and down her back, he was painfully aware of the bones he could feel beneath her skin.

"Did I hurt you?" he asked.

"Lord, no! If I could, I would be purring," she mumbled.

He smiled, satisfied that she was still in his arms. They lay without moving until he was hard inside her again. And this time he took her deep and fast through a climax that left them shaking.

She fell asleep in his arms as the rainstorm passed. He didn't mean to sleep, but he did, dreaming of bombs about to explode, too close for him to get to safety.

He was mumbling in his sleep when Lainey woke. It was instinct that made her move off him as quickly and quietly as she could. She was wrapped up in a robe and sitting in her rocker when he cried out, then flew out of bed with both hands curled into fists.

She reached over and turned on a lamp.

"You were dreaming," she said calmly.

Sam's heart was hammering. The fact that she

wasn't in bed beside him scared the shit out of him. Had he hurt her? Was she afraid of him now?

"Did I hurt you?"

"Of course not," she said. "I heard you talking in your sleep, so I just got out of bed."

"Jesus," he whispered, then sat down on the side of the bed and shoved his hands through his hair.

She moved from the rocker to the bed and curled herself around him. "It's okay. You're okay. *We're* okay."

He was still trying to wrap his head around being here with her and not under fire. Then she tossed her robe aside and crawled back under the covers with him.

"Lie down with me, Sam. It's cold."

He eased back onto the pillow and she rolled toward him, pillowing her head on his shoulder and wrapping an arm around his chest.

"You're so warm," she said softly.

Sam caught her hand and held it like a lifeline as she settled against him and fell back asleep.

He lay without moving, absorbing the sweetness of being beneath the covers with the only woman he'd ever loved. She'd seen his body and not been disgusted, and now she knew that he never really slept. Awake, Sam Jakes lived in this world, but when he closed his eyes, the devil took him back to the desert. He hadn't realized how tired he was from fighting battles day and night until a little bit of heaven brought him home.

He was suddenly conscious of holding Lainey too tight as she shifted in her sleep. He eased his grasp, and then kissed the curls at the top of her head before pulling the covers up around them. The rain on the roof was like the feet of a thousand running children. He closed his eyes, and when he woke it was morning. The house was warm. The aroma of brewing coffee was in the air, along with the smell of bacon.

He dressed quickly and followed the scents all the way to the source, then kissed the back of Lainey's neck as he entered the kitchen.

"Good morning, sweetheart."

The deep voice in Lainey's ear sent a shiver all the way up her spine. She'd gone down the hall twice since she'd been up just to reassure herself that last night had not been a dream. Seeing Sam Jakes in her bed each time had given her heart a sweet jolt.

"Good morning," she said. "I didn't wake you. I was hoping you didn't have early plans."

"My early plans are you," he said, and snitched a piece of bacon from the plate and popped it in his mouth. "What can I help you do?" he asked.

"Umm, put butter and jelly on the table, and then make some toast?"

"I can do that," he said, and then picked up another piece of bacon, but instead of putting it in his mouth, he lifted it to hers. "Open wide, pretty girl."

She grinned and took a big bite. "Trying to fatten me up, aren't you?"

"Just helping you follow doctor's orders," he said, and then headed for the refrigerator.

A few minutes later they sat down to eat. Lainey was reaching for the butter to put on her toast when Sam paused and looked at her from across the table. Like Lainey, he was still pinching himself that this was even happening. And the sad part of it was, she'd been right. If his mother hadn't been murdered, he would never have come home. He would have settled for less.

Lainey saw the expression on his face and laid down her fork. "Are you okay?"

He blinked. "What? Oh, yes, baby, I'm fine. I was just thinking of how easy it is to be derailed by life. Last week you were with me only in dreams, and now here we are. I shared a bed with you last night and a meal with you this morning, and as shattered as we are about my mother's murder, I haven't been this happy since before 9/11."

For a moment Lainey had been afraid he was regretting last night, and now she breathed an easy sigh of relief.

"If it helps, I know how much Betsy wanted us back together. She told me so more than once."

Sam reached across the table to hold her hand.

"My only reservation is scaring you or making you afraid of me," he said.

She shook her head in denial.

"I love you. You love me. We'll figure it out as we go, Sam."

"Deal," he said and gave her hand a quick squeeze.

Greg Standish was contemplating calling in sick. It wouldn't be a lie. He was literally sick to his stomach from the stack of bills before him. But he was the president of the bank, and unless he was dead or dying it was his job to be present, so he pushed the bills aside and went back to his room to get ready for work.

He had showered and was shaving when he heard the bedroom door open, and then the sound of footsteps moving across the carpet. Expecting someone to call out, he was surprised when everything stayed quiet. On impulse, he opened the door just a crack to see who was in the room and saw Carly going through his wallet.

He threw his razor in the sink and came out of the bathroom, shouting, "What the fuck do you think you're doing, young lady?"

Carly jumped like a scalded cat and began shrieking, "Daddy, Daddy! I just need to—"

"You didn't ask!" he shouted. "You were stealing from me! How many other times has this happened? Huh?"

"Well, Mama does and—"

"Oh, my God! Like that's supposed to make it right?" he roared.

She covered her face and cried louder. She was still wailing when Gloria came rushing into the room. She took one look at Greg half-naked, with only a bath towel wrapped around his waist, and her daughter backed against a wall screaming her head off, and added her own shriek to the mess.

"Gregory! What is the meaning of this? What did you do to Carly?"

He froze.

Carly was still screaming, and his wife was about to accuse him of some immoral act. He could see it in her eyes.

He pointed at his daughter. "Shut the hell up!"

She sucked in the last shriek, and then hiccupped on a sob.

"Don't talk to our daughter like that!" Gloria screamed.

Greg pointed at her next.

"And you shut the hell up, too! I've about had it with the both of you. I am trying to get ready for work and find my daughter in *our* bedroom going through my wallet like the sneak thief she is!"

Gloria's indignation sputtered like a quickly doused fire, but her husband was just getting started.

"And do you know what her excuse was? Mama does it! Do you, Gloria! Do you steal from me, too? Have you no shame?"

Gloria's face reddened. "Carly, go to your room!" she snapped.

"Oh, hell no!" Greg said. "She's not going anywhere, and neither are you." He pointed to the foot of the bed. "Sit, the both of you, and listen, because I'm not going to say this but once."

Gloria grabbed her daughter and shoved her down on the bed, and then plopped down beside her, muttering something to the effect that it was all Carly's fault.

"So talk," Gloria said.

Greg grabbed a towel from the bathroom and wiped the shaving cream from his face, and then tossed the towel on the floor at their feet, well aware it would tick his wife off that it was there.

"Here's the scoop," he said. "We're broke! I earned it. You spent it. It's gone. I cannot earn enough to cover your debts if you never spent another penny for the rest of this year. You are both selfish, wasteful and unappreciative, and part of that is my fault for letting it go this long."

Carly's mouth had dropped open when she heard the word *broke*, and it had yet to shut.

Gloria had a hand at her breast, as if ready to feign illness, and Greg saw it.

"If you die, you'll be buried in a pauper's grave, so I'd advise you to get over it."

Gloria gasped, and then started to weep.

"Cry all you want. It's not going to change the facts. This house is going on the market today. We will be renting, and you better pray to God I don't get fired. Every credit card is being canceled today, so don't try to use them, because you're going to be very embarrassed when they're rejected."

"No, no," Gloria wailed. "How will I face my friends?"

Carly added to the racket. "You can't, Daddy! I need a dress for the Harvest Ball!"

Greg just stared at them.

"*You're* worried about your friends," he told his wife, then said to his daughter, "and you are actually sitting there telling me you need a new dress, when I've just explained that we're broke—as in 'can't buy food' broke! I'm done. Both of you…get out! If you so much as open your mouth and argue with me again, I'm stopping off at the lawyer's office on the way to work and filing for divorce. It would be an utter relief to be rid of the both of you."

"You'll have to pay me alimony!" Gloria shrieked.

"And child support!" Carly wailed.

"With what?" he shouted. "Get a job! Both of you! Now leave!"

Carly flew out of the room, but Gloria stood, still unwilling to yield the floor.

"Why are you still here?" Greg drawled, and then

dropped the towel. "Or is it this? I'm willing to be late to work if you're up for a quickie."

"Cover yourself," she yelled, and stomped out the door, slamming it shut behind her.

"That's what I thought," he muttered, then picked up his wallet and took it with him into the bathroom to finish shaving.

It was a hard thing to accept after all the work he'd gone to in an effort to realize his dream of being mayor, but that dream clearly wasn't going to come true.

Nine

Marcus Silver was waiting on a conference call and had wandered into the library of the family mansion to study the portraits of his paternal ancestors. It was something he did when he felt unsettled, a way of connecting with his past and strengthening him to handle what needed to be done.

His four times great-grandfather, Jarrod Silver, who had emigrated from England, had been a big, strapping man with a square jaw and a steady gaze. The dog at his side was a mastiff. Marcus knew its name had been Zeus from reading family history.

The portrait of Geoffrey Silver, his three times great-grandfather was hanging next to Jarrod's. The artist had captured the intent and determination in Geoffrey's wide face and high forehead, considered a sign of high intelligence in those times. The dog at his feet was a large bloodhound named Thunder that, according to family history, had been used to track down runaway slaves.

He shoved his hands into his pockets as he gazed intently at the next portrait. Aaron Silver, his two times great-grandfather, was displayed as grandly as the others, but he had a severe underbite, which left him with a less than commanding appearance. Marcus smiled. This grandfather had invested heavily in railroads, which had contributed greatly to the family coffers, proving looks were no predictor of success or failure. The dog in the portrait with him was a cocker spaniel, a beautiful dog but without the macho cachet of the first two.

He turned to the opposite wall, where the portrait of his great-grandfather, Delacroix Silver, was hanging. Delacroix had lost a good deal of the Silver fortune during the stock market crash early in the last century. But instead of bemoaning his losses, he'd soon replenished the family coffers by turning a blind eye to the law, buying and selling illegal whiskey and then delivering it to the speakeasies in the bigger cities of Chicago and New York. By the time prohibition had ended, the Silver fortune was healthy once more. The English pug in Delacroix's lap looked as defiant as its master.

A quick flash of tears blurred Marcus's vision as he moved to the portraits of his grandfather, Montgomery Silver, and his black Lab, Striker, then to his father, Thomas John Silver, and his English setter, a dog named Royal. Marcus remembered many happy hours playing with old Royal when he was a boy.

Marcus knew it wasn't manly to be enamored of one's own appearance, but seeing his portrait hanging next to his father's gave him a huge sense of pride. He came from good blood. The dog in his portrait was a German shepherd named Hunter. They never replaced him after he died. He and T.J. weren't all that keen on pets.

Thomas John's favorite byword had been "blood will out." Marcus wondered if, by the time T.J. reached his age, his impressive bloodline would hold him steady, and if his portrait would be hanging among the others. It was going to be up to T.J. to carry on. Marcus had sacrificed so much and done what had to be done to keep their heritage secure. He hoped T.J. was up to the task of safeguarding it for the future.

Fresh from his night with Lainey and the goodbye kiss they'd shared, Sam walked with the stride of a man who'd shed a great burden. He moved across the hospital lobby toward the elevator, anxious to see if there was any change in Trina's condition. When he saw the elevator doors beginning to shut he grabbed them, then strode in, nodding to the other man in the elevator, who was holding a small potted plant.

"How's it going?" he said and pressed the button for the third floor.

"Oh, I'm fine," the killer said. "Are you going to see Trina?"

"Yes," Sam said as the door opened to the second floor.

"Then, give her my best," the killer said, and headed down the hall carrying the potted plant before him like a shield.

"Will do," Sam said, and then promptly forgot all about it.

He got off on the third floor and walked swiftly toward ICU.

Clarice Powell was on duty when Sam stopped to sign in.

"Good morning, Clarice. Has the doctor already made rounds?"

"Yes, he was in early." She pulled the chart. "No changes noted, but she's stable, no fever, which means no infection, which means she's healing."

Satisfied, Sam went inside and headed straight to Trina's room. Cain Embry was still on duty when Sam walked up.

"Morning, Cain."

"Good morning, Sam."

"Everything okay here?" Sam asked.

"Yes."

"Good," Sam said and entered Trina's room. He leaned down and kissed the side of her cheek, and then spoke softly close to her ear.

"Hey, little sister, it's Sam. You're safe and you're healing. I love you, baby."

Then he sat down in a chair beside her bed, laid his hand on her arm and started talking. When he'd been hospitalized for so long, there were things that had worn on his nerves, and one of them was the strident tone of people's voices. Regardless of whether Trina could hear him or not, he was intent on keeping the tone of his voice soft and even.

After reminiscing about some of her childhood mishaps, and how he and Trey used to sneak her extra cookies when she was little, he shifted to holiday memories.

"Do you remember the last Christmas that Dad was with us? You wanted an air rifle, and Mom wanted you to have a Barbie playhouse. They had the biggest argument I ever heard them have, and it was over your present. It got so intense Trey and I were afraid they'd forget about buying us anything, but you were oblivious to the undercurrents. Dad took you out to the mountain to target practice, and Mom began teaching you how to cook. By the time Christmas came, Mom and Dad had made up and you got a puppy. That was Boomer. He was a good old dog, wasn't he?"

He watched her face intently for any sign of movement but saw nothing, so he told himself to be satisfied just to be with her. He noticed her lips looked dry and got up to put some glycerin on them. He was washing his hands when he got a text from Trey that ended the visit. He stopped by her bed to tell her he was leaving.

"Trina, honey, I have to go now, but I'll be back. Love you."

He left ICU and met Lee getting off the elevator.

"Hi," Sam said. "I'm going to the precinct. She's stable. No change."

"Thanks," Lee said. "I took my lunch hour early so I could spend it with her. See you later."

Sam drove straight to the precinct, and then hurried down the hall to Trey's office.

"What's going on?" he asked.

"I have a social security number on Donny Collins. I was about to start running his name through the computer to see if he popped up anywhere, but I have a prisoner who's being transferred, and the US Marshal just arrived. You probably know more about running traces than I do. Are you willing?" Trey asked.

"Absolutely," Sam said. "Should I use your computer?"

"Yes. I left you the log-in info," Trey said. "Work your magic, brother. I need to know this guy's status ASAP. The minifridge has cold pop, and there are snacks in my desk drawer. Sorry I can't offer a better lunch."

"I'm good," Sam said. "I had a big breakfast with Lainey."

Trey's eyes widened, and then he smiled.

"I'll be damned. Well, I'm happy to hear that. Text if you need me."

As soon as Trey left, Sam shed his coat, rolled up his sleeves, sat down at the computer and got to work.

The killer was on a mission.

All the old roadblocks had disappeared with the death of Betsy Jakes. Now he had a new one, but he was working on correcting his one mistake. There was a man he knew who used to work for Colquitt Mining in Kentucky until he retired and came back home to West Virginia. His name was Moses Ledbetter, and he was a demon with explosives. After a brief phone call on a throwaway phone, an amount of money was agreed upon and delivery was due in three days.

Yesterday he'd taken a late lunch and gone to the local library to see what he could find on the hospital layout. He'd logged on to a library computer to see what was available, and when he found a site with the original blueprints and a story on the date they broke ground, he was elated.

He began studying the layout, even taking a few pictures with his phone. After he returned home for the evening he studied the pictures some more, taking note of stairwells, air shafts and the hospital lab, and where they were in relation to ICU.

Satisfied that he had the important locations fixed firmly in his mind, he'd headed for the hospital that morning to see if the layout was the same or if, over the years, remodeling had changed it. He'd bought a potted plant to use as cover, so it would seem as if he was on the second floor to visit a patient, when in actuality he was checking out what was directly under ICU.

It was a fluke that he'd ridden up in the elevator with Sam Jakes. He had to admit, the man made him nervous. He was so big and, from what he'd heard, very unpredictable. He didn't want to have to go head-to-head with the man in a fight. He would lose hands-down. So he kept walking the hall, needing this to be over, but so far all he'd seen were patient rooms, which weren't what he wanted.

He was headed down the west hall when he saw a man he recognized from church walking the halls in his hospital gown and pushing a pole holding his IV.

"There you are, Mr. Berry! They mentioned your name on the prayer list at church. Looks as if you're doing well now, up and walking about."

Sherman Berry smiled. "Why, I am doing better, thanks, but I wouldn't wish hemorrhoid surgery on my worst enemy."

The killer chuckled. "Ouch! I'm glad to see you're doing well. If you'll tell me which room you're in, I'll just set this plant on a table and be on my way."

"Are those for me?" Sherman asked.

"They sure are."

"That's wonderful! I appreciate the thought. I'm

just down the hall in 224. Bed A. I have a roommate, but they have him out running tests," Sherman said.

"It's great to see you up and about," the killer said, and strolled on down the hall as if he owned it.

He left the plant in the room, and then continued down the corridor in the other direction, but he found nothing suited for what he needed. He paused, trying to picture the blueprints again, and decided to go down one floor and see what was below him.

The force of the bomb he'd bought would take down an entire building. He just wanted to cover his bases and be sure that the force of the blast was directly under ICU. The damned woman had already survived a bullet in the chest. He needed to be sure her luck finally ran out.

Instead of going back up the hall to the elevator, he backtracked a couple of doors to the stairwell and went one floor down, then stepped out of the stairwell to look around.

It was the door right in front of him that caught his eye. He crossed the hall, went inside the chapel and walked down the aisle to the altar. He looked up, imagining the location of the ICU, and smiled. This was the perfect place from which to send a few more souls winging their way to heaven. He left the hospital in haste, anxious to get back to what he'd been doing. Time was running short.

The first trace Sam ran on Donny Collins was the work history associated with his social security number, and he was a little shocked by what came up. Sometimes an answer came easy, but not often. This was one of those times that it had, and it felt good to be helping find their mother's killer.

He sent Trey a quick text.

No work history on D. Collins after May 1980

Then, just to be thorough, he ran the same number through military records, then checked for legal name changes and still came up empty. Gut instinct told him that the body his mother dreamed about seeing at the bottom of some mine shaft was Donny Collins. The puzzle was why it had happened and who'd done it.

The phone rang and he answered without thinking. "Chief Jakes' office."

"This is Sheriff Osmond. Is the chief there?"

"Hello, Sheriff. This is Sam Jakes, Trey's older brother. I'm here helping with the case. He's here but away from the phone for a bit. Can I give him a message?"

"Well, hello, Sam. I'm sorry about your mother. She was a fine lady. You said you're helping with the case?"

"Yes, I own Ranger Investigations out of Atlanta."

"The reason I called was to let Trey know I got clearance to begin searching the old Colquitt Mining site west of Mystic tomorrow."

Sam's pulse kicked. "Am I allowed to be there?"

"It's fine with me," the sheriff said.

"I'll give him the message. Thanks for letting us know," Sam said.

"Then, I guess I'll see you tomorrow," Sheriff Osmond said and disconnected.

Sam jotted down the message and left it on Trey's

desk, then he went back to the computer to check a few more sites to see if Donny Collins popped up.

Another twenty minutes passed. He sent a text to Lainey reminding her of their dinner date that night and saying he would pick her up at six thirty. A few moments later he got a text back with nothing but a heart emoticon on the screen, which made him smile. Yeah, he loved her, too.

Sam was still at the desk when Trey returned. Sam handed him the note from Sheriff Osmond.

Trey scanned the note with interest. "Osmond is going to the mine tomorrow?"

Sam nodded. "He said I could go, too."

"Good. I'll make arrangements before I leave here tonight," Trey said, then glanced at the computer screen. "So you've found nothing else anywhere?"

"His social security number hasn't been active since May of 1980. There are thousands of Donald Ray Collinses in the US, but none that match the one we're looking for. I even checked the registry for legal name changes on the off chance that he would have changed his name for some reason. There's nothing, Trey. It's as if he dropped off the face of the earth."

"Or down a mine shaft," Trey said.

Sam shuddered. "So where to now?" he asked.

Trey picked up a pen and started pacing as he talked. "My gut tells me the gossip about cheating has something to do with what happened," he said.

Sam remembered Lainey standing up, holding the diaries. "Where are those diaries Lainey brought? She said there were names."

"There are, but not given names. Her mother either used nicknames or wrote them in some kind of teenage code talk."

"What do you mean?" Sam asked.

Trey dug the diaries out of his desk drawer.

"See for yourself. They've already been entered in as evidence. I'm reading them on my downtime."

"I can read them for you," Sam said.

"Good. Take them with you and make notes," Trey said and handed them over.

"Okay, but in the meantime, who in the senior class had the most to lose by being found out?" Sam asked.

Trey paused. "Someone who might not graduate?" he finally said.

"I don't think so," Sam said. "When we were in school, the kids who barely slid through knew they were on shaky ground. One test wouldn't have made that much difference to them. Most of them were going to get jobs anyway, with or without a high school diploma, right?"

"Right," Trey said and started pacing again. "So who *did* have the most to lose if they failed that test?"

"Let's ask ourselves that question another way. Who had the most to gain by acing it?" Sam asked.

"The same ones who would lose big if they failed," Trey said. "The valedictorian and salutatorian."

"But would you really kill someone over that?" Sam asked.

Trey paused again. "What if it was an accident? What if you didn't mean to, but it happened? What would you do then?" he asked.

Sam stood. "Hide the body."

"But what if there were witnesses?" Trey added.

Sam stared across the desk at his brother.

"Then you would have two choices. Either run for your life or try to stop them from telling."

"And the witnesses had only one choice," Trey added. "Tell what they'd seen."

Sam shuddered. "What if this is it, Trey? What if this is the reason Mom and her friends were even in that wreck?"

"But three of them lived," Trey said. "Why wait this long to silence them?"

"Because the killer lucked out. None of them remembered what had happened," Sam said.

"So why now? Mom's memories were triggered by Dick Phillips' death. If Dick hadn't died, she would have likely grown old with those memories forever locked in her mind," Trey said. "So why did the killer go after Dick in the first place?"

"Something must have changed for the killer," Sam said.

Trey's eyes widened. "That's it! We have to figure out whose life is changing and let that lead us to our killer."

"It would have to be something big," Sam said. "Something that would throw him into the public eye in some way."

"I want to talk to Marcus Silver," Trey said.

"But he already said winning that money wouldn't have changed a thing about his life, and no one challenged that statement," Sam said.

"Winning isn't always about the prize. Sometimes it's about the honor."

"Are you going to talk to him now?" Sam asked.

"Yes. I don't want to give him a heads-up. I want to see how he reacts when I show up at his house."

"I'm going with you," Sam said, then grabbed his jacket and hat, followed Trey out the back door and then slid into the passenger seat of the cruiser. "Impressive layout," he added, eyeing the dash cam, the radio and the in-dash computer the department used to run checks and warrants.

"It serves most of our needs," Trey said as he drove out of the parking lot and headed down Main Street. "So talk to me about Lainey. Last I knew she threw a coffee cup at you."

"I went back," Sam said.

Trey grinned. "You always were a glutton for punishment."

Sam sighed. "And slow to admit I'm wrong."

"I wasn't going to mention that. So you two really made up?"

"She's willing to give me another chance," Sam said.

"Then, don't blow it."

"I won't do it intentionally," Sam muttered. "My main concern is not hurting her or scaring the shit out of her."

Trey nodded.

"Hey, Trey, did you know she was diagnosed with breast cancer last year?" Sam asked.

Trey looked startled. "Hell no! Is she all right now?"

"They took both breasts, and she finished the chemo treatments not too long ago. She's way too thin, but her hair is growing back and for now she's cancer-free."

Trey gave his brother a quick glance and saw tears in his eyes. "So she's okay. That's great!"

"Yes, it is," Sam said. "But she said something to

me that I haven't been able to forget. She said if Mom hadn't been murdered, I wouldn't be here and we would most likely never have seen each other again."

"Wow," Trey said. "She didn't cut you any slack, did she?"

"No, and rightly so, but it made me think how random life can be. Mom wanted us all to be happy. Our happiness was all she talked about, like hers didn't matter anymore, but if none of this killing had started, where would we be?"

Trey thought of how far apart he and Dallas had been before Dick was killed. "She was overjoyed when Dallas and I got back together."

Sam nodded. "She told me when she called to talk to me about giving you Dad's pistol on your birthday. I could hear the joy in her voice."

Trey smiled. "Yes, and thank you for being okay with that. It meant a lot."

Sam shrugged. "It should be yours. Both of you were in the same profession. I know how proud he would be." Then he added, "She left a message to all three of us in my letter. I think she expected to be the next victim, despite anyone's efforts. She wanted us to know that she was okay with dying. She said she missed Dad so much, and that by the time I read the letter, she would already be in his arms."

"Oh, God," Trey said and took a slow, shaky breath.

Sam ran a finger around the crown of his Stetson as he tried to think how to say what he'd been feeling.

"I guess what I'm getting at is that fate did what none of us could do for ourselves. Mom is where she wanted to be. Dallas came home to you. Tragedy threw Lainey and me together again," Sam said. "I keep telling myself this whole mess feels orchestrated by a higher power. Back in 1980 someone got away with murder. The way things are unfolding, we might be able to bring him to justice."

"You amaze me, brother."

"How so?" Sam asked.

"You're different now. More thoughtful, I guess. I don't have any other way to describe it."

Sam shrugged. "Like I told Lainey, the boy she knew died in a war. I'm all that's left."

Trey squeezed Sam's shoulder. "You are more than enough, and I'm damn glad you're still here."

As they drove through Mystic, Sam couldn't help but notice how many people waved at Trey as they passed. His brother belonged here. He'd found his place, his calling. A couple of times Sam saw someone do a double take when they realized he was with Trey. It felt surreal to be sitting in the car with his brother and driving around town again. It must be strange for the locals as well, to see him when he had been gone for so long.

Finally they reached the iron gates marking the entrance to the Silver estate. The gates were wide-open today, but Sam remembered a time when they hadn't been. When a visitor had to either call ahead to let someone know they were coming with a delivery, or wait at the entrance for someone from the big house to let them in.

"Hey, Trey, remember when these gates used to be closed all the time?"

Trey frowned. "No, not really."

"Well, they were. I came here with Dad one time when I was little. He'd picked me up from school because it was snowing and the roads were getting bad, but he had to deliver something to the Silver estate, so we came here before we went home."

"Where was I?" Trey asked.

"I don't think you were old enough yet to go to school. Anyway, I just remember when we drove up, Dad rang the house on some kind of intercom, and then we sat in the car with the heater blasting, waiting for someone from the big house to open the gates."

"Weird," Trey said.

Sam nodded. "I didn't think anything of it then, but now it seems like overkill. I mean, Mystic is hardly LA. No one thinks of this place as the Silver Estate. It's just the Silver place."

"Well, today they're open and we're going through," Trey said, and they drove up to the main house.

They were on their way to the front door when T.J. drove up behind them and parked beneath the portico.

"Hey, guys! What's up?" he said, walking toward them.

"We need to speak to your dad. Is he in?"

T.J. frowned. "He was going out of town this morning. I don't know if he's back yet or not. Come in and we'll find out, okay?"

"Thanks," Trey said and followed him inside.

T.J. paused a moment in the foyer, listening, and then pointed to a room just up the hall.

"That's the library," he said. "Why don't you two make yourselves comfortable in there, and I'll find Cook and see what she knows."

"Thank you," Trey said.

He walked toward the library as T.J. headed in the

opposite direction. Sam lagged behind Trey, watching until T.J. disappeared around a corner, then followed his brother into the room.

Trey was moving around the room, looking at the portraits.

"I didn't know the Silver family had been on this land that many years. Look at this! The first Silver was born in the late 1700s, so he would have been the first to settle here. And this one lived here during the Civil War," he said.

"There's Marcus," Sam said, pointing to the latest portrait, which was hanging on the other side of the room.

Trey turned, thinking Marcus had entered the room, and then saw the portrait Sam was pointing at.

"Quite a legacy," Trey said.

Sam's eyes narrowed. "Also a lot of weight to bear on your shoulders."

Before Trey could comment, T.J. was back.

"Sorry it took so long. Today is the maid's day off. Cook wasn't here, so I had to call Dad to see where he was and how long it would take for him to get home."

"So he's not here," Trey said.

"No, and he said he won't be back until late."

"Well, then, just tell him I'll come back another time."

"I sure will. Is there a message or anything?" T.J. asked.

"Not really. Just more stuff regarding the murders."

T.J.'s expression fell. "I'm so sorry about your mother. She was a nice lady. I lost *my* mother a few years back, and I still miss her every day."

"What happened to her?" Sam asked.

"Oh, she hated living here in Mystic. Kept wanting Dad to move to the capital, somewhere with some life and dignity, she would say, but Dad wouldn't go, so she divorced him. She was killed less than six months later in a wreck."

"Sorry to hear that," Sam said.

T.J. nodded. "Thanks. You know, sometimes you have to do the hard stuff, even when you don't want to. If she'd stayed, she might still be alive."

"I can see how you would think that, but try not to beat yourself up," Trey said. "We'll see ourselves out."

He and Sam left the library. They were on the way to the cruiser when Sam spoke.

"So now we know why the gates aren't closed anymore."

"Huh? Why?" Trey asked.

"Mrs. Silver didn't like Mystic. I'm guessing those gates gave her a feeling of superiority. She could shut out the rabble and hide behind the facade of her little palace."

"Oh, right," Trey said. "It's weird what matters to people, isn't it?"

"Kind of like cheating. Some people would be humiliated to get caught. Some would laugh it off and probably try it again another time," Sam said.

They drove away without answers today, but there was still tomorrow.

T.J. watched from the library window, frowning, wondering what the brothers knew that he didn't. He didn't like surprises, especially when his dad was getting ready to announce his bid for a Senate seat.

Ten

Lainey was in tears. She'd been through her entire closet looking for something nice to wear for her dinner date, and everything was so loose, she looked like she was wearing a sack. Sam would be there in a little over an hour, which didn't give her any time to drive into Mystic to shop. She was verging on panic mode when her phone rang. When she saw it was him, she sat down on the side of the bed to talk.

"Hello," she said.

"Hey, honey, it's me. We still on for tonight?"

"Nothing fits," she said, and then burst into tears.

Sam frowned. "Oh, hey, hey, no tears," he said. "I can fix that. You just get all prettied up and wait for me to get there, okay?"

"I'll be prettied up in blue jeans. Maybe we should just go to Charlie's for burgers," she said.

"It's gonna be fine. See you soon."

Lainey hung up, and then fell backward onto the bed with a frustrated thump.

"My first real date in ten years and I have nothing to wear."

* * *

Sam dressed in five minutes, checked to make sure he had his gun, grabbed his hat and headed for the motel office at a lope. Delia was sitting behind the counter watching TV when he ran in.

"Where would you go to buy something pretty for a date?" he asked.

Delia turned down the sound, and then grinned. "Is this an invitation?"

"I'm serious, and I don't have much time," he said.

"Okay, honey. I had to tease you a little. Look, there's a really nice boutique here in town. It's called Le Chic."

"Oh, I saw that the other day. Would they still be open?" Sam asked.

"You head that way, and I'll call and tell them to hang around."

"Thanks, Delia. I owe you," Sam said and headed for his SUV.

He drove with an eye on the traffic, hoping he could get there in time, and breathed a quick sigh of relief when he saw the open sign was still lit.

When he walked in, he brought the outside with him. A stiff breeze rattled the bell over the door and blew a handful of scarves off a rack.

"Oh, sorry!" he said, and started to retrieve them when a young woman came running.

"It's not your fault. I need to move that rack," she said. "Are you Sam?"

He nodded.

"I'm Shawn. Delia called. Said you needed some help. What can we do?"

And just like that, his anxiety eased. He eyed the girl, judging her size against Lainey's.

"I need to get something pretty for my girl. We're going out to eat tonight, and nothing in her closet fits her anymore."

Shawn giggled. "That's the complaint of every girl," she said.

"Not her. She's been sick. Everything is too big."

"Oh, I'm so sorry. I didn't mean to be thoughtless. What do you think she would like…a dress, or slacks and a top?"

"Slacks and a top," he said.

"Can you guess her size?"

"What's yours?" Sam asked.

"I usually wear a six or an eight," Shawn said.

"Maybe a two or a four."

Shawn nodded. "Okay, we can look at both sizes, and you can be the judge."

Sam followed her to the pants section, where she began pointing out different fabrics and styles. He thought of how thin Lainey was and how cold it would get when the sun went down, and opted for a heavier fabric.

"Here's something in black velvet," Shawn said. "You can't go wrong with black, and velvet is comfortable to wear. This is a size four." She took the pants off the hanger, and then held them up. "And this is the size two," she said and held them up as well, so he could compare waist sizes.

"The size two," Sam said. "But she's taller than you," he added.

She held the pants up to her waist, and then pointed. "These are way too long for me. They should be about right for her. Now, what about a top? Maybe a pretty sweater to hug her dainty curves?"

Sam took a deep breath. "She doesn't have any of those right now," he said.

Shawn's eyes widened, and then filled with tears.

"I'm sorry. I keep saying that, don't I?" She wiped her eyes and tried a shaky smile. "Let's start over, okay?"

"Look, it's okay. It's a tough situation, but she's still alive and that's all that matters to me. I want a top that makes her feel good about herself without calling attention to the obvious."

"Of course, and if I have it in a small, I know just the one," Shawn said and headed for the other side of the store, where jackets and blouses were hanging.

He followed with a lump in his throat.

"How about this?" Shawn said, holding up a white silky blouse. The neckline dipped to a slight V, and the front was edged from button to buttonhole with large floppy ruffles.

Sam imagined those ruffles disguising the fact that Lainey was missing both breasts.

"I'll take it, along with the pants," he said.

"How about this black velvet jacket to finish off the look? If she's a bit thin right now, the peplum waist will give her a little definition, and the one button at the waistline will leave the ruffles on the blouse free to fall on the outside of the jacket. See?" She held the jacket up over the blouse to demonstrate.

"Yes," he said, and pulled out his wallet.

"Do you want me to leave them on the hangers? I mean, since she's going to be wearing them shortly, the velvet would be fine, but we wouldn't want to put a wrinkle in the blouse."

"On the hangers," he said.

Ten minutes later he was on his way out of town.

It was just after six when he pulled up to the front of Lainey's house and parked. He grabbed the plastic garment bag and headed for the house.

Lainey opened the door, and then shivered as the wind whipped in.

"It's cold," she said as Sam came through the door.

She shut it quickly behind him, shivering as he wrapped her up in a one-armed hug.

"You smell good," he said, and then kissed her. "Mmm, and you taste good, too. Here you go, Cinderella. I'm not your fairy godmother, but I like to think I have an eye for fashion, especially when it's on you."

Lainey's heart skipped. "I won't be long," she said, and made a run for her bedroom.

"Yell if you need help!" he said. "We can be late."

He heard her laughing as her bedroom door swung shut. That was all he needed to hear.

He took off his hat and coat, and then sat down and turned on the TV to see if he could catch a weather report. Since they were going to search the Colquitt Mining site tomorrow, he was hoping it would stay clear.

A few minutes passed and he was listening to the end of the weather report when he heard footsteps behind him. He turned off the TV and stood up.

"Oh, wow. Oh, Lainey," he said.

She was beaming, and Sam couldn't stop staring.

The straight-leg pants made her legs look even longer than they already were, the little black jacket with the flared waist put a much-needed curve on her backside and the fall of white ruffles from the blouse beneath was like icing on a cake. He saw the black half boots with hammered silver on the toes, the cap of red curls and the smile on her face, and knew he'd hit it out of the park. She looked like she'd stepped out of *Vogue* magazine.

"You look beautiful."

"It fits. It all fits," she said, so happy she couldn't stand still. "I can't believe you picked this all out by yourself, but I love it."

"I had help. A girl named Shawn saved the day for both of us," Sam said, trying to take it all in. "You are going to set heads to turning tonight. Just remember you're with me."

She laughed and all but leaped into his arms.

"Thank you, Sam! I haven't felt this good about myself in such a long time."

He kissed her forehead and then both cheeks, saving her pink lips for last.

"Don't want to mess up any makeup," he said. "Are you ready to go?"

"I just need my coat out of the hall closet."

"Do you want the long gray one?" he asked as he opened the closet door.

"Is it cold enough for that?"

"Yes, the wind is sharp, and the sun is about to go down."

"Then, yes, the gray one," she said.

He held it out as she slipped it on. She grabbed

her purse as he opened the door and turned on the porch light.

Lainey locked the door, then turned to face the wind, pulling the coat up around her neck as she looked out across her yard and the road beyond.

"Everything okay?" Sam asked.

She nodded, thinking what a gift this was.

Her.

Sam.

On their way to somewhere else.

She'd waited a long time for this moment.

"Everything is perfect," she said, and then smiled.

They walked off the porch together, and minutes later were on their way to Cutter's Steakhouse.

Will Porter exited the hospital, his thoughts in free-fall.

Rita was dying. She had suffered a stroke, and her organs were shutting down.

All these months he'd wished her dead, and now it was happening. He didn't know whether to drop to his knees and pray to God for forgiveness, or dance. This was not the time to file as a candidate for state superintendent of schools, but he almost didn't care. When this was all over, he had the rest of his life to do as he wished.

He thought about going home to eat, but there was no food in the house. He considered picking up something on the way home, then decided to stop off at Cutter's. He was in the mood for a good steak, and he always saw people he knew there. Maybe someone would ask him to join them. Either way, he wasn't ready to go home. His conscience was already there, waiting for him.

* * *

Greg Standish had been out of town all day, but he knew the for-sale sign would be on the front lawn when he got home. He'd signed the papers with the Realtor this morning and let the man in to take pictures. The man had called him around noon to tell him that he'd put the lock box on the front door and the for-sale sign up in the front yard.

Greg could only imagine the hell he was going to catch, but he didn't really care. Just the simple act of finally deciding to cut off the money his wife and daughter were bleeding from him was a start.

The sun was setting when he drove back into Mystic and headed for home. The streetlights were on, and as he neared the house he saw the for-sale sign in the yard. He felt a moment of regret, and then it was gone. The house was nothing but a weight around his neck.

He pulled up in the drive and went around to the back door to go in, as was his habit. The house was dark; the rooms were chilly. He frowned and began turning on lights as he went, and turned up the thermostat when he got to the hall.

It wasn't until he got to the bedroom that he noticed things were missing. Gloria's jewelry box that always sat on the top of the dresser was gone. His first thought was that they had been robbed, and then it hit him. He ran for the closet. Her clothes were gone, shoes and purses, too, underwear missing from the dresser drawers.

"Son of a bitch," he muttered and headed to Carly's room. He found the same thing. All her stuff was missing, too.

He walked back through the house with a heavy

heart. So it had come to this. The first time shit got hard, she ran away. He went back into the kitchen and saw the note on the island. He picked it up.

> *We've gone to Charleston to Mother's house. I took Carly out of school. She'll finish out the year there. I saw the bills. I'm sorry. I don't know how to do without. I won't fight the divorce.*
> *Gloria*

"Well, hell," Greg mumbled, and then dropped the letter and turned to face where life had taken him.

His stomach grumbled. He would have been pissed off that no one had cooked him any food, but he couldn't remember the last time Gloria had cooked anyway. He checked his wallet for money, and when he saw he had just enough to eat on, he walked back out of the house and drove away. There was food in town. All he had to do was pick a place.

Sam and Lainey entered Cutter's to find the standard Friday-night crowd. The hostess, Cherry Adams, saw them and smiled. Sam had come in with Trey and Dallas the other night, but without a date. It appeared he was revisiting old times.

"Good evening, you two. Lainey Pickett! It's been ages since I've seen you. Where are you living now?"

"I'm still living on the home place," Lainey said.

Cherry's eyes widened with surprise, but she kept her curiosity to herself.

"Well, whatever you've been doing, you look stunning. I love your hair, and that outfit is to die for."

Lainey's smile froze. She had almost died to get it.

"Thank you. Sam picked it out for me. He has a good eye, don't you think?"

Sam was grinning. A little embarrassed, but soaking up the attention just the same.

"I think the Jakes brothers always know what they like," Cherry said. "So let's get you seated. Would you like a booth or a table?"

"Booth, please," Sam said, and then took Lainey's arm as they followed Cherry across the room.

The killer walked into Cutter's right behind Sam Jakes and a tall, slender redhead. He watched as Sam removed her overcoat and handed it to the girl in coat check, then pocketed the stub she gave him.

All he could see was the back of her head, but from where he was standing she looked good. Then she turned sideways, and when Sam leaned down to whisper something in her ear, he recognized her. Lainey Pickett. Their reunion must have been a result of her presence at the meeting at City Hall. Then the hostess appeared and took them over to a booth on the west side of the room.

His eyes narrowed as he watched them go. Sam couldn't keep his hands off her. He seemed to remember them being a couple before Sam left for the military. From the way they were behaving, they might be leaning toward that relationship again. Whatever. He had more to worry about than who Sam Jakes chose to fuck.

The hostess came back to greet him, and when he also asked for a booth, she seated him right behind Sam. Apparently, they were sharing a waitress, which was fine with him. As long as she kept his coffee hot and the conversation short.

Unaware he was close enough to the killer to reach out and grab him, Sam directed his focus entirely on Lainey.

She was beaming, and the way her eyes flashed as the waitress walked over and she recognized yet another friend from her past made him happy.

She and the waitress, a girl named Jennifer, had gone to school together. Jennifer seemed so happy to see her that she kept giggling while taking their order.

As soon as Jennifer left, Sam reached across the table and held out his hand. Lainey grasped it as if it were the gold ring on a merry-go-round and held tight.

"Oh, Sam, this is wonderful. Thank you for bringing me here."

"Believe me, it's totally my pleasure," he said softly. "So tell me, how was your day? Did you have classes?"

"World history at 2:00 p.m. and that was it. I'm off until Monday, but that day is pretty full. What about you?"

"There was a lot going on that had to do with the investigation," he said. "And I've got a big day tomorrow, but I won't go into that here."

"Do you know if there was anything of value in Mom's diaries?" she asked.

"Yes. Just the revelation about the cheating scandal was huge. It's opened up all kinds of leads."

"Mom kept diaries all her life. There are more if you think you might need them," she said.

"My mom did the same thing. She called them

journals, but she was still writing in them up until she was murdered. In fact, what she wrote, combined with what we gleaned from your mother's diaries, has given us most of what we know right now."

Lainey leaned forward and lowered her voice.

"I stayed in your meeting until I felt I had nothing more to share, and then I left, so I don't know what all was said afterward about the cheating thing, but I can't imagine committing murder over something like that. As for the names in her posts, they weren't the real names, were they? They read like code to hide people's real names. I can't imagine why, other than it being Mom's way of being cute as a teenager."

"I haven't had a chance to read them yet, but I have them. Trey gave them to me today."

"She wrote about things like Tom Collins and Betty Boop being lovers, and everyone thinking Betty Boop was helping someone cheat, but it wasn't her boyfriend TC. The gossip was, someone else paid her a lot of money for the answers to a final."

Sam's heart skipped when she said the name Collins. Tom Collins was the name of a mixed drink, but *Donny* Collins was MIA. Then he wondered if Donny Collins had a girlfriend in school. It was something to investigate.

He shrugged. "Cheating has a whole lot of repercussions. A cheater's status and honor would take a big hit if he was found out, and some people will do anything to keep their name clean, you know?"

"You're right. I didn't think of it like that."

"Oh, good, here comes our appetizer," Sam said.

Lainey leaned back with her hands in her lap as Jennifer set the hot baked-artichoke dip in the middle of the table, and then asked, "May I top off your drinks?"

"We're good for now," Sam said.

"Enjoy," Jennifer said, and moved on to the next booth.

The killer looked up when the waitress stopped by his table. While he'd been waiting, he had gotten an earful of information he didn't like, and now he was so distracted he could barely focus enough to order. By the time the waitress left, Sam and Lainey were talking about food and he'd missed his chance to hear the end of the conversation. He didn't like knowing there were even more diaries that could screw up everything. What the hell was it about girls in the '80s writing everything down?

The steaks they'd ordered came cooked to perfection, although Lainey got full before her food was gone. Sam obliged by finishing off the last four bites of her small filet, and then had the audacity to ask if she wanted dessert.

"Maybe crème brûlée or a slice of cheesecake?" he asked.

"I have poppy-seed cake with cream-cheese icing at home," she said.

"That sounds even better," Sam said. "We can go home, have dessert, then eat cake."

Lainey laughed, and he grinned. Hearing that sound would never get old.

He signaled for the check, left a handful of bills that included a big tip and took Lainey's arm as they turned to leave. But their appearance together had the curious wondering, and they were stopped a couple of times before they got back to the lobby to retrieve her coat.

"Did you enjoy your meal?" Cherry asked.

"It was delicious, and it was so good to see you," Lainey said.

"Come back and see us anytime," Cherry said, and then left to seat another couple as Sam helped Lainey on with her coat.

As he'd predicted, the air had turned much colder while they'd been inside, and Lainey was very glad for the weight and length of her coat. They were on their way across the parking lot to the car when a loud explosion rocked the ground on which they were standing, followed by a huge fireball shooting up into the air.

Eleven

Sam reacted without thought. He pulled his gun with one hand and shoved Lainey behind him with the other. One explosion and he was thousands of miles away, fighting a war.

Lainey saw the fire, and then she saw Sam's face and knew he was mentally no longer with her. All of a sudden it no longer mattered what had caused that explosion. She needed to focus on how to defuse the situation. For a moment she was uncertain how to react, and then all she could think to do was defuse the situation.

She slipped out from behind him and carefully put a hand on his arm.

"Sam, it's okay, honey. You're in Mystic. You're home."

He glanced down at her, and when the front door to the restaurant opened and people began filing out to see what had caused the explosion, his focus shifted to them.

In that moment Lainey grabbed his face with both hands. "Sam! Look. At. Me!"

Sam's heart was pounding, and despite the cold, he was sweating. He was already trying to regain his sense of self when he heard Lainey's voice. He looked down and saw the worried look on her face, and his gut knotted.

"I'm sorry," he said.

"Put the gun up," she said.

He looked surprised that he was holding it and put it back in the shoulder holster, but his gut was still in knots. "Damn it. Now you see why—"

She interrupted him before he could say it.

"What I see is a man who has a right to be jumpy because of loud, unexpected noises. I'm cold. Let's get in the car, okay?"

He sighed. The only good thing about what happened was that she'd gotten a dose of the other side of his life and hadn't freaked out.

He unlocked the door for her, and then circled the car and got in. As soon as they were inside, he started the engine so he could turn on the heater, and then clasped her hand.

"I'm sorry. This is what happens sometimes. Did I scare you?"

"No, you didn't scare me. You're my Sam."

He threaded his fingers through hers, and then leaned back against the seat with his eyes closed, trying to regain his sense of self. His heart was pounding so hard it was difficult to breathe, and all he could think was that he'd ruined a perfect evening.

"But that's just it, Lainey. Sometimes I'm *not* your Sam. Sometimes I'm the bomb tech who got blown up."

"I get what you're saying, but you aren't hearing

me. When I see this, I just think it's because of something that happened to my Sam. Of course your ways of reacting to things will be different because your life experience has been different, and if you will remember, I know next to nothing about what happened, because you never told me. I only knew the bits your mom shared."

"What do you want to know?" he asked.

"Where were you when it happened? How did it happen?"

"In Iraq. Fallujah, to be exact. One of the men from our unit, a man named Carlos Olvera, had stepped on a mine. If he moved off it, it would explode. I was on my knees trying to defuse it. I had on all the padded gear a bomb tech wears, and was digging down in the sand when I stopped and turned to grab a tool. As I did, Carlos suddenly yelled, 'Sniper! Get down!' I heard a burst of gunfire as I threw myself away from the bomb. Carlos fired back, but he had already been hit. Everything blew up when he fell. Because I wasn't facing the bomb when it went off, I took most of the shrapnel and the blast in my back. Carlos died. I didn't. Loud noises still rattle my cage."

"Lumps under my skin rattle *my* cage, too. Let's just agree that we're part of the walking wounded and let it go."

He exhaled slowly. "I can do that," he said, and before she could answer, the notes of "Amazing Grace" filled the car.

Sam answered his phone. "Hello?"

It was Trey. "Where are you?" he asked.

"Just leaving Cutter's with Lainey, why?"

"I got a call about an explosion."

"Yes, we heard it. It was loud...really loud."

And in that moment Trey got it. "Oh, shit. Are you okay?"

"Mostly. So what's up?"

"I was going to tell you that Trina's condition has been upgraded from critical to serious, and they're going to start weaning her off the drugs that are keeping her asleep."

"That's wonderful news. Did they give you a timeline as to when they expect her to wake up?" Sam asked.

"Maybe in a couple of days."

"That's great," Sam said.

"As long as you're okay, I'll get over to the scene, see what the hell happened. Talk to you later," Trey said.

Sam slipped the phone in his pocket and turned to Lainey.

"That was Trey. He called to tell me Trina's improving and they're going to begin weaning her off the drugs."

Lainey gasped. "Sam! That's wonderful! Did they say how long it would take for her to wake up?"

"Maybe a couple of days."

"And then you'll know your killer!"

He nodded, but his gaze was still focused on the fire above the rooftops.

"That was one hell of an explosion," he said.

She turned to look at the skyline and saw huge orange flames above the roof of the nearest building.

"I hope no one was injured."

Sam looked at the sky. "It would be a miracle," he muttered.

She squeezed his hand. "Miracles happen, don't they?" she said.

He looked at her then, with the streetlights painting shadows on the contours of her face and was struck once again by her singular beauty. Despite everything she'd gone through, for him, she was still light in the dark.

"Would you mind if we stopped off at the hospital for a quick look in on Trina before we go home?" he asked.

"I would love to see her," Lainey said. "Do you want me to drive?"

He slid a hand beneath her chin, then leaned over and kissed her.

"No, baby, I'm okay, but thank you for asking." He steered out of the parking lot and headed to the hospital.

The killer walked out just as they were driving away. He was still bothered by the fact that Lainey Pickett had more of her mother's diaries. It stood to reason that no specific names had been mentioned or the cops would already have made an arrest, but it left him with an unsettled feeling. This had started out simple; now there were too many things beyond his control.

He drove out of Cutter's parking lot and followed Sam's car to see where they were going. When they drove into the hospital parking lot, he guessed they were going to visit the sister. He thought about trying to find Lainey Pickett's house, but he didn't know where she lived and let that slide for now.

The truth was that he was tired of the whole mess. His original targets had been necessary, and he'd thought of it as "them or me." It was when Trina Jakes had entered the picture that everything began going wrong. He'd shot her point-blank. He thought he'd shot her in the heart, but obviously he had missed. Now he was involving someone else in his attempts to get rid of her, which meant that once Moses Ledbetter gave him the bomb, he couldn't let Ledbetter live, either. The stakes were getting higher and the cost so much greater. After all he'd gone through, this had to work out.

Lainey was holding Sam's hand as they stepped off the elevator, and she could tell he was still trying to shed the remnants of the flashback. When she slid her thumb over his wrist and felt the ragged thump of his heart, a slow anger washed through her. What he'd been through—what all soldiers went through fighting other men's wars—was unconscionable. She was beginning to get a feel for Sam's mind-set, for his sense that he needed to distance himself from the people he loved, and she understood something now that she hadn't understood before. PTSD was like a scar. In one form or another, it was there forever.

Sam glanced at the time as they walked into ICU. Clarice was at the desk when he stopped to sign in.

"Good evening, Sam. Who's your pretty friend?"

Lainey smiled. "I'm Lainey Pickett," she said as she took off her coat and draped it over her arm.

Clarice's eyes widened. "Well, my goodness, honey. I know you, but I didn't recognize you."

"My hair's a lot shorter," Lainey said. It was an easy way to shift the subject away from her waiflike appearance.

"Hey, Clarice, I'm adding Lainey's name to the visitor list," Sam said. "And I understand they're going to start weaning Trina off the drugs that are keeping her asleep."

"I saw that," Clarice said.

"If you can keep it quiet, that would be great. We don't want to make it public knowledge. If the killer thinks she's still unconscious, she'll be safer," Sam added.

"Understood," Clarice said. "I'll make sure all my nurses are alerted to that."

"Thanks," Sam said, and then took Lainey's hand. "Come on, honey. Let's go say hello."

As they neared 12B Sam noticed Cain Embry was gone and Mike Cantrell was back on guard duty.

Cantrell stood when he saw Sam coming. "Evening, Mr. Jakes."

"It's Sam, remember? This is Lainey Pickett, and she has visiting rights with the rest of the family, okay?"

Mike eyed Lainey and nodded. "Ma'am, nice to meet you."

Lainey smiled.

"We won't be long," Sam said. "I just wanted to see her before I ended the day."

"Yes, sir," Mike said, eyeing Lainey again, and then sat down as they walked into Trina's room.

Lainey froze. "Oh, sweet Lord," she whispered, then dropped her coat on a chair and walked straight to the bed. She leaned over the bed rail, laid a hand on Trina's forehead and gently smoothed down her hair. "Hey, Tink. Hey, darling, it's me, Lainey."

Sam was startled. He hadn't expected this immediate tenderness, and had forgotten how close Lainey and Trina had once been. Trina was just a kid when he and Lainey were a couple, and he had completely forgotten Lainey used to call her Tinker Bell.

Just thinking of Trina as a young girl, remembering her and their mother head-to-head, laughing and planning what they were going to do next, was a painful reminder of what they'd lost. Trina had been his mother's surprise baby and, after being the only female in a house full of men, a delight for Betsy Jakes.

He took a deep breath, and then walked up behind Lainey and put his hands on her shoulders.

"So many machines," Lainey said as she looked up. There were tears on her face.

Sam hugged her. "She's getting better, remember?"

Lainey nodded. "I know. I was just thinking of everything she saw," she whispered.

Sam shuddered. That was part of his nightmare, too. "I want a name. That's all. I just want a name."

It was the soft, almost calm manner in which he spoke that gave Lainey a start. Of all the times Sam feared he was going to frighten her, this was when she saw the soldier—the warrior—that he'd been, the one who wanted justice for his family.

Then he took a deep breath, and when he reached for his sister, the look had disappeared and he was her Sam again.

He leaned over the bed rail and ran a finger along the side of Trina's cheek. "It's me, Trina. It's Sam. We're just waiting for you to wake up."

They heard footsteps at the door and turned around to see Lee walking in.

"Lee, how goes it, buddy?" Sam asked.

Lee's expression was solemn, his eyes hollow from worry and lack of sleep.

"Just waiting for my girl," he said, and gave Lainey a curious look.

Sam put an arm across Lainey's shoulders.

"Lee, this is Lainey Pickett. Lainey, this is Trina's boyfriend, Lee Daniels."

"It's nice to meet you," Lee said.

Lainey went one better. She walked over and hugged him.

"Lee, I'm so sorry. When Sam and I were together before, Trina was always special to me. I'll be glad when she wakes up to say hello."

Lee liked the sweetness of Lainey's manner. "This one's a keeper, Sam Jakes."

Sam shrugged. "Yeah, I know. I just didn't think she would still want me."

"Which was stupid," Lainey added.

"And that's true, too," Sam said.

Lee glanced at Trina. "I guess you heard the good news?"

"About Trina being weaned off the drugs? Yes."

"Trey said we shouldn't talk about it," Lee said.

"I just told the head nurse the same thing," Sam said.

"I want her to wake up with that son of a bitch's name on her lips," Lee said. "I want his name to be the first words she utters."

Lee's voice was shaking, and Lainey could tell by the way he kept touching Trina's face that he wanted to be alone with her.

"Sam, I'm ready to leave whenever you are," she said.

Sam nodded, told Trina goodbye and then gave Lee a quick hug.

"Hang in there, Lee. She's closer to coming back to us than she was before, right?"

"Right," Lee said. He was already pulling a chair up to Trina's bedside as they left the room.

"Bless his heart," Lainey said as they walked back toward the elevator.

"Yeah. They'd been fighting and were on the verge of making up when this happened. It's tearing Lee apart that he hurt her feelings."

"As long as we live, we have a chance to make things right," Lainey said as she punched the button at the elevator, and then turned around and kissed him.

It was brief but heartfelt, and Sam knew it. Instead of letting her go, he pulled her close and held her.

When the door opened, Will Porter stepped out.

"Good evening," Will said. "I trust you've been visiting your sister."

"Yes," Sam said. "You're here pretty late, aren't you?"

"My wife is here."

"I'm sorry. I hadn't heard," Sam said. "I hope she's healing."

Will shook his head. "Unfortunately, her prognosis is poor. They moved her into ICU this afternoon. I expect they'll move her to hospice soon."

Sam's heart skipped a beat. One of his mother's classmates was now moving in and out of ICU with a perfect excuse. It didn't give him a good feeling.

"What room is she in?" he asked.

"10B, but she isn't able to communicate. She had a stroke."

"Oh, no, I'm so sorry," Lainey said.

The elevator doors had already gone shut, so they had to hit the button and wait for them to open again as Will Porter walked away.

"I feel bad for him," Lainey said.

Sam had a different feeling about him. He had both guards' phone numbers on his contact list, and without explaining himself, he sent Mike Cantrell a quick text.

One of the 1980 graduates has a wife in 10B. Watch him. Don't let him anywhere close to Trina.

He got a brief text back.

Noted. Eyes on him.

The elevator car returned.

Sam slid a hand on Lainey's back as they got on, and then punched the button for the lobby.

"It's been a long day, baby. I think it's time to get you home."

She turned into his arms.

"You are my home, Sam, and it's been the best day. Good news about Trina. A wonderful evening with you. The only downside of any of it was that explosion. I sure hope no one was hurt, whatever it was."

Trey drove up to an inferno at the far end of Main Street. Someone had driven into the gas pumps in front of the minimart, and the explosion that ensued had nearly flattened the building.

The clerk and two customers had seen the car careening out of control and, fearing it would either hit the station or the pumps, they had all run out the back door.

They were still running when the pumps exploded, knocking them off their feet and sending burning debris showering down around them.

The driver was a lost cause. Trey hoped he'd died on impact, because burning to death was a hell of a way to die. It made him think of Sam, and he hoped they had gone back to Lainey's from the hospital instead of to his motel, because they would have had to drive right past this.

The officer on duty tonight was Earl Redd, but Trey had their night dispatcher call his extra men in to help control traffic, and he also had the streets blocked off to keep the curious away.

His fears that the night clerk and any customers were inside the burning building were soon eased when they came walking up behind him.

"Hey, Chief, we need some first aid here."

Trey turned just as the clerk, Carl Morris, bent over and clasped his knees, as if trying to catch his breath.

Trey ran to his aid. "Carl! I am so glad to see you. We thought you were inside."

"We would have been if it hadn't been for Johnny Pryor here. He was on his way out of the store when he saw the car and yelled at us to run. It was a toss-up as to whether it would hit the pumps or the building. Either way, we didn't want to be inside. We ran out the back and were in the alley and still running when the pumps exploded."

Trey eyed the other three people with Carl.

"Is anyone hurt?" he asked.

Johnny was shaking. His face was streaked with

dirt, and Trey could tell he was in shock. The other two, an older couple, were shaken and clinging to each other. All of them had burned spots on their clothing and hair.

"Let's get all of you checked out," Trey said. He took Johnny and the woman by the arm and walked them over to the ambulance that had just arrived.

While the EMT was checking Johnny's vital signs, Trey took the moment to question him.

"Johnny, I understand you're the one who initially saw the car. What made you think it was going to hit the station?"

"The driver was going really fast, and when I saw the car suddenly veer toward the gas pumps, I didn't think he'd be able to pull up in time."

"Did you recognize the car or the driver?" Trey asked.

Johnny wiped a hand across his face as if trying to wipe away the memory of what he'd seen. "Yeah, I saw the driver clear enough."

"Who was it?"

"A teenage boy. Don't know his name, but he sacks groceries at the supermarket. I think they call him Speedy."

Trey's heart sank. He turned around and stared at the car engulfed in flames and the firemen still trying to put it out. He knew who Speedy was. Speedy's dad, Randy Powell, grew tobacco and raised hogs. His mother, Clarice Powell, worked in ICU at the hospital—the same nurse who signed them in and out when they went to visit Trina. He was sick to his stomach. This was going to be a really bad night for their family.

* * *

Lainey fell asleep on the way home, wrapped up in her long gray coat with her head against the window. Sam drove slowly so as not to wake her. He still felt like he was living a dream.

The night was dark, but the sky was clear. The security lights in the yards of farmhouses along the way lit their own little portions of the world. Lights burned brightly inside the houses, and he began counting off their names as he drove past, remembering who used to live where and wondering how many were still left.

He thought of Lainey's parents with sadness. They'd both passed, and he hadn't known. It hurt even more to think of her going through all of that on her own. But if he'd been here, he would have made everything worse. He'd done what he'd done for a reason. His gift was that she'd waited.

As Sam came around a curve in the road, the headlights flashed on a panther just coming out of the trees along the roadside. He tapped the brakes, and as he did the big cat hunkered down, opened its mouth in a snarl and slunk back into the trees.

Sam's eyes widened as the cat disappeared. The sight of the magnificent animal was stirring. This was part of what he missed about his home. There was wildlife in Atlanta, but there it walked on two legs.

Lainey shifted in her sleep.

He glanced down to make sure she was okay and accelerated out of the curve. Only a couple more miles to the house.

He caught a glimpse of movement from the corner of his eye and watched as a falling star burned out above them. How long, he wondered, had that star been falling? Since before he was born? Was it a message for him that the past was gone? Or was it a warning?

He drove over the hill and looked down at the security light in the yard of the house below. He'd done this so many times in the past. Back then this house had been his second home, and the people in it part of his family, and Lainey the soul mate he'd been given to love.

Thank You, God, for keeping us alive. I won't let her down again.

He took the turnoff into the drive and slowed down as he headed toward the house.

It was the familiar crunch of gravel that woke Lainey. She sat up to see where they were. "We're already home?"

"You missed seeing a panther," Sam said.

She shuddered. "Really? I thought I heard one a couple of days ago. That shriek they make sounds like a woman screaming. Really eerie."

"Got your key?" he asked.

She dug it out of her purse and handed it to him. When they reached the house, Sam unlocked the door, then walked in ahead of her, turning on lights as he went.

Lainey paused to lock the door. "Can you stay?" she asked.

"Long enough to love you to sleep," he said.

Lainey hung up her coat, and then held out her hand. "'Come into my parlor,' said the spider to the fly."

Sam's eyes darkened. "You had me at 'come,'" he

drawled, and picked her up in his arms and carried her to her room, raining kisses on her face, on the back of her neck, behind her ear. By the time they reached their destination, she was shaking.

"Put me down, Sam. I need to get naked."

Twelve

"Last time we did this, we did it in the dark," Sam said. "But I want to see your face. Can you handle that, baby? Can you handle me? I'm not so pretty, but I'm damn good."

Lainey's hands were shaking as she continued to undress.

"Do I look like I'm all of a sudden shy? I waited a long time for you to come home, and I don't intend to waste a single moment now that you're here," she said in a soft, shaky voice. "Get your clothes off before I die where I'm standing."

Sam had never stripped so fast in his life. He was hard and aching, and as he was pulling a condom up over his erection, all he could think about was being inside her.

When Lainey turned her back to pull down the bedcovers, Sam grabbed her from behind and slid a hand between her legs. Her clit was hard and throbbing, her breathing deep and ragged, like she'd been running for miles. He splayed one hand across her rib cage to steady her and made her scream with only two fingers.

Lainey was riding the high with no thought of anything but the blood rush in her body. She couldn't think, couldn't talk and had no notion of wanting anything but that climax she was chasing. It hit her so fast she jerked. When her legs went out from under her, Sam kept her from falling.

She was still shaking when Sam laid her down. He parted her legs and slid deep into the wet heat between them, then grunted from the pleasure. As he began to rock against her, one deep thrust after another, over and over, he could feel her hands stroking his back, tracing the scars, cupping his backside, holding him tight, keeping him deep.

Time rolled on.

Lainey's head was pressed against the headboard, and he could feel the muscles coiling within her, pushing her toward a second climax. Her lips were slack, but her gaze was fixed on his face.

"See me, Sam," she whispered. "I see you." And then she wrapped her legs around his waist.

He pushed harder, faster.

"You feel so good," he whispered.

He laid his face against the curve of her neck, trying with everything he had in him not to come without her, but he couldn't hold on. It rolled over him and pulled him under. He didn't know until it was over that she'd gone with him. She was lying beneath him, her arms around his neck, and both crying and laughing.

"Oh, my God, oh, my God. You should be declared a lethal weapon. You rocked my world, melted my bones and you make love like a stud. You followed me home. Can I keep you?"

Sam grinned, then began kissing her, leaving the imprint of his lips all over her body, from right beneath her chin, down her chest, across the scars, to the middle of her belly, until he heard her sigh.

"Are we good here?" he asked.

"We are *so* good," Lainey said.

"Can I take a rain check on round three? I have to be up early to meet Trey. We're going to check out a mine."

"I couldn't manage a round three right now if you begged," she said. "Just don't make me get up to see you out."

He kissed her one more time, and then reluctantly got up and went across the hall to the bathroom. When he came out, she was curled up on her side with the covers pulled up around her neck, sound asleep beneath the lights.

He dressed slowly, taking his time just so he could watch her sleep, and then turned on a night-light before he turned off the ones overhead. Just before he left, he tucked the covers up behind her neck so she wouldn't be cold, then leaned down and whispered in her ear.

"I know you can't hear me, but getting you back is worth all the pain I suffered when I gave you up."

He turned off lights as he went through the house, and then turned the lock before he let himself out. He didn't know if she usually left the porch light on at night, but he did it anyway, just in case.

It was after 3:00 a.m. before Trey verified that the vehicle that had hit the gas pumps was registered to

Randy Powell, and by then Randy Powell had already come to town looking for his teenage son, who'd missed his curfew.

Randy had come to Mystic ready to be furious with his kid, but instead, when he heard what had happened, he headed for the station. When they wouldn't let him drive any closer, he got out and headed there on foot. The closer he got, the faster he went, until he was running. And when he reached the scene and recognized his old car, he screamed.

Trey caught the man in his arms and had to walk him away. His heart was breaking for the family, especially the mother who had yet to know what had happened to their child.

The father's appearance hastened his need to notify Clarice before someone else broke the news, and he took Randy with him to do it. The couple was going to need each other even more before this night was over. The boy had been their only child.

Trey watched Randy trying to hold it together, but by the time they got to the third floor of the hospital, where the ICU was located, he knew the grieving man wasn't going to make it any farther.

"Randy, take a chair here in the waiting room. I'll bring Clarice out to you, and we'll do this together, okay?"

"Yes, okay," Randy said, and then grabbed Trey's arm. "Why?"

Trey ached for his sadness.

"I'm coming to realize there is no answer to why bad things happen. All I know is that after a tragedy, our job is to get through it. You and Clarice will have to be strong for each other. Just give me a couple of minutes to get her," Trey said, and then left the waiting room.

It was only a few more yards down to the ICU, but the closer he got, the slower he walked. Once he stepped through those doors, he was going to change a mother's life.

He pushed through the double doors as quietly as he could, cognizant of all the seriously ill people asleep on the other side. No one was at the front desk, but there was a nurse coming out of a room just to his right. She looked startled to see the police chief on the floor at this time of the morning and immediately stopped what she was doing.

"Chief Jakes?"

"I need to speak to Clarice Powell. And you will need to get someone to cover for her for the rest of this shift."

The startled expression on the woman's face said what she was thinking. "Yes, sir," she said.

"Just tell her I need to talk to her. No more."

The nurse nodded, and then hurried away.

Moments later Trey saw Clarice come out of a room and head toward him with a slight smile on her face.

"Chief Jakes? This is a little late for a visit, don't you think?"

"I didn't come to see Trina. Will you please step out in the hall with me a moment?"

Her eyes widened, and he could hear a note of panic in her voice when she asked, "What's wrong?"

He took her by the elbow and gently led her out of the unit.

"Please, Chief. Is it Randy? Has something happened to Randy?"

Before Trey could answer, Randy Powell walked out of the waiting room and started up the hall toward her. It was the tears on his face that gave him away.

Suddenly Clarice gasped. Everyone in Mystic had heard the explosion. All they knew was that someone had driven a car into the gas pumps at the minimart. She moaned.

"No, no, no. Not my Jack. Please tell me it wasn't Jack!" she cried.

"I'm so sorry, Clarice," Trey said, and then caught her as her eyes rolled back in her head.

Trey stayed in the waiting room with them until Randy's mother, Beth Powell, arrived. She was pale and staggering when she walked in, and then gathered them both in her arms as they began to cry all over again.

Trey was exhausted. It was almost four in the morning. The search at the mine site was supposed to begin around nine. This was going to be a long-ass day, and he still had paperwork to write up on the accident.

Sam was sleeping with his gun in one hand and his phone in the other when someone knocked on his door. He woke up with a start, then realized he was getting a text and glanced at his phone.

It's me, Trey. Let me in.

Sam stepped into his jeans and zipped them up, then took his gun to answer the door.

"What the hell?" he said as Trey walked inside. He locked the door behind him, and then watched Trey taking change out of his pockets and kicking off his boots. "Trey. What's going on?"

Trey didn't even look at him.

"Can I use your shower? There's no time to go home and clean up before we have to go to the mine. I had a change of clothes at the precinct, but I smell like smoke."

Sam could tell that whatever had caused the explosion must have been bad.

"Of course you can use the shower. My shaving stuff is on the counter, too. Use what you need."

Trey stripped where he stood, then walked into the bathroom and shut the door.

Sam sat down on the side of the bed and turned on the television, then kicked back to watch. It was the comfort of knowing his brother was in the next room that made him relax enough to close his eyes.

Trey came out with a towel wrapped around his waist and water drops running down his forehead. He glanced toward the bed and realized Sam had fallen asleep, then saw the scars and froze. He'd never seen his brother like this, only wrapped in bandages while he was still healing. This was far worse than he could ever have imagined. And except for whatever help he'd accepted from their mom, Sam had dealt with it alone. Trey took a slow, shaky breath and turned away just in time to catch the early-morning weather forecast on the still-running TV. The day was supposed to be clear.

Sam woke up as Trey was putting his boots back

on. He scooted into a sitting position and reached for his shirt.

"Don't do that because of me," Trey said.

"Do what?" Sam said.

"Put on a shirt," Trey said.

Sam hesitated, and then laid it aside. "Force of habit. So enough about the shirt. Talk to me."

Trey stomped his feet into the boots, then got up and started to pace. That was when Sam knew he was trying to come to terms with what had happened the night before.

"You heard the explosion?" Trey asked.

"Yes."

"You know Clarice, the RN who's usually at the front desk when you walk into ICU? She's married to Randy Powell."

"I didn't know that's who she married. Randy was the team's best wide receiver our senior year in high school. He was one fast dude."

"Yes, well, their only son, Jack, aka Speedy, drove his car into the gas pumps at the minimart last night."

Sam flinched. "Oh, my God, that's awful. And they blew up with Jack still in the car?"

"Yes."

"Sweet mercy," Sam said. Just thinking about all the flames and heat made his gut knot. "Do you know why? Was he drunk or—"

"We don't know, and the body was burned so badly I don't know what the coroner will be able to figure out. Honestly, I'm not sure how much it even matters. All his parents care about is him, and he's gone. How it happened won't change a thing."

"Are you okay?" Sam asked.

Trey shrugged, and then suddenly stopped pacing and sat.

"No, I'm not okay. This just added to the huge knot in my chest. I can't remember the last time I woke up without it, and I won't be okay until the killer is caught and Mom is laid to rest." He grabbed his towel and started drying his hair. "This is making me crazy, Sam. I don't have a fucking clue as to who's doing this, and only a half-assed reason that may or may not be why."

"Trina is going to wake up and put all this uncertainty to an end," Sam said.

"It won't be any too soon," Trey said, then tossed the towel and started finger combing his hair.

"So what time do you want to leave for the mine?" Sam asked.

"Eight thirty?"

Sam nodded. "I'll follow you out there so I'll have my car just in case you get pulled away on a call. Oh, one other thing. I took Lainey to see Trina last night after dinner. We met Will Porter getting off the elevator as we were leaving. He was there visiting his wife…in ICU."

Trey frowned. "Since when did that happen?" he muttered.

"I don't know, but from the way he was talking, I got the impression she's dying. And she's in room 10B."

"I don't like that," Trey said.

"I didn't, either, so I gave Cantrell a heads-up that the guy was from the same class as our three murder victims, so he needed to keep an eye on him and make sure he didn't get anywhere near Trina."

"Good call," Trey said. "I'm going to check out the situation and confirm his story. In the meantime, tell me what's happening with you and Lainey? Are you official again?"

"Yes," Sam said.

"I'm happy for you," Trey said.

"Happy doesn't quite cover how *I* feel," Sam said, grinning. "On another note, I was talking to Lainey about her mother's diaries, and how she thought the names her mother wrote down in her diaries were a kind of teenage code for the real names."

"Yes, I got that," Trey said.

"Well, there was something I noticed when I was reading them. One of the couples she mentioned was Tom Collins and Betty Boop. That got me to wondering if Tom Collins was Donny Collins, and if he had a girlfriend. If he did and we can figure out who she is, she might know a lot of what we're trying to find out."

Trey's eyes widened. "Well, hell, that's why it's good to bring fresh eyes into an investigation. I never thought of that. There was no Betty in that class, so—"

"'Betty Boop' could simply mean we're looking for someone with the initials BB, although there are countless other reasons to use that nickname, and she could easily have been younger, too. I read some more in the diaries before I went to bed last night but don't know anything else that would help. You need to find someone who remembers those kids and those years."

"I still have Will Porter's yearbook. I'll go through it again and check out the lower grades for a Betty or a girl with the initials BB first before we move on to a different interpretation of the nickname," Trey said, and then glanced at the clock.

"So do you want to go back to bed, or come eat breakfast with me?"

Sam reached for his shirt again. "I want to eat with my brother," he said. "Give me a few minutes."

Trey wanted to look away when Sam stood. He didn't want to stare at the scars, but God help him, he couldn't help it. And when Sam went into the bathroom, the burn scars on his back held Trey prisoner. It wasn't until the door closed between them and broke the connection that Trey realized he'd been holding his breath.

Trey scrubbed at his face with both hands as if trying to wipe away the sight from his mind. Sam's trip home had revealed so much more about him than any of them could have imagined. Trey had thought he knew his brother. He'd thought he understood why Sam had stayed away. But he'd been wrong. He didn't know this man at all. This Sam put him in awe. After what he had endured and survived, Sam was like some damn superhero. All he needed was a big *S* on the front of his chest.

Lainey woke up just after 7:00 a.m., needing to go to the bathroom, then remembered Sam and last night and shivered. He hadn't lied. He was good—really good—at making her lose her mind.

Still as naked as he'd left her, she dashed across the hall to pee, then turned up the thermostat as she came out. She went back to her room and crawled into bed to wait until the house was warmer, and fell asleep.

The next time she woke up it was almost 10:00 a.m.

She didn't have classes, but there were tests to grade, so she made herself get up.

But Sam was still on her mind. She thought about him while she was taking a shower and realized something about their situation that neither of them could have planned. Sam would never trust himself to be a father, and she'd been told chemo had probably ended her chance to get pregnant. But if they could just grow old together, she would never ask God for anything more.

Later, as she was making herself a sandwich, she got a text from Sam.

Missing you. Love you. I'll call you later today.

She sent a text back.

Love you and miss you, too. I'll be waiting.

Sam smiled as he put the phone back in his pocket, then saw Trey waving him over.

"What's going on?" Sam asked.

"Sheriff Osmond just got here, so we're ready to go," Trey said as he tied a long length of climbing rope onto his belt.

"Good. I brought my spotlight," Sam said as he headed for the entrance to the mine.

Sheriff Osmond had two deputies with him. "Sorry about the delay. Crime waits for no man, and I'm shorthanded because of it. It's just me and two deputies. I'm leaving one on the radio and one keeping the locals off-site."

"No big deal, Sheriff. I doubt there's a need for a

large search team. We shouldn't need to look beyond the most obvious shafts. I don't think anyone would have had time to go deep," Trey said.

Sheriff Osmond nodded. "I agree, so let's get started. Get a mask before you go in, and keep your radios on. GPS won't work in there, so we stay together and watch our footing. This mine has been shut down since 1978."

The three men walked in about twenty yards until the tunnel branched off in several different directions.

Sheriff Osmond pointed. "Sam, you have the biggest light source, so you get the lead. Just take it slow."

Sam nodded and headed into the first tunnel on their right, with Trey and the sheriff behind him. Within moments it was evident a lot of shifting had occurred since the mine had been shut down. The roof sloped farther on one side than the other, and a lot of the shoring was broken. Sam paused to sweep the area with his spotlight. His gut knotted at what he saw. When the shoring broke, the floor of the tunnel had shifted a good six inches down on one side, displacing the track that the coal cars had run on. The track was bent in some places and raised above the ground in others, making passage dangerous.

"You see what I see?" Sam said. "This is a bad tunnel, so whatever you do, don't touch any of the shoring. If this bothers anyone, now is the time to say so." No one spoke. "Okay, then, it's going to get dusty, so mask up and follow me."

Each of them was carrying a flashlight, but they were depending on the brighter spotlight ahead of them to light the way.

Old spiderwebs coated with dust dangled like

shredded fabric above their heads. The air was cold and still, and there was no sound except for their footsteps. Every step they took stirred the dust below their feet until the air was thick and hazy.

Just as the tunnel began to slope downward, Sam stopped.

"Hold up," he said.

They all saw it at once. It was a cave-in.

"Damn it," Trey said.

"I'd say this is as far as we go here, but there are still three more tunnels to check," Sheriff Osmond said. "So let's go back and search number two."

Sam passed his light back up to Trey, who took the lead on the way out. When they returned to the main passage, they were silent, their mood less hopeful.

Sam retrieved his spotlight and led the way into the second tunnel.

The shoring there was still in place, but the tunnel was barely wide enough for the coal cars to have passed, and the track they would have used was missing.

He paused and gave the area ahead of him a three-sixty sweep with the light, and as he did, he saw a large dark space between where he was standing and the continuation of the tunnel.

All of a sudden, he realized what it was.

"Get back," he said urgently.

Trey swung his light toward Sam. "What's wrong?"

"There's a big hole in the floor just ahead of me," Sam said.

"Let me see," Sheriff Osmond said.

"No, both of you stand back. Until we know what

we're standing on, we don't want to put too much weight on the rim."

Osmond shuddered and backed up past Trey.

Sam stopped about six feet from the hole. "Give me a few minutes to check this thing out," he said.

"What the hell do you think you're going to do?" Trey demanded.

"Crawl up on it belly down and look over the edge."

"Not until I tie this rope around you," Trey said, unhooking the rope from his belt as he stepped forward, then quickly fastening one end around Sam's waist. He and the sheriff took the loose end.

"Okay, we're good here," Trey said. "Just go slow, and if you feel something give, roll toward the wall. We'll pull you back."

Sam nodded, then got down on his belly and began to inch toward the edge of the hole with his spotlight clutched tight in one hand. It didn't take long, and then he scooted forward just enough that he could see down as he aimed the spotlight into the hole.

It took a few moments for him to see the bottom, and when he did, he reacted with a jerk. A weird feeling went through him, and he wondered if his mom and her friends had stood on this very spot so many years ago. He thought of how scared they must have been, and how desperately they had tried to get back to tell someone what they'd seen.

"Hey, Trey."

"Yeah? What do you see? Is there anything there?"

"I would bet good money that we just found Donny Collins."

Sheriff Osmond gasped. "Are you serious?"

"I see a skull and most of the bones to go with it."

"Well, son of a bitch," Sheriff Osmond said softly. "I'll be honest. I didn't think anything was gonna come of this."

"Get back," Trey said and tugged on the rope.

"I'm coming," Sam said and scooted backward until he was far enough away to stand up and untie himself.

Sheriff Osmond was already on his radio.

"Target located. Tunnel number two. We're coming out."

"10-4, Sheriff."

Trey gathered up the rope and reattached it to his belt, and then looked at his brother. All he could see were Sam's eyes, and they were welling.

Then Sam pulled down his mask. "She could have been here to see this happen, you know," he said. "She and her friends saw something bad go down and tried so hard to tell. Now we have to finish it."

"It may take a while to identify the body," Sheriff Osmond said.

"If we're lucky, there could be identification down there with him," Sam said.

"I vote for lucky," Trey said.

Thirteen

Even though they tried to keep the find quiet, by the time the sheriff's department contacted search and rescue from the Forest Service to lower the coroner down the shaft to examine the remains in situ, half the county knew what was happening. Most of Mystic knew it had something to do with the murders, but they didn't know how, or who the body would be.

The killer was in a panic.

He tried to call Moses Ledbetter to see if he could get the bomb any sooner but didn't get an answer. He left word for Moses to call, then went home and began to withdraw what money he could get his hands on in case he needed to make a run for it. For him, it was all about timing. Once the witness against him was silenced, even if they dragged the remains of a hundred bodies from the mine, there would never be a way to pin the murders on him. Come hell or high water, he had to find out why Ledbetter wasn't answering. The guy was an old man after all. He could be sick…he could be dead. He needed to know where he stood.

* * *

Lainey's date with Sam had prompted her to do something she should have done months ago. She had cleaned out her closets.

It was midafternoon when she finished packing up what she was giving away and carried the last box to her car. She shoved it in the backseat beside the other one, then ran back to the house to get her jacket and purse. She paused to lock up and heard Dandy raising a ruckus. She walked off the porch and looked toward the pasture.

Dandy was running with his head up and his mane and tail flying. She laughed. He hadn't done anything like that in ages.

The beautiful fall day must be agreeing with him.

"Hey, Dandy! Apple treats for you when I come back!" she yelled.

The grullo kept running, and for a moment Lainey wished she was on him, riding with the wind on her face and her hair in tangles. Without thinking, she touched her head, then let her hand drop. No hair to blow in tangles. No time to play on a horse. But she could still bring the little pillow-shaped horse treats Dandy loved.

She headed for the car. Once she gave away the clothes she could no longer wear, she was going shopping. It had taken Sam coming back to make her care about how she looked, but nothing could have changed her heart. She would have loved Sam Jakes for the rest of her life even if she'd never seen him again. The difficult part was finding a way to accept that it had taken death to bring them back together. There had to be a way to reconcile her joy with that tragedy. She drove away while Dandy was still kicking up his heels.

* * *

It was after 2:00 p.m. when they brought up the remains. Trey was outside in his police cruiser talking to one of the officers back in town, and Sam was inside the mine with the search-and-rescue team.

The first person to come up was the coroner, Marv Addison. He was masked up to the bridge of his nose and had goggles over his eyes. He had suited up in coveralls before he went down, which was fortunate, because he came up coated in what looked like a layer of gray silt.

They unhooked his rigging and sent it back down into the hole. The next thing to come up was the recovery basket, holding a body bag with the remains. Then the others were brought up one by one.

Sam helped search and rescue carry the basket with the remains to the coroner's van. They transferred the body bag to the back and went to return the rescue basket to their truck while Sam waited for Dr. Addison to return from talking to Trey and Sheriff Osmond.

When Dr. Addison finally came back to toss his coveralls in the van, Sam took him aside.

"I know you aren't going to release details until you've done an autopsy, but can you tell me if you found any identification with the body?"

Dr. Addison knew Betsy Jakes had been the latest murder victim, and he also knew her daughter, if she woke, would finger the killer. He knew what was at stake and, for once in his life, broke protocol.

"We recovered a wallet with a driver's license issued to a young man named Donald Collins. There was nearly five hundred dollars inside, so it wasn't a robbery. We also recovered a suitcase with clothing and a bus ticket to Los Angeles. And the bones are consistent with a young male Caucasian. I cannot confirm that the bones are those of Donald Collins. But I *can* confirm that those items were found with the body."

"Oh, my God," Sam mumbled. "Mom was right."

"Mom was right about what?" Trey asked, as he walked up behind his brother.

Sam repeated what the doctor had just told him.

"Did you find anything that pointed to cause of death?" Trey asked the coroner.

Dr. Addison shrugged. "Back of his skull is crushed, but I won't venture a guess as to how it happened. Could be pre- or postmortem. You'll have to wait for my autopsy report."

Trey smiled grimly.

"Well, since Donny Collins had a bus to catch, I can vouch with some certainty that he didn't intend to catch it out here. However he died, it wasn't by his own choice. I think we've just found the reason for our three murders. Now all I need to know is who killed the kid and we can find our killer, too."

Dr. Addison grabbed some wet wipes and began cleaning his hands, then wiped the dust from his shoes.

"I'll make sure you and Sheriff Osmond both have copies of my report as soon as it's ready," he said, then got in the van with his crew and drove away.

Sam looked at Trey. "What next?"

"I need to swing by the precinct," Trey said.

Sam nodded. "I'm going to talk to Will Porter again. See if he knows if Donny Collins had a girlfriend."

"What do you think about a killer leaving all that money on a body?" Trey asked.

Sam frowned. "I would say the killer didn't need

money or he would have looked, even if the death was an accident. It's human nature. And since Mom said she saw the body in the shaft, they must have seen the killer throw the body down there. If there was anything the killer wanted, he would have taken it before he dumped the body."

Trey nodded. "Kind of what I was thinking."

"I think we need to avoid talking to Marcus Silver just yet," Sam added.

"Why?" Trey asked.

"He already stated he didn't need the scholarship money. We know his family was loaded. I'm not saying he's guilty, but it *is* a factor to consider," Sam said.

"Agreed, so we wait for more information before we draw any conclusions," Trey said.

"I think so. I'll let you know what I find out about the girlfriend," Sam said.

"Talk to you later," Trey said and left the scene.

Sam went to his car, but as soon as he closed the door, he called Lainey.

Her phone rang enough times that he thought it was going to voice mail, and then she answered with a breathless catch in her voice. "Hello?"

"Hey, honey, it's me. Did I catch you at a bad time?"

She laughed. "No, I'm just trying on clothes."

He smiled.

"A most important task, I would say. Be sure to find something easy for me to take off."

She laughed again, and the sound settled in his heart.

"I'm headed back to Mystic. Is it okay if I come out tonight?" he asked.

"Only if you stay," she said. "Bring your toothbrush and your rock-star self."

He chuckled. "How did I become a rock star?"

"Because you're good, remember? At the risk of overstroking your ego, you're actually *really* good, Sam Jakes."

"You can never overstroke, honey. It's when you quit too soon that makes it hurt."

She laughed again. "I'm hanging up on you now. I'll see you around seven?"

"Yes, you will."

Sam was still smiling as he started the car and drove back into town.

Will hadn't gone to the hospital that morning. Everyone in town knew about his wife now. After all his years of trying to keep her weakness a secret, this kind of news traveled fast no matter what the origin. Now everyone knew she was an alcoholic and that she was dying because of it. He'd stayed home not to be at her side, but because he couldn't face people's curious stares and questions.

But sitting still for long periods of time had never been Will's strong suit. It had been months since Rita had cleaned their house, and even though he knew she was never coming home, he began going room by room, gathering up the liquor bottles from all her hiding places and taking them to the kitchen.

Then he stood at the sink, opened them one by one and poured the contents down the drain. Every so often he took a drink for the hell of it. Since she was dying, he could hardly drink to her health, so he drank to dull the pain of his guilt.

It was late afternoon when his cell phone rang. All the bottles were empty and long since carried out to the trash, and he was pretty close to drunk when he answered the call.

"Hello."

"Mr. Porter, this is Dr. Fielding. Your wife's condition has worsened, and I think you need to get to the hospital as quickly as you can."

Will shuddered as he wiped a shaky hand across his face.

"Yes, thank you. I'll be right there."

He disconnected, and then walked to the kitchen, got the leftover coffee from the coffeemaker and drank it cold straight from the carafe.

He drank until it was empty, then shuddered and gagged from the quantity and the bitterness. He stood there for a few moments, then staggered to the bathroom and threw up his guts. After a few minutes he washed his face and brushed his teeth, then put on clean clothes and left the house.

Since it was Saturday, Sam knew Will Porter wouldn't be at school, but the man also wasn't answering his phone. Since the man's wife was in ICU, he sent Mike Cantrell a text.

Have you seen Will Porter today?

Porter is here. His wife is dying. Family has been called in.

Okay. Thanks.

Once again, death was keeping the investigation at a crawl.

* * *

Since Sam couldn't talk to Will Porter, he went back to the police precinct and got Porter's yearbook. He grabbed a cold pop from Trey's minifridge, got a package of cheese crackers from the machine and kicked back on the sofa in Trey's office. He got up once to get a pad of paper and a pen, then went to work.

He popped a cheese cracker in his mouth and started with the freshman class, searching for girls with the initials BB or the first name Betty. There was only one Betty. He moved to the sophomore class and found one girl with the initials BB, but her first name was Barbara. He took a drink of the cold pop, and then ate a couple more crackers before he started on the junior class. There was one girl named Beth Bradford who had the right initials, and one named Betty. He stopped there, since he already knew there weren't any Bettys or BBs in the senior class. So if their theory held water, he had four names that might or might not have been the Betty Boop mentioned in Billie Conway's diaries. And Betty might or might not have been Donny Collins' girl, which meant there were still too many unknowns. He needed to find out if any of the four still lived in the area and decided to ask Delia, since she'd lived here all her life. He dumped his trash, emptied his cold drink and headed for the motel with the old yearbook in hand.

Delia was filling the cold-drink machine in the motel lobby when Sam walked in. He laid the yearbook aside, took off his jacket and hat and started helping her fill in the slots with bottles of pop without comment.

She looked a little surprised. "You don't have to do this."

"I know, but I already owe you for helping me with Lainey's new clothes, and when we get through here, I'm going to bug you for more information. This is the least I can do."

Delia was pleased, and it showed. When Sam squatted down to fill in the lower slots, she saw the burn scars on the back of his neck, and her first thought was to hug him, then she felt like crying. She had to look away to regain her composure. By the time they were finished, she had pulled herself together again.

"So what can I help you with?" she asked.

"Come sit beside me," he said, sitting on the sofa and patting the other cushion.

She eased down with a slight groan.

"Getting old sucks," she muttered, and then immediately thought of Betsy and wished she could take that back. "I'm sorry. It was a thoughtless comment. Getting older is a gift, because it means I'm still here."

His sadness had been instantaneous. His mother's choices had ended with a bullet to the brain. He was struggling to regain his composure just as Delia was mumbling her apology.

"Don't feel bad. I keep thinking it's not real," he said.

She nodded. "Okay, what's going on?"

"You weren't in Mom's class, were you?"

"No. I was two years behind her. We didn't become friends until after we were grown and married."

"Okay, but you *were* in high school when she was a senior. Now for the questions. Do you remember Donny Collins?"

She frowned. "The name is familiar."

"He was the salutatorian in the graduating class of 1980."

"Oh, right! I knew I knew it. Marcus Silver was valedictorian, right? All of us girls had a crush on him. He wasn't all that cute, but he was smart and rich, which made up for it."

"Yes. So by any chance do you remember if Donny had a girlfriend?"

"Oh, gosh…that was so long ago I can barely remember what he looks like."

Sam opened the yearbook. "This is him," he said, pointing to Donny's senior picture.

"Oh, yes! Now I remember him."

"What about a girlfriend? Does anyone come to mind?" he asked.

She frowned. "I don't know, honey. It's been so long."

"What if I show you some pictures of other girls and see if anyone rings a bell?"

"Sure, I don't mind."

Sam opened the book to the freshman class and pointed out the girl named Betty.

"Do you remember her?"

"Not at all. Sorry."

"That's okay. We're moving up to the sophomore class. That was your class, right?"

Delia nodded. "Okay, who's next?"

"This one."

"Oh, that's Bobbie Bennett. I remember her just

fine, but she wouldn't have been Donny's girlfriend. She was gay. She died before our senior year."

Sam's hopes were dimming.

"Okay, that's fine. We're eliminating them, which helps. These last two were in the junior class. Just think back and try to remember if you ever saw either one of them with Donny." He pointed to the first girl. "Do you remember her?"

"Yes. Betty Farris. I don't remember who she dated, though. I'm so sorry, Sam."

He was trying to stay positive. Maybe Donny Collins didn't have a girlfriend and the diary entry wasn't about him. It didn't matter. They would still find out who'd killed him when Trina woke up.

"Okay, one more, and then I'll let you get back to work. What about this one? Do you remember Beth Bradford?"

"Of course I do. She's Beth Powell now."

"Beth Powell? Is that someone I should remember?" Sam asked.

"You went to school with her son, Randy."

Sam's expression stilled. "Oh, no. Her grandson is the boy who was killed last night?"

"Yes. Such a tragedy," Delia said.

"So do you remember anything about her personal life in high school?"

Delia's frown deepened. "She had a boyfriend. I remember her wearing his class ring, but I can't say who it was. It might have been Donny Collins, but I can't say. You'll have to ask her."

Sam sighed. Once again life was slowing down an investigation. He couldn't talk to Will Porter because his wife was dying, and this was hardly the time to approach Beth Powell about anything, though he might have to break protocol and do it anyway. He didn't give a shit about manners if it kept his sister alive.

"I'm sorry I wasn't more help," Delia said.

"No, no, that's not true. You were a lot of help. Investigating is often about eliminating people. Finally finding who you're looking for is always at the end of the investigation."

"Okay, then," Delia said, and pushed herself up from the sofa. "And thank you for helping me refill the pop machine," she said.

"Totally my pleasure, and thanks again."

Delia watched him leave, then went back to work. She didn't know who was killing her friends, but she hoped they found him before anyone else had to die.

Fourteen

The killer was parked on a dirt road at the foot of the mountains surrounding Mystic. Moses Ledbetter lived up there somewhere. If he knew where, he would already have been knocking on his door. He was so pissed off he could barely focus.

He stared up at the mountain and the long shadows already spilling down the side toward the flatland. It would be sundown soon, and he would have to go home.

"Okay, old man. I'm going to call you one more time, and if you know what's good for you, you'll fucking answer your phone," he screamed, and pounded his fist against the steering wheel.

Then he picked up the burner phone and, one more time, punched in the number he'd used to call Ledbetter before, then listened to it ring. And ring. And ring.

"Son of a fucking bitch," he said, and had started to hang up when he heard a voice.

"Hello? Who's calling?"

The killer gasped.

"Moses?"

"No, this is his grandson."

"I need to talk to Moses," he said.

"Were you a friend of Grandad's?" the man asked.

"No, I hired him— Wait! What do you mean, *were*?"

"Grandaddy passed two nights ago."

The killer leaned back against the seat and closed his eyes. Damn it all to hell; lately he couldn't catch a break.

"Was it a heart attack?"

"No. He blew himself up out in his shop. We still don't know what was going on, but he's gone, and we sure are gonna miss him."

"I'm sorry to hear this," the killer said.

"About this job he was doing for you?" the man said.

"What about it?" the killer asked.

"We found a package sitting on his kitchen table. There's a note on it. He wrote 'a thousand dollars owed,' but no name or contact information. If that was you, we could sure use the money to lay him to rest."

The killer sat up straight in the seat. Things were actually looking up.

"Yes, that's me, and that's the amount we agreed on. Can you deliver it to me?"

"I reckon I can, but not before tomorrow afternoon."

The killer wanted to scream. "There's no way you could get it to me tonight?"

"No, sir. I'm sorry, but the family is laying Grandaddy's remains to rest tomorrow morning, and tonight is family night."

"Of course. I understand. So can you meet me at the foot of the mountain on the Pike Trail…at Lassiter's Corner?"

"Yes, and you'll have the cash money, right?"

"Right."

"Then, I'll see you tomorrow afternoon around 2:00 p.m.," the grandson said.

The killer was shaking by the time he disconnected. Once again, things were out of his control, and he so needed this all to be over with.

T. J. Silver was just finishing a late dinner alone when he heard his father's footsteps in the foyer. He wiped his mouth and got up to go meet him.

"Dad! I was beginning to worry. I expected you home long before this," he said.

Marcus hung his coat in the entryway closet.

"I was at the capitol all day, and then got delayed coming home."

T.J. gave him a quick hug. "You must be starved. Cook can bring you a plate. I just finished."

"I grabbed a bite on the way home," Marcus said.

"Okay, so tell me how it went today. Did you talk to your backers? How do they feel about your chances?"

Marcus frowned. "I talked to them. We didn't get into specifics, because I have yet to announce my candidacy."

T.J. rubbed his hands together with glee. "Then, we need to finalize that party, don't we? Are you excited? I am. This is going to be a whole new way of life for both of us, right?"

"Not unless I get elected," Marcus said.

"Ah, come on, Dad. You're a shoo-in. They all said it. Senator Gold is retiring, and it will be all newcomers on the ticket. I've been planning your campaign tour with your manager and—"

Marcus frowned again and interrupted as he began sorting through the mail on the hall table. "I haven't officially hired him," he said.

T.J. grinned. "Well, I've been meaning to tell you about that."

Marcus turned. "Tell me what?"

"I already hired him. He's been on the job for a little over two weeks now. We've been mapping out a strategy for—"

Marcus's face turned a dark, angry red. "Who's running for this seat—you or me?"

T.J.'s heart skipped a beat. "Well, you, of course, Dad. But you told me to work on it, and I *have* been, every day with—"

"I still haven't decided if I'm even going to do this," Marcus said, and flung the mail onto the floor as he stomped up the stairs.

A few seconds later T.J. heard him slam the door to his bedroom.

"What the hell was that all about?" he muttered, and began picking up the mail.

It was nearing sundown by the time Lainey got home. She jumped out of her car and began gathering up her purchases. The first thing she unloaded was the sack of apple treats for Dandy. She left them on the back porch, then glanced toward the pasture but didn't see him. He was probably ticked off at her for being late. She thought about calling him up to the barn and shutting him in one of the stalls for the night, then headed back to her car. She gathered up the sacks with her new clothes and took them to her bedroom, then began to change.

Wanting to get her chores done so she could start dinner for herself and Sam, she changed into work clothes, dropped her phone in a coat pocket, along with her flashlight, and started out the door, then stopped. Because it was so close to nightfall, she decided to take her daddy's rifle with her to the pasture, just as a precaution.

She picked up the bag of apple treats, juggling it and the rifle as she headed for the barn. The security lights were already coming on, and she was debating with herself about throwing a half bale of hay out in the corral instead of carrying oats and sweet feed out to the pasture. If Dandy got hungry enough, he would come looking for dinner.

But by the time she reached the barn, her conscience got the better of her, and she decided to take the feed to him. She dumped the bag of treats in the granary, opened it to put a handful in her pocket, then mixed sweet feed and oats in the feed bucket and headed toward the pasture, whistling for Dandy as she went. Normally he would answer with a neigh and come running, but when he didn't, she frowned.

"Dang it, Dandy. Where are you?" she muttered and glanced toward the grove of trees at the edge of the pasture, then she walked on out to the feeding trough and poured in the oats.

She laid the rifle down at her feet and paused to pull up some thistles growing beneath the trough, and when she looked up again, it was almost dark. Frowning, she turned on the flashlight and whistled for Dandy again, and then started walking. It wasn't like him not to come, and she was beginning to worry.

She was halfway between the barn and the creek when she saw him lying on his side. The blood coming out of the scratches on his haunches looked black in this light, and the huge tear in his side told the rest of the story.

"No!" she screamed, and immediately swung the flashlight in a 360-degree arc, desperate to find the big cat that had done this.

When she saw light reflecting off a pair of eyes less than fifty yards away, she froze, realizing she was now standing between the cat and his kill, a dangerous place in which to be. Then the big cat let out a scream of displeasure that had her heart pounding in sudden fear. She kept staring at the eyes, trying to decide if she should shoot or run.

Before she could make the decision, the cat leaped and began running toward her, closing the distance between them in mere seconds.

She raised the rifle and took aim, but in the growing darkness she couldn't see the panther. One second, two seconds, she stood without moving, waiting for another look.

All of a sudden he was right in front of her. He leaped and she shot. The animal's squall of rage and pain echoed in her ears, and she was backing up when she took the second shot, unable to tell if she'd hit him or not.

All of a sudden she was flat on her back. She could hear the cat still squalling and guessed that she'd hit it, but when she tried to get up, the pain that ran up her leg nearly made her faint.

The first thing that went through her mind was that she had to call Sam.

* * *

Sam was on his way to Lainey's for the night when his phone rang. He glanced down as he picked it up, saw it was from her and put it on speaker so he could talk without holding it to his ear. "Hello, baby."

"Sam, where are you?"

He frowned. "On my way to your house, why?"

"How close are you?" she asked.

"About two miles away. What the hell's wrong?"

"I need you to hurry. I came out to feed Dandy, but he didn't come, and when I went to look for him, he was dead. That panther killed him, and then came after me. I shot it, but I didn't kill it, and I hurt my leg and can't get up. I'm scared, Sam. I'm afraid it will—"

Sam stomped the accelerator while she was still talking.

"Are you in the pasture behind the barn?"

"Yes. Oh, God, Sam. I think it's coming back."

"Shoot at it again," he said, and went airborne as he came over a rise in the road and landed hard about five yards downhill. The back wheels fishtailed, but he steered out of the skid and kept driving, flying past her neighbors' properties, lit up now against the dark.

Lainey swung the flashlight toward the pasture in front of her and could no longer see eyes. The panther had moved. She didn't know if it was stalking her or just watching her light.

All of a sudden she saw it just a few yards away.

"No, no, no!" she screamed, and shot again.

Sam thought the cat had taken her down. He shouted her name aloud as he topped the hill above her house.

He caught a glimpse of light out in the pasture and drove down the hill and up her driveway with his hand on the horn.

When his headlights swept across Lainey lying in the grass, his heart nearly stopped. He got on the run with his gun drawn, using his headlights to see.

He saw the big cat lying on its side just a few feet away and put one last shot in it to make sure it was dead, then dropped down beside Lainey, frantically running his hands across her body, searching for signs of life.

Suddenly, she gripped his arm. "I'm okay."

"Oh, my God," he groaned, then scooped her up in his arms and carried her to the car, where he set her down in the passenger seat beneath the light. "Did he bite you? Are you scratched anywhere?"

"No, but I hurt myself. My ankle and my left wrist both hurt. I think I stepped in a hole when I fell backward. Dandy is dead." Tears were rolling down her face now. "If I had come home sooner, I might have saved him."

"No, you just would have gotten yourself hurt, maybe killed," Sam said. "Let me go get the rifle and your flashlight, and then I'll take you back to the house."

She was sobbing and shaking by the time Sam got back to the car. He slid in behind the wheel, and then reached for her hand.

"What about Dandy?" she asked.

"There's nothing to be done before tomorrow."

She was shaking so much it was hard to catch a breath, and she couldn't quit crying. Part of it was sadness for Dandy, and the rest was still the adrenaline rush of fear from when the cat had run at her.

Sam drove all the way up to the back door, and then carried her into the house. As soon as he got her into the light, he saw the true extent of her injuries.

There were leaves and grass in her curls, and her ankle was swollen. She kept favoring her left wrist, so he checked it more closely. After feeling the joints and seeing her wince in pain, he shook his head.

"I'm taking you to the ER, so if you need to go to the bathroom or wash your hands and face before we go, say so now."

"The bathroom," she said.

He picked her up and carried her there.

"I'll be outside. Just call out when you're ready," he said, and then closed the door.

As soon as the door went shut, he heard her start crying all over again. He took out his phone and called Trey.

"Hello? Sam?"

"Hey, I'm bringing Lainey into the ER," Sam said.

"What's wrong? Did she get sick?"

"No, but she had a run-in with a panther out in the pasture behind the barn. She's okay, but I need to get her wrist and ankle X-rayed."

"Oh, my God, what happened? How did that happen?"

"She went to feed the horse. When he didn't come, she went looking for him, and that's when she met up with the cat."

"Good Lord! I didn't know we had a big cat down here. They usually stay up in the mountains."

"I saw it the other night when I was taking her home."

"Did she find her horse?"

"The horse is dead. The panther is dead. She shot it when it came at her. And I'm heading to town with her now."

"Do you need me?" Trey asked.

"No, but I need to tell you that I may or may not have found Donny Collins' old girlfriend. However, we can't question her right now."

"Why not?"

"Because it's Beth Powell, Randy Powell's mother, Jack Powell's grandmother."

Trey flashed on the dead boy in the burned-out car and closed his eyes. "What a nightmare this is turning out to be," he said.

Sam heard the toilet flush. "I've gotta go. Talk to you tomorrow."

"Call if you need me," Trey said.

"Go to bed, Trey. Get some rest. I've got this."

Sam dropped the phone in his pocket as the bathroom door began to open. As soon as Lainey saw him, she started crying again. He just picked her up in his arms and held her.

"You're going to have to quit crying or I'll be crying, too," Sam said. "I was so damned scared that I wouldn't get to you in time. All I could think was I just got her back—that you had to be okay."

"I know. I was scared, too. Let's go do this and say prayers that nothing is broken. I don't want to think about being in a cast for six weeks when I just finished all those trips to the doctor."

"Whatever it is, it's gonna be okay, baby. I let you down once, but it will never happen again. Whatever we go through now, we go through it together," Sam said and kissed her cheek.

Grateful for his presence, she hugged him.

"Okay, ready to go?" he asked.

"I need my purse. It has my medical info in it."

"Where is it at?" Sam asked.

"On my bed."

He carried her to the bedroom to get the purse, then carried her out through the back door and over to his car.

"Hand me your keys and I'll lock up for you," he said, once he had her settled inside.

She dug the key ring out of her purse and tossed it toward him. He caught it in midair, ran back to lock up, then loped back to the car.

Lainey's eyes were closed when he got in.

"Are you hurting much?" he asked.

She nodded.

"Damn it, honey, I am so sorry," he said, and then dropped the keys into her purse and drove away.

The emergency room was quiet when Sam carried Lainey in, but when news began spreading about a panther killing her horse before she killed the panther when it attacked her, her exploits became the news of the night.

The lab tech was the son of one of her neighbors, and as soon as he finished with Lainey, he was on the phone calling his parents.

The woman in X-ray had a friend who lived on Lainey's road, and when she was through with Lainey's X-rays, she called her friend with the news.

When the orderly brought Lainey back from X-ray,

Sam jumped up from the chair and helped her out of the wheelchair and back into bed.

A nurse had followed Lainey into the cubicle. "As soon as the doctor reads the X-rays he'll be in to talk to you," she said. "Is there anything I can get for you?"

"I'm freezing," Lainey said.

"I'll bring you another warm blanket," the nurse said and quickly left.

Sam sat down beside her and pulled the single lightweight blanket up over her arms. She was so pale and looked so tired. It was a reminder of how fragile her health still was, and it scared him.

"What can I do?" he asked. "Do you need a drink? Are you still in a lot of pain?"

Lainey heard the fear in his voice and understood so much more than he could imagine. She'd been so afraid for him when he was hurt, though like the girl she'd been, she'd run from it. She reached for his hand and just held it. "You're here. That's all I need."

"You look so tired," he said.

"I *am* tired. I did more today than I've done in ages."

"So close your eyes, baby. The doctor will wake you when he arrives."

Just then the nurse came back with the blanket.

"Here you go. Nice and warm," she said and covered Lainey up from chin to toes.

"Oh, that feels so good," Lainey said. "Do you think I'll be here much longer?"

"The doctor is looking at your X-rays now. He'll be here soon. Do you need anything?" the nurse asked.

"Just to go home," Lainey said.

The nurse left, and once again they were alone.

"Close your eyes," Sam said.

She did, and fell asleep so quickly it was startling. Sam realized he was witnessing the effects of his sudden reappearance in her life. The turmoil it had created for her—the loss of sleep, not eating properly—she had no reserve for this kind of upheaval, and he'd caused all of it. By the time the doctor showed up, Sam had come to a conclusion. She just didn't know it yet.

"Good evening," the doctor said as he strode in.

Sam stood up as Lainey opened her eyes.

"Am I broken?" she mumbled.

The doctor grinned and popped a couple of X-rays onto the screen, then turned on the light behind them.

"No, you're still in one piece," he said, pointing at the images. "You have a hairline fracture here in your wrist and another in your ankle, there, just above the joint, but they're minor. I understand you just finished chemo for breast cancer, is this right?"

"Yes," Lainey said.

The doctor's eyes narrowed.

"I think both of these fractures are due to loss of bone density from the chemo rather than the impact of your fall. Are you taking vitamins and calcium along with your other meds?"

"Yes."

"Then, I'd suggest you up your calcium by at least five hundred milligrams, get some weight back on you and no more midnight meetings with a panther."

"No more," she said. "Do I have to wear casts on my ankle and wrist?"

"I'm not going to cast them, but I'm sending you home with a soft boot to stabilize the ankle, and I want you to go back to your GP in a couple of weeks to see how it's healing. We'll wrap your wrist, too, and don't do any heavy lifting."

"Deal," she said.

The doctor glanced at Sam. "Are you related to Chief Jakes?"

"Yes, I'm his brother. Why?" Sam asked.

"No reason. You just look like him, so I was curious."

"I'm the eldest. I live in Atlanta."

"Nice family. I'm very sorry about your mother."

"Thank you," Sam said. "So can I take Lainey home now?"

"Yes, just make sure she takes it easy for a while."

"I'll monitor her every move," Sam said.

Lainey looked up at him, but he wasn't looking at her. She could tell he was up to something.

Fifteen

Lainey was in the car and still shivering as Sam pulled a blanket from the back of his SUV and tucked it around her.

She pulled the blanket closer and snuggled down in the seat.

"Are you comfortable, honey?" Sam asked.

"Yes, thank you."

He got in the car and turned the heat up as he drove away, but instead of leaving town he headed for his motel.

"Where are we going?" Lainey asked.

"To get my stuff. I'm staying with you. If it scares the shit out of you to sleep with me, I'll pick another bed and be fine."

She started to cry.

"Are you upset with me?" Sam asked.

She wiped the tears off her cheeks. "Have you ever had a dream come true?"

Sam took a deep breath and reached for her hand.

"Together, Lainey. You and me. This is part of what

that means to me. And when this nightmare is over, will you come to Atlanta with me?"

Tears were rolling again.

"Oh, honey…" Sam said.

"Just another one of those come-true moments," she said and used her blanket to wipe away her tears. "Go check out of your motel. It's check-in time at the Pickett Inn."

He accelerated into the parking lot, then drove to his room.

"I'm going to leave the car running so you'll be warm. It won't take me more than five minutes to pack. I'll check out as we leave."

She watched as he got out of the car. When he paused a few moments to scan the parking lot, she frowned, wondering what had caught his attention. Then when he turned and went into his room without further concern, it dawned on her that this was most likely normal behavior. The soldier had learned to scan the landscape before moving away from cover. If it reassured him to do that, then it worked for her.

She leaned her head against the window and tried not to think of how afraid Dandy must have been. She tried to get it out of her mind, but the horror of such an ignoble death for such a wonderful companion hurt her heart.

A few moments later she saw the motel door open again, with Sam silhouetted against the light behind him.

Before his return she'd almost forgotten the exact curve of his lips and the strong jut of his chin. She'd forgotten what it felt like to hold his hand, and how protected she'd always felt within his embrace. He'd

gone away from her a young man and returned as a
battle-scarred warrior. As much as she missed who
he'd been, she was beginning to think she liked this
Sam better.

Then the lights went out and he walked into full
view in the headlights before he kept moving and
dumped his things in the back of the SUV. A cold
blast of wind swirled through the interior and then
disappeared just as quickly when he shut the hatch.

"One more stop, and then we're going home," he
said as he got in and circled the motel. He stopped
at the office and gave Lainey's arm a brief pat. "Are
you still with me?" he asked.

She nodded.

"It won't take long to settle up," he said, and once
again she watched him walk away.

When he came out the second time, Lainey was
sound asleep. As he got in and closed the door, she
barely reacted. He put the car in gear and drove away.

Going back down the same road he'd been on hours
earlier felt weird—almost like letting air out of a bal-
loon. The band of muscles across his chest was so
tight it was hard to breathe, and he was struggling to
maintain composure. It felt like he was on autopilot
as they covered the miles, but when he topped that
last hill and saw the security light in the backyard and
the porch light shining to show him the way home,
the pain in his chest finally eased. Sanctuary awaited.

Lainey woke up as the car turned onto the gravel.
She sat up, and then laid a hand on Sam's arm, but
she didn't say anything.

Sam glanced at her. "What, honey?"

"Nothing...just centering my world."

He swallowed past the lump in his throat as he parked. "I'm going to open the front door first, then I'll come back for you."

Too weary to argue, she quietly waited for his return.

The air was cold when he opened the door, but he picked her up, blanket and all, and carried her indoors. The warmth and familiarity of the old farmhouse welcomed her home.

"Tonight was awful," Lainey said as Sam carried her to her room. "But you know what my mother would have said? She would have reminded me that this too shall pass. It's what I held on to tonight. It's what I thought after you saved me. I still have to bury Dandy, but it will be done, and then this will all be a memory."

He sat her down on the side of her bed, and then cupped the back of her head with a shaking hand and kissed her.

"For a few seconds tonight I thought I had lost you. It was the worst feeling in the world. I get what I did to you by staying away. Just know I never intended to hurt you, and that I grieved not being with you, too."

"I know, Sam. In a way, we became collateral damage. Now we're two new people finding our way through the chaos of our situations, and I can't wait for our future to unfold."

"Me, too," he said, then leaned forward and kissed her. "Are you hungry?"

"Not really."

"How about hot chocolate?"

"I only have packets of the instant stuff. Maybe it would warm me up," she said.

"Can you manage to undress on your own?" he asked.

"Yes."

"Then, I'll go make the hot chocolate and bring you some."

"Thank you, Sam. I don't know what—"

"Don't say it," he said. "It's over, okay?"

She nodded. "Okay."

She could hear him in the kitchen banging cabinet doors as he looked for what he needed and smiled as she began to undress. By the time she got into her nightgown and slid into bed, he was back.

"Thank God for microwaves and instant mixes," he said.

She smiled as he handed her the mug of cocoa.

"It smells wonderful," she said and took a careful sip to make sure it wasn't too hot, then she curled her hands around the warm mug and sipped while watching Sam get ready for bed. By the time she had finished the hot chocolate, he was turning out the overhead light.

"Are you hurting a lot?" he asked as he sat down on the side of the bed.

"No, the pain meds they gave me at the hospital are enough."

Sam helped her ease down beneath the covers. "Do you need a pillow under your foot? I think it would help."

"Maybe," she said.

He pushed a pillow beneath her ankle, then slid

into the bed beside her, turned over onto his side and put his arm over her waist.

"Do you think you can sleep okay?"

"I think I could sleep anywhere as long as I have you," he said and closed his eyes.

Then he proved himself right by sleeping all through the night without a moment of panic or one bad dream.

It was barely daylight when Sam heard a tractor out on the road. When it turned and came down the driveway he got up and looked out. The tractor was an old John Deere with a big box blade on the front end. It was hard to tell, because the driver was bundled up against the cold, but he thought he recognized her neighbor Larry, the one who'd run through her fence. When the man passed the house and then the barn and drove into the pasture, Sam knew what he was about to do.

He'd come to bury Dandy for her.

Sam glanced back at Lainey, but she was still asleep, curled up on her side. He grabbed his clothes and got dressed in the living room, then headed out the door, got in his car and followed the tractor to the pasture.

The old man had found the horse soon enough and was out checking to see where the best place to bury him would be. When he saw Sam drive up, he stopped and waved.

Sam walked up with his hand out. "Larry, it's been a long time," he said and shook his hand.

Larry pumped Sam's hand with a smile on his face. "I'll be damned. If it ain't Sam Jakes! Boy, it's good to see you again." Then he motioned toward the horse. "I heard what happened. I knowed how much Lainey loved this old fella and wanted to get him buried before he got scattered all over."

"That's very thoughtful of you," Sam said.

"Well, I tore up her fence some the other day, so I thought this might even us up. I was thinking of pushing out some dirt right here, and then dragging the carcass into the hole and covering it back over. I brought a rope to tow it. Now I see there's a panther to bury, too. I really don't need no help unless you want to stay," Larry said.

"No, I won't stay. She got hurt some last night, and I don't know how sore she's going to be today."

"Is she gonna be okay?" Larry asked.

"Yes. She'll heal. So I'll go back to the house if you're sure you don't need me."

Larry waved him off. "I've buried many a cow like this. One horse and one panther can't be no different."

"Thanks again," Sam said and drove away, leaving Larry to finish what he'd come to do.

By the time Sam got back to the house, Lainey was in the kitchen with the soft boot on her injured ankle and a slipper on the other. She was wearing her bathrobe and making coffee.

There were tears in her eyes when Sam walked in, but she smiled. "Good morning, sweetheart. Did you sleep well?"

He wrapped her up in a big hug and kissed the top of her head. "Yes, I slept well. You must be the magic that was missing in my life. Did you see Larry?"

She nodded.

"He was worried about you. He heard what happened and wanted to do this for you because of the mess he made with your fence."

"I appreciate it," she said, and then kissed him good morning. "What would you like for breakfast?"

"I would like for you to go get dressed in something warm while I make breakfast. Can you do that?"

"Yes, but—"

"No buts. I can make eggs and bacon."

She smiled.

"Then, I would like mine scrambled," she said.

"Good, because it's the only kind I make that turns out right."

She stroked the side of his face. "I love you," she said softly.

"I love you most," he whispered and brushed a kiss across her mouth.

She was still smiling as she went to get dressed.

Trey arrived at the precinct with a plate full of blueberry muffins and set it in the break room before going into his office.

Earl Redd came in the back door, smelled the muffins and snagged one before heading to the chief's office. He was chewing and licking his fingers when he walked in.

"Man, these are good, Chief. I'm gonna assume they're from Dallas, so tell her thank you from me."

Trey smiled.

"You know *I* didn't make them. She'll be pleased you enjoyed them. So what's going on this morning?" he asked.

"It's a slow Sunday. Everyone will probably get

ready for church later, but right now Charlie's is humming about what y'all pulled out of the mine."

Trey frowned. "How so?"

"Word has gotten around that we've been looking for Donny Collins, and there's a lot of talk that it might be him."

Trey thought of the Harper women. He should have known they would talk about Sam's visit. And Will Porter could have mentioned it in passing.

"Then the 1980 graduates start talking about their meeting with you and that you were trying to find every graduate, and how he was the only one still unaccounted for when the meeting was over."

Trey sighed. "Well, Earl, this could work for us. Maybe this will shock someone into coming forward."

"Maybe so," Earl said, and finished off the muffin while waiting for Trey's orders.

"Maintain your usual patrol route," Trey said. "Radio in if you need assistance. There's another cold front coming in tonight, so there'll probably be a lot of business around the grocery store after church. We don't need any more traffic deaths."

Earl frowned. "That was really rough," he said. "I feel so bad for the whole Powell family."

"We all do," Trey said.

"See you later, Chief," Earl said. He took another muffin with him as he left the building.

While Trey was getting a cold drink from his minifridge he heard his fax machine kick on. He took a quick sip, and then set the can aside as he went to get the papers the machine was spitting out. One quick glance and his heart sank.

It was from the coroner's office. He read the name

Betsy Jakes, and his hand started to shake. When he first took this job, he never imagined he would be reading an autopsy of his mother's body.

As expected, there were no surprises. She'd died from a gunshot wound to the head. Hell, he'd known that when he found her body. Now the reality was official, though. He filed the fax and walked out of the office.

Larry buried the horse and the panther. When he drove out of the pasture and started back up the driveway to go home, Lainey was standing on the back porch. She waved and blew him a kiss.

He saw the wrap on her arm and the soft boot on her leg, and felt so bad at what had happened to her. He tipped his hat and kept driving. Just one neighbor helping another.

When she went back inside, Sam was waiting for her with a blanket and a kiss.

She put her arms around his neck and leaned into his embrace. Something bad had happened, and now it was over. Life went on, and so would they.

"Are you getting ready to go into Mystic now?" she asked.

"If I do, will you promise me that you won't go outside and start some project, no matter what, and that you'll call me if you need help? The doctor said no lifting, and I'm saying stay off your ankle."

"Yes, I swear."

"Okay, then yes, I'm going into Mystic now. So do you want to go lie back down in bed or on the living room sofa?"

"The living room, please. I'll watch TV until I get sleepy, and I'll be careful and call if I need to."

He walked with her into the living room, and then settled her on the sofa. He handed her the remote and propped her foot up with a pillow, then left her with a last kiss."

"I'll be back with lunch at noon," he said. "And if I'm going to be late, I'll call. I'm really anxious to check on Trina and see if she's showing any signs of regaining consciousness."

"Let me know."

"I will. Love you, Lainey."

She smiled. "Love you, too."

He locked the door behind him as he left.

Marcus Silver was drinking whiskey before breakfast.

Will Porter was at his wife's side, watching her take her last breaths.

Greg Standish was debating the wisdom of going to church. He guessed Gloria had told her friends that she was leaving him before she left town, but he was pretty sure she hadn't said why, because that would have made her look bad. The fact that she'd taken their daughter out of school so suddenly had left him looking like the bad guy. He was frustrated by the gossip he knew had to be circulating but was determined to hold his head up and go on about his business. He'd given up too much to quit now, and he needed to maintain propriety in order to keep his job. And because he was in too deep to crawl into a hole and hide, he made himself get dressed. Church was the perfect place for a man to relieve himself of his burdens, and the Good Lord knew he had plenty to shed.

Beth Powell felt as if she'd aged ten years overnight. The grief of learning her only grandson was dead had nearly killed her. If it hadn't been for staying strong for her son and daughter-in-law, she didn't know what she would have done.

Randy was distraught to the point of having to be medicated.

Clarice had cried for hours, and when she stopped, she also stopped talking. Now she just walked around like a zombie.

Beth didn't know what was going to happen to her family in the coming months, but today they had to go to the funeral home and pick out a casket for Jack, and she was the only one composed enough to be behind the wheel.

She left her house with a heavy heart and picked them up just after 10:00 a.m., and they drove all the way into town without a single word passing between them.

They arrived at the funeral home without incident, but as soon as they walked into the lobby, Clarice moaned and then sank to the floor on her knees. It took both Beth and Randy to get her on her feet and seated on a sofa. Randy looked at his mother with tears running down his face, and she could do nothing to help but hug him.

Ted Martin, the funeral director, appeared within seconds and knew it was going to be a difficult visit. The circumstances of the boy's death were horrific, the tragedy made worse because he'd been an only child. And since it was obviously going to be a closed-casket ceremony, he couldn't even use his skills to make the deceased look at peace, which might help to soothe his grieving family. He needed to pull out all the stops this morning to get through this.

"Mr. and Mrs. Powell, my deepest sympathies. Beth, I am so sorry for your loss. How can I help you?" he asked.

"We don't know where to begin," Beth said.

"Then, I would suggest we begin with choosing a casket. We have a large number from which to choose, and of course can order any color you want if we don't have it in stock. Would you follow me?"

Randy helped Clarice up, and then walked with his arm around her waist in case he needed to catch her. Beth walked beside her son, because his expression was breaking her heart.

When they entered the display room, Beth was struck with such a strong sensation of déjà vu that she stumbled. She'd been here before when she'd buried her husband, Tom. She'd never thought of having to help bury a grandchild.

Randy choked on a sob when he saw all the caskets, and Clarice's eyes went blank. Beth sighed. At least Clarice had removed herself from the equation. It would be up to herself and Randy to get this done.

"Do you know if you would prefer a wood tone, a marble effect or maybe something like this?" Ted asked, pointing to a metallic gold-and-black casket.

"I don't know," Randy mumbled, then wiped his eyes and blew his nose with a handkerchief. "Mom, what do you think?"

"I think since Jack loved to hunt and fish so much,

something in a wood-grain finish would fit. Clarice, honey, what do you think?" Beth asked.

Clarice blinked.

Randy hugged her and turned to Ted. "Sorry. I don't think Clarice is up to this, so Mom and I will choose."

Ted nodded and took them through the display room. They finally chose a dark oak with a plain white interior.

"So it won't clash with the color of his suit," Beth said.

Then Randy insisted on a vault, so they chose that, as well. When they adjourned to the front office to do the paperwork and choose a date for the service, Beth sat down with great relief. Her heart was pounding, and her legs were shaking so hard she could barely stand. Randy's face was too red, and she feared his blood pressure was too high, while Clarice was too pale. Beth wondered if she would ever come back to them.

Ted had the contract finished in no time, and Randy was busy writing out a check for the service costs when two other employees walked through the lobby just outside Ted's office. The door was open, and even though the women were speaking in undertones, their voices carried.

"Did you hear about the authorities finding that body out at the old Colquitt Mine?"

"Yes! Isn't that something? Supposed to be some kid from the 1980 graduating class."

"How do you suppose they'll prove that? I mean, there's nothing there but bones."

"Oh, the identification and everything was there,

didn't you hear? A suitcase. A bus ticket to California. Even a wallet with a bunch of money still in it."

The room tilted in front of Beth's gaze. She moaned, and then reached out for the corner of the desk to keep from falling out of her chair.

Randy caught her. "Mom. Mom! Are you all right?"

She wiped a shaky hand across her face. "I'm fine. Are we nearly done here?"

Ted Martin gave a receipt and copies of the paperwork to Randy, and then told them he would let them know when he was ready to open the viewing room for visiting hours.

"No viewing," Randy said.

Ted nodded. "Yes, of course. What I mean is that I will have your son in the casket. It will be locked and then brought to a viewing room where you can receive your family and friends."

Randy sighed. "Oh. Right."

Beth was shaking. The men's voices were just a roar in her ears. She couldn't have repeated a word of what they were saying to save her soul.

"Okay, then. We'll wait for your phone call," Randy said as he stood up.

Ted nodded. "Since you still have to consult with your pastor, if you need to change the date or time for any reason, all you have to do is call."

Randy nodded again, and then helped his wife up and out of the room, while Beth brought up the rear. They got in the car and then sat without talking.

Beth was operating on autopilot. "We need to do flowers," she said.

Randy shuddered. "Will you just take us home, Mom? Clarice can't do that, and I don't know how."

"I'll come back and order the flowers if you'll call your pastor from home," she said.

"Yes, I will. Thank you. Thank you so much, Mom. I couldn't have done any of this without you."

Beth's vision blurred. "You are my heart, and it's breaking for you right now. I am so sorry for you and Clarice. So sorry. Life can hit us with some really ugly blows, and this is one of those times."

Randy leaned against the backseat, put his arm around Clarice and closed his eyes.

Beth drove them home without talking.

When she reached their farm, she got out and hugged them both, then turned around and drove back into Mystic, but it wasn't just to order flowers. She needed to talk to Chief Jakes. She needed to know if what she'd heard those women saying was true, and if it was, she was about to mess up someone's life in a very big way.

Sixteen

Beth ordered a blanket of white roses for the casket and a matching spray from herself. She wrote her check in a fog, listened to condolences with a deaf ear and walked out of the florist while the man was still talking to her.

She felt as if she was going to throw up, but the rage in her was strong enough to keep her moving. She drove straight to the police precinct and walked in with one thought on her mind.

"I need to speak to Chief Jakes," she said.

"He's not in right now but he's on his way," Avery said.

"I'll wait," Beth said and sat down in a straight-back chair at the front.

She took a deep breath, trying to slow down her heart rate, but it didn't work. God, she hoped she got this said before she dropped dead.

Five minutes passed.

"Do you think it will be much longer?" she asked.

Avery Jones was the day dispatcher and also served

as a desk clerk. He could tell by the way Beth Powell was sitting that she was upset.

"No, ma'am, I don't. I'm surprised he's not already here. Chief Jakes is—"

There was noise in the back of the building, and Avery grinned.

"That's the chief coming in now. I'll let him know you're here," he said, picking up the phone.

Beth took a tissue out of her purse, and wiped her eyes and blew her nose as Avery was speaking to the chief, and when he hung up she stood.

Trey hurried down the hall, and when he saw her through the doorway he could tell something was very wrong. "Mrs. Powell?"

"I need to talk to you," she said.

"Certainly. Let's go to my office," he said and took her elbow and led her back down the hall.

As soon as Beth saw the man sitting in the office, she recognized him as the eldest of Betsy Jakes' children.

Sam also knew who she was and began gathering up his things.

"Mrs. Powell, I'm so sorry for your loss. Just give me a second to get my stuff, and I'll give you two some privacy."

"No, stay. This has to do with you as much as it does with Chief Jakes."

Sam leaned against a wall with his arms folded across his chest, leaving the chair for her.

Beth sat down, but she was on the edge of the seat, looking as if she was about to eject herself from the chair.

"How can I help you, Mrs. Powell?" Trey asked.

"I need you to answer me one question, and it's really important that you tell me what you know."

"I'm listening," Trey said.

"Whose body did you find in the Colquitt Mine?"

"Well, the coroner hasn't given me a—"

"No!" she shouted, and then shuddered. "I'm sorry, but don't hedge. I heard you found identification with the body. Did you?"

Trey glanced at Sam, who nodded.

"Yes, we did," Trey said.

"Who?"

Trey sighed. "There was a wallet with the body. The driver's license had Donny Collins' name on it."

Beth screamed, then moaned and doubled over in the chair, covering her face.

Trey jumped up, but Sam was quicker and knelt down beside her, worried she was going to faint and fall out of the chair.

"What is it, Mrs. Powell? What do you know?" Sam asked.

Beth couldn't stop sobbing. "I thought he dumped me. I thought he was too chicken to tell me, so he strung me along till he left, then forgot all about me."

Sam's heart skipped a beat. This was it. This was the break they'd been waiting for.

"So Donny was your boyfriend in high school?"

"Yes. I loved him so much. I was two months' pregnant when he graduated. He was planning to go to college with the scholarship money he was certain he expected to receive, but then he didn't get it. Plan B was to go to California to find a job and a place to live, and then he was going to send for me."

Trey's eyes widened. "And when you didn't hear from him?" he asked.

"I thought he blew me off. I thought he skipped out on me and our baby."

Sam pulled up a chair beside her, and then reached for her hands. "Mrs. Powell… Beth, look at me."

She lifted her head.

"What do you know about the cheating?" he asked.

She began to sob all over again. "I was the one who got the answers and five hundred dollars for my trouble. I didn't know it would end up cheating Donny out of the scholarship. I didn't know. I just needed to get money for us to leave."

The moment Sam and Trey heard that, they knew why Donny's wallet had held five hundred dollars, and they knew who the cheater had to be—Marcus Silver, the only other contender for the scholarship, but they needed her to say it. Sam squeezed her hands gently, trying to tug her back to the moment. "Who asked you for help in cheating?"

"Marcus Silver."

"Did Donny know?"

"No. I didn't know until Marcus was awarded the scholarship the night of graduation. I was too scared to tell Donny what I'd done, but I think someone told Donny that Marcus had cheated. Probably other kids saw him doing it, you know? I think now that he and Donny must have argued after graduation. I didn't see it happen, but if anyone had a reason to keep Donny quiet, it would have been him. His father was a tyrant, and we all knew it. He had to be perfect all the time or he was in trouble. It wasn't winning the money but being valedictorian that mattered. If he didn't get it, his father would probably have beaten Marcus to within an inch of his life for disappointing him."

"Will you testify to this in a court of law?" Trey asked.

"Yes," she said.

But there was one thing still left unspoken, and Sam wanted to know the answer. "What happened to the baby?" he asked.

Beth blinked as if surprised that he'd asked something she assumed was obvious.

"I gave birth to him on my own. I didn't marry Tom Powell until Randy was about six months old. Tom adopted him, but Randy is Donny's son, and Jack was his grandson."

"Wow," Trey said softly.

Sam got a box of tissues from Trey's desk and handed them to Beth. She pulled out a handful and wiped her face.

"I guess that's all I have to say," she said.

Trey hesitated. "Out of curiosity, how did you access the answers to the exam?"

Beth sighed. "I was a teacher's aide to Mrs. Henry, who was the physics teacher."

"Okay, then. I want to thank you for coming forward."

"Am I in trouble?" she asked.

"No," Trey said.

"Are you going to be all right to drive yourself home?" Sam asked.

She clutched her purse against her breasts. "I endured being an unwed mother when it was considered an unforgivable fall from grace. I feel like I have been given a blessing just knowing Donny did love me. That he didn't abandon me after all."

"You do know this is all going to come out eventually?" Sam asked.

"I know."

"I don't know what Randy knows about all this, and he's going through a lot of hell right now on his own, but it would be best if he heard it from you first."

She nodded.

"He knew Tom wasn't his birth father, but that was all. I didn't want him to grow up thinking he wasn't worth loving, that his father abandoned the both of us, which is what I thought all along. We'll figure it out. I'm just devastated about Donny. He might have been dead for the past thirty-six years, but in my heart he just died today."

Then she started crying all over again, but it was a quiet, broken kind of weeping that spoke to the burden of the blow.

"I need to call Sheriff Osmond," Trey said.

"I'll walk Beth out," Sam said, then helped her up and walked her out of the precinct.

"Are you sure you're okay to drive home?" he asked when they got outside. "It wouldn't take me long to drive you. I could get Trey to follow and bring me back."

Beth paused at her car, and then impulsively hugged him.

"I promise I'm okay. My son needs me, and I need to see a killer brought to justice. Are you going to talk to Marcus Silver?"

"Yes, ma'am. You can count on that."

"Is he going to be arrested?"

"I can't speak for the sheriff or for the chief, but it is my professional opinion as a private investigator that Marcus Silver is in a whole lot of trouble."

Satisfied with that answer, she nodded, then got in her car and drove away.

Sam ran back to his brother's office.

Trey was just getting off the phone.

They stood there for a few moments just staring at each other, then Trey high-fived his brother. "I knew something would break on this case."

"What did Sheriff Osmond say?" Sam asked.

"He's pretty pumped about the information. I told him we were going to bring Silver into the precinct for questioning. He wants to be here. I told him we'd be happy to set Silver's ass in an interrogation room until he can get here. He said he'd be here in less than two hours."

Sam glanced at the time. It was almost eleven.

"Then, we need to go get Silver, and I need to call Lainey and tell her I'm not going to make it home at noon."

Trey nodded. "You ride with me."

"Happy to oblige," Sam said.

Lainey was in the bathroom when her phone rang. By the time she got back to answer it Sam had sent a text. She read it with growing shock.

Break in the case. Can't come home at noon. Going to bring Marcus Silver in for questioning. Please keep that to yourself. Trina is being moved out of ICU sometime today, although she has yet to wake up. Love you most. See you later. Call if you need me.

Marcus Silver? Was he the one responsible for the body in the mine? Did that mean he'd also killed Betsy and all the others?

Lainey sent a text back to Sam.

Best news ever about a break in the case. Justice for the murders and Trina will be safe. I'm fine. Do your thing. I love you.

Trey and Sam drove back through the gates at the Silver estate in a much different frame of mind. Trey cautioned Sam all the way there about not losing his cool. They needed Marcus to admit to the cheating, because the physical evidence they had on him added up to zero. All they had right now were Beth Powell's statement and the assumptions they'd drawn regarding it. They still didn't know for sure why he had panicked and murdered three of his classmates after all these years—though they had a pretty good guess—but they were going to find out.

It was starting to sprinkle when they got out of the car. Sam glanced up at the sky and frowned. Another cold, wet day. He was missing the milder weather of Atlanta and guessed Lainey would appreciate it once she moved there.

They knocked.

A maid answered.

"We need to speak with Marcus Silver," Trey said.

"Just a moment and I'll see if he's receiving visitors," she said.

Trey stopped her. "No, ma'am, we're not visiting. We're here on an official capacity. Either he comes to us or we go to him."

Her only reaction was a tightening of her lips as she brought them into the foyer, and then scurried off.

They heard some thumping and a loud voice from upstairs, and then the maid came back on the run.

"Mr. Silver asks you to come up. He's in bed."

"Fine with me," Sam said.

Trey and Sam followed the maid up the stairs, then into the bedroom. It was immediately obvious that Marcus wasn't ill. He was sitting on the side of the bed in his pajamas and bathrobe, seriously drunk.

"What the fuck do you want?" Marcus asked.

"We need you to get dressed and come down to the station with us to answer some questions."

The shock on Marcus's face was clear as he jumped up and walked away, mumbling about disrespect.

Sam took hold of the man's arm and turned him around to face them.

"Did you hear my brother ask you to get dressed?" he said softly.

Marcus began to bluster. "I don't have to—"

Sam yanked his arm just enough to unsettle his stance. Marcus staggered and would have fallen but for the firm grip Sam had on him.

"Yes, you do have to," Sam said. "Do you want me to yank those pajamas off your ass for you, or are you going to do it?"

Marcus began to realize they were serious. "I wanna call my lawyer," he said.

"You haven't been charged with anything," Trey said. "Did you expect to be? Is that why you're drunk… because you knew you were going to jail?"

"I didn't do anything," Marcus mumbled.

"Then, come down to the precinct so we can clear this up," Trey said.

Marcus thought about it, but he thought too long.

"Forget about his clothes, Trey. Just get a coat and we'll take him down in pajamas. That will look good in the morning paper."

Marcus's bravado died where he stood. Appearance was everything, and he couldn't let himself be humiliated that way.

"I'm changing," he said and stumbled into his walk-in closet.

Sam followed.

"I don't need an audience," Marcus said.

"You have one anyway," Sam said. "Hurry up."

Marcus stumbled all over the closet before he got himself decent, and when they started down the hall he was barely able to pick up his feet.

The sprinkles of rain had turned into a steady drizzle. Trey put Marcus in the backseat, and Sam slid in beside him. Despite the chilly weather, Marcus was sweating profusely and eyeing Sam with growing horror.

"I don't understand what this is all about," he said.

"Sure you do," Sam said.

Marcus wiped a shaky hand across his face and didn't utter another word.

They took him in through the front door because Trey wanted the man to be seen and to worry about being seen. They needed him as unsettled as possible, and they needed him sober. They didn't want a lawyer to come back on them later and accuse them of leading an inebriated man to confess to something he hadn't done. The wait for Sheriff Osmond should take care of that very conveniently.

Avery Jones' eyes widened perceptibly and his mouth dropped open when he saw who they had brought in, but he quickly looked away.

Trey walked Marcus all the way through the police station to the interrogation room at the back next to the jail.

"Have a seat," Trey said, and turned to leave.

"Wait! What's going on? I thought you said you wanted to talk."

"Well, yes, we do, but I'm waiting on Sheriff Osmond to get here. Since we're both working the case, we've been sharing information. It's just simpler for him to hear you give your statement, and then we'll be done."

Marcus shrugged.

"I'm going to bring you some coffee," Sam said. "I suggest you drink it. It would be to your advantage to be sober when this begins."

Marcus paled and started to shake as Sam left the room.

Sam returned a few minutes later with two large cups of hot coffee and put them both down in front of Marcus. "Knock yourself out," he said and shut the door firmly as he left.

Marcus reached for the first cup with a shaking hand and took a sip. Tears were running down his face, and the knot of fear in his gut was growing bigger by the moment.

Sam paused outside in the hall to look at Marcus through the one-way glass. "He's gonna lose it," he said.

"It can't happen soon enough for me," Trey replied.

* * *

It took another forty-five minutes for Sheriff Osmond to get there, but he came in the door smiling. "Do you really think you've got our man?" he asked.

"What I know is that I have a very strong, very reliable witness who can speak to motive and who knows where that five hundred came from, and I'll bet if we run a bluff, it will send Marcus over the edge," Trey said.

"So let's do this before he lawyers up. Is he sober enough?"

"He's had about two quarts of coffee and I imagine he needs to take a piss," Sam said.

"Then, let's go make him a little more uncomfortable. I'm going to stay quiet while Silver gives his statement," Sheriff Osmond said. "I think having Betsy Jakes' sons take the lead will be pressure enough." Then he followed the Jakes brothers down the hall.

After Sam texted to tell Lainey he wasn't coming home at noon, she shifted her focus to other things. She had already decided to call the university and get someone to take her classes tomorrow, and once she told them what had happened they were understanding. They wished her a speedy recovery and told her to let them know when she was ready to return.

She puttered around the house with another cup of hot chocolate in hand, then added a couple of cookies and called it lunch. She was folding laundry when she noticed the box of her mother's diaries she'd brought down from the attic. After the laundry was put up she went back to the box and picked through some of them. Reading the entries was poignant, but also fun. It was like visiting with her mother again.

She brought a couple of diaries with her to the sofa, covered up beneath a blanket and opened up the one that began after her mother had graduated high school and begun dating the young man who would eventually become Lainey's father.

It had been a long time since she'd looked through this one, and when she ran across a handful of pictures slipped in between the months of September and October of 1980, she started to set them aside until two names jumped out at her.

There were three pictures that appeared to have been taken out in the high school parking lot right after the graduation ceremony. Nearly all the people in the photos were either still wearing their caps and gowns or had them over their arms.

The pictures were joyous, capturing the elation of young men and women on the verge of becoming adults. Her mother had made notations of who was who with the same code she had used in the diaries.

There was one of a girl kissing a boy and another that was a group shot of good friends with several sets of parents. And the last one was a very clear view of two boys driving out of the parking lot together. Lainey grinned when she saw it, thinking that her mother must have been standing directly in front of the car to get that shot. Both boys looked startled to see her standing in the way, and the driver was glaring and waving at her to move out of the way.

She laughed. Then she saw the notation.

Silver Spoon in his daddy's car and Tom Collins riding shotgun.

She stared at it for a long moment in disbelief. Silver Spoon was an obvious reference to the richest boy in school, the one who'd been born with a silver spoon in his mouth. And there was Tom Collins again. She didn't remember what Donny Collins looked like, but if Sam and Trey had just brought Marcus Silver in for questioning, this might be really important. She started to give Sam a call, and then remembered they were most likely interrogating Marcus Silver, something she didn't want to interrupt. And they needed to see what she'd found, not just hear about it. Despite her ankle, she had to take it to the precinct while the man was still being questioned.

She got a coat and her purse and headed out the door with the photo, hobbling as she went. It wasn't the smartest thing she'd ever done, but it wasn't going to kill her.

As she started up the drive, she reached down to turn on the windshield wipers, and when she looked up she was facing toward the pasture and the big mound of fresh dirt. She looked away quickly. Life had taught her some hard lessons, but her rule of thumb was that if she survived it, then it was over.

The urge to speed was strong as she drove toward Mystic. Just like when she'd found the story about the cheating scandal in her mother's diaries, she had the feeling of anticipation that something her mother had done was going to be crucial to solving these crimes.

Marcus had a roaring headache, but he was mostly sober. When the door to the interrogation room opened, he jumped to his feet.

"I need to use the restroom," he said.

"After we're finished," Trey said. "Please sit down."

Marcus was stunned, and it showed. He was used to his every whim being catered to, and the simple act of refusing him a trip to the bathroom seemed preposterous.

"Now, see here, I—"

Sam pushed him down in the chair and kept a hand on his shoulder until he grew quiet.

"Is there anything you would like to tell us?" Trey asked.

"How about that there is a very likely possibility that you people will lose your jobs over this?" Marcus snapped.

"We had a witness come forward today in regard to the cheating scandal," Trey said.

Marcus's belligerence settled into sarcasm. "I don't see what some high school prank has to do with any of this," he said.

"Don't play stupid. It was important enough for someone to murder three people," Sam said.

Marcus blanched. "I had nothing to do with that."

"That remains to be seen. According to my witness, you gave her five hundred dollars for the answers to an exam. The grade on that test was the tipping point between valedictorian and salutatorian, not to mention the deciding factor on who won a scholarship, only she didn't know that," Trey said.

"I don't know what you're talking about. I keep telling you people I didn't need that scholarship money."

"No, but you needed the honor and glory that went with it, didn't you?" Sam said. "We saw those paint-

ings on the wall in your library. I'll bet Daddy was a
stickler for perfection? Am I right?"

Marcus glared.

"Look, we already know you cheated. All we want
to know is, did Donny Collins know it, too?" Sam
asked.

Marcus frowned. "He didn't know anything. He—"
All of a sudden he realized he had admitted to the
cheating with that slip of the tongue and stopped in
midsentence.

Sam smiled. "That's better. Doesn't it feel good to
get rid of that little burden? Hell, Marcus, it was just
a test. Like you said, it happened a long time ago. It's
over and done with, right?"

Marcus didn't look up.

Sam looked at Trey and grinned.

Sam pulled a chair up to the interrogation table,
sat and then leaned forward. "Was your father abu-
sive?" he asked.

Marcus shifted in the chair. "I still need to pee,"
he said.

"In a few minutes," Trey said. "Answer the question."

"I guess you could say he was, but that doesn't
mean I did something wrong," Marcus mumbled.

"I didn't say you did what you did because you
were afraid of your father. I didn't say why you paid
Beth Bradford to cheat. She told us she didn't know
why you did it, either. But she needed money, and
she got you the answers to the test because she was
Mrs. Henry's aide, and you gave her five hundred
dollars, right?"

Marcus wiped his face with both hands.

"It doesn't matter," Trey said. "She'll testify in court to all of it, including her part in it."

"No one will believe a word of it," Marcus blustered. "I am a valued member of the community."

"Back then you were just a senior in high school," Trey said. "Kids are always making mistakes. No doubt people assume you made some, too."

"I need to pee," Marcus said.

"I need the truth," Trey said.

Marcus moaned. "Oh…hell. Yes, I paid to get the answers. I didn't want to listen to my dad shout at me for not having a perfect score. It's no big deal. It's over and done. Now can I pee?"

"So how did Donny Collins take it when he found out?" Sam asked.

"I told you. He didn't know. No one knew."

"That's not the truth, and you know it," Sam said. "Beth knew. She's the one who gave you the answers. And Beth was dating Donny, wasn't she?"

Marcus's eyes widened. "I don't know."

"Oh, sure you do," Trey said. "Every teenager knows who's hooking up in high school."

"So you paid Beth five hundred dollars," Sam said.

Marcus shrugged. "I guess. I don't remember the exact amount. What does it matter?"

Sam put his hand on the table in front of Marcus, then marked off every word he spoke with a tap of his finger.

"There was five hundred dollars cash in the wallet we found with the body we pulled out of the Colquitt Mine. The driver's license in that wallet belonged to Donny Collins. That five hundred dollars was what you paid Beth for the answers. Isn't it something, how one thing leads to another, then backward and forward again and ties itself up in this neat little bow?"

The scent of urine suddenly filled the air.

"Well, well," Sam said. "I think you just pissed yourself out of a trip to the john. Now we can get down to business."

Marcus moaned.

"I didn't do anything to Donny Collins. I didn't hang out with him. I was not his friend. I would have had no earthly reason to be anywhere in his company. I don't know what you're talking about. I think I want—"

Before he could finish there was a knock at the door.

Trey frowned. "I told Avery not to bother us," he said, and then went to the door.

Avery was standing in the hall with Lainey Pickett at his side.

"I know you said not to bother you, but I think you need to see this, Chief."

Seventeen

Lainey handed Trey the photo. He looked at it, grinned and then yelled at his brother from the hall.

"Hey, Sam, could you come out here a minute?"

Sam was stunned to see Lainey in the hall.

"Lainey, honey, are you okay? What's wrong?"

"Nothing's wrong," she said. "I was reading more of Mom's diaries when I came across that picture." She pointed to the photo Trey was holding. "It was one of several my mother took after the graduation ceremony. Look at what she wrote. The passenger is Tom Collins and the driver is Silver Spoon. That has to be Marcus Silver. He looks just like T.J. looks now."

Trey was grinning as he handed Sam the picture.

"Just see what your pretty lady did. This certainly refutes Marcus's claim that he didn't hang out with Donny Collins."

"So that *is* Donny Collins?" Lainey asked.

"Yes, and you're right that it's Marcus driving," Sam said, then hugged her. "Your mother was amazing, and so are you."

She smiled.

"We've got to get back inside," Sam said. "This might be the tipping point."

"Is Trina still in ICU?" Lainey asked.

"No. They moved her into a private room. The guard is still there, and I think Lee is, too. He was when I was there this morning."

"Would it be okay if I dropped by before I went back home?"

Sam frowned. "Are you okay moving around that much?"

"I won't be there long."

"If you feel like it, then by all means it's okay. You're part of the family. Besides, your name is on the list. Just be careful, okay?"

She nodded.

Sam bent down and kissed her quickly, then hurried back inside the interrogation room with Trey.

Lainey felt good. Yet another bit of history that was helping them make their case.

All the way home from church, T.J. thought about his father, hoping he'd ended his drinking binge before he passed out on the floor. The drizzle was turning into rain as he parked beneath the portico and went in through the French doors that led straight to the library.

The scent of roast beef wafted through the hall as he headed for the stairs. He hoped Cook had made something good for dessert. He was in the mood for sweets.

His foot was on the bottom step when the maid came running toward him from the back of the house.

"Mr. T.J., Mr. T.J., your father isn't here."

T.J. frowned. "His car is out front."

"Chief Jakes and his brother came this morning. They took your father with them when they left."

T.J.'s heart skipped a beat. "Why?"

"I didn't know. And I don't know what to do."

"Christ almighty! You could have called me."

She ruffled like a pissed-off hen full of righteous indignation. "Your number has never been made available to the staff, sir."

He flushed. It was true. He considered the running of the house his father's business.

"So what can you tell me?" he asked.

"He left the house in disarray," she said.

T.J. frowned.

"What do you mean?"

"I mean, he was not his usual dapper self."

T.J. stifled a moan. "Had he still been drinking?" She nodded.

"Was he drunk?"

"I would guess so."

"Son of a bitch," T.J. muttered, and headed back out the way he'd come in.

The scent of urine was ripe inside the interrogation room, and Marcus Silver was in extreme discomfort and horrified it had happened. He looked everywhere but at the sheriff still in the room with him.

When the Jakes brothers came back in, he could tell by the looks on their faces that something had happened. Instinct told him it was not in his favor. And when they walked over to Sheriff Osmond and showed him what looked like a photo, he tried not to worry.

"Sorry for that interruption," Trey said.

"Have you no mercy?" Marcus mumbled. "I need a bath and fresh clothing."

Trey ignored him. "So tell me again how you and Donny Collins got along."

Marcus slapped the flat of his hand on the table. "He was a nobody. I did not hang out with people like him. Ever! I want my lawyer!"

The thought went through Sam's head that he was so going to love Lainey into exhaustion. It wasn't just the fact that her mother had kept track of her childhood like an IRS CPA, but that Lainey had been thoughtful enough to search through a lifetime of mementos to help them solve this case. Especially when she'd started out hating his guts.

Trey laid the photo down in front of Marcus.

Marcus glanced down and then froze. He felt a blood rush of panic as his life began flashing before his eyes. Then he put both hands on the table and looked up.

"I want my lawyer."

"Why am I not surprised?" Sam drawled.

T.J. entered the precinct in a rush, bringing cold wind and blowing rain with him.

"Where's my father?" he shouted.

Avery held up one finger while he finished a dispatch. When he was through, he turned to meet T.J.'s eyes. "I'm sorry. What did you say?"

T.J. leaned over the counter and screamed in the dispatcher's face. "Where the hell is my father?"

Footsteps sounded in the hall, and then Chief Jakes walked into the lobby. "Hello, T.J. What the hell is wrong with you? Do you want to be arrested for disturbing the peace?"

T.J. took a deep breath. "No."

"Then, stop yelling at my dispatcher."

"I'm sorry, Avery. I was upset about my father and took it out on you," T.J. said.

Avery shrugged.

Trey glared.

T.J. started over.

"Our maid said you came and got Dad this morning."

"And she was correct," Trey said.

"May I speak to you in private?" T.J. asked.

"Follow me," Trey said and led the way back to his office.

Sam was on the phone when they walked in. He saw who it was and hung up just as T.J. lost his cool again.

"I meant in private!" he shrieked.

Sam stood up.

Trey pointed at his brother. "You stay."

Sam sat back down.

T.J. opened his mouth, and then shut it again.

"Have a seat, T.J.," Trey said.

It sounded more like an order than an invitation, which made T.J. nervous. "Where is my father?" he asked.

"In jail," Trey said.

T.J. leaned forward, the expression on his face one of disbelief. "He can't be. Why? Have you booked him already? Where was our lawyer in all this?"

"He is, and his lawyer came when he requested one," Trey said.

T.J. groaned beneath his breath and leaned back in the chair.

Sam had been silent, but the questions T.J. asked seemed curious to him, especially the one about being booked. "Why does it matter to you if he's already been booked?"

"The senate seat. Dad is going to announce his candidacy for a vacant senate seat," T.J. said. "Whatever is wrong, surely it can be cleared up without all this."

"And now we have the motive for the rest," Sam said softly and looked up at his brother.

T.J. frowned. "What do you mean?"

"Is there anything else we can do for you?" Trey asked.

"I'm calling our lawyer!"

"He's already been here and gone," Sam said. "Maybe you should call *him* for your answers."

T.J. pushed himself upright and stumbled toward the door. He paused once and looked back. "It's all ruined," he mumbled, then shook his head and walked out.

"You need me for anything else?" Sam asked.

Trey grinned. "Nope. Go find Lainey and give her a kiss from me—and one from Mom."

Sam felt his brother's pain. "I will be happy to do that," he said, and left the room.

Trey sat down, and then stared across the room at the picture of his father in his highway patrol uniform. He could almost imagine that stern expression on Justin's face morphing into a smile. Within an instant the feeling was gone, but it felt like a sign—a brief acknowledgment of a job well done.

The news was spreading all over Mystic.
Marcus Silver was in jail, under arrest for murder-

ing Donny Collins in 1980, and charges were pending for the murders of Dick Phillips, Paul Jackson and Betsy Jakes, and for the attempted murder of Trina Jakes.

Word was that Marcus adamantly denied all of it, of course.

Beth Powell heard the news from one of her friends and wondered how long it would take for the news of her involvement in the cheating scandal to surface, and then she shrugged it off. In the grand scheme of things, being stupid as a teenager was a given. Look at Jack. He'd gotten shit-faced drunk and burned himself up in his daddy's old car. His daddy's heart was broken, and his mama was in the process of having a nervous breakdown. As far as Beth was concerned, nothing worse could happen to their family than what they were going through now.

She stared off into space for a few moments, and then picked up her phone and called her son.

He answered on the third ring and sounded breathless, as if he'd been running. "Hello?"

"It's me, honey. How's Clarice?"

"Her mother and sisters are here. I think it's helping."

"I need to talk to you," she said.

"Okay, shoot."

"No, honey. I need to talk to you face-to-face."

"Are you okay? Are you ill? What's wrong, Mom?"

"I'm not sick. You'll find out the rest when you get here."

"I'll be right there," Randy said.

She disconnected, then got up and went to her bedroom, where she began digging through her cedar chest. She dug all the way to the bottom before she found the picture she was looking for, then pulled it out and hugged it to her breasts.

About fifteen minutes later she heard Randy coming in the back door.

"Mom?" he called.

"I'm in the living room," she said.

His stride was quick as he entered the room, and he had a look of concern on his face. It wasn't the first time Beth had seen the resemblance between him and Donny, but it *was* the first time she was proud it was there.

"Hi, honey. Come sit by me," she said.

Randy dropped down beside her, and then reached for her hand. "What's wrong?"

She handed him the picture.

He frowned as he looked at it, then handed it back. "Who's he?"

"Your father."

Randy gasped, and then slowly reached for the picture again, this time studying every facet of the young boy's face.

"Why now, Mom? After all of these years, why are you showing me this now?"

She started to cry.

"Because this is who they pulled out of the Colquitt Mine. All these years I thought he'd abandoned us, but he didn't, Randy. He didn't. Your father was murdered the night he graduated high school."

Randy looked past the tears on his mother's face to the light in her eyes, and he got it. She was happy— happy to know that she'd still been loved.

He put the picture down and hugged her.

"I don't even know what to say," he said. "Do they know why he was killed?"

"Part of it is my fault, but I had no idea when it was happening how it would turn out."

Then she began to explain the panic she'd felt when she'd learned she was pregnant and the downward spiral her life had taken from there.

Lainey looked up as Lee walked into Trina's room, carrying two bottles of Coke. He handed one to her and set his to the side.

"I already broke the seal on that for you," he said.

She smiled. "Thank you, Lee." She popped an over-the-counter pain pill she'd found in the bottom of her purse, and chased it with a drink of the Coke.

"Do you hurt much?" he asked.

She thought of her real pain pills in the console of her car and sighed.

"It's not bad. More of a dull ache, you know?"

They both glanced at Trina, making sure their talking wasn't disturbing her before they continued.

"Sorry about your horse," he said, "but I'm glad you're okay."

"So am I," Lainey said, and then took another quick sip of the pop. "What did the doctor say about Trina's condition this morning?"

"That her vital signs were much stronger, the wound is healing well, fever is minimal."

"When do you think she'll wake up?"

He shrugged. "I don't care how long it takes, as long as it happens. I just want my girl back."

Lainey patted his arm. "I know. This has been such a scary time for all of you."

Just then her phone signaled a text. She glanced down, saw it was from Sam and read it.

Silver under arrest. Your picture sealed it. Your help and your mother's diaries put a killer behind bars. I love you so much.

Lainey gasped.

"Lee, look at this!" she said and handed him the phone.

"Oh, my God! *He's* the killer?"

"I guess so," Lainey said.

"But why?"

"I don't know, but I'll bet the authorities do. I am so relieved this nightmare is over," she said.

Lee stood up and leaned down near Trina's ear. "Hey, baby," he said. "They caught the man who did this to you. Marcus Silver will never hurt anyone else again."

Trina turned toward his voice and exhaled.

Lee gasped. "Trina? Honey?"

She took a deep breath.

Lainey stood up. "Is she waking up?"

"I don't know, but this is the most movement I've seen from her since they put her in ICU, and it happened after I told her they caught the killer."

Trina's eyelids began to flutter, then a finger moved.

"Thank You, God," Lee said as he clasped her hand. "Trina? You heard me, didn't you? They caught the man who shot you. Marcus Silver is behind bars."

Trina's lips parted.

"Look!" Lainey said.

Lee was holding his breath.

Lainey leaned forward.

"Hey, Tink. It's me, Lainey. You're safe. Lee is here. Everyone loves you. The man who hurt you is in jail."

Trina sighed, and when she did, they heard her breathe a single word.

"What?" Lee said. "What did she say?"

Lainey frowned, then said in disbelief, "It sounded like she said no."

Trina's eyelids fluttered again.

Lainey leaned closer. "Honey, did Marcus Silver shoot you and your mama?"

Trina sighed, and again the single word emerged with her breath. "No."

"Oh, my God!" Lainey said.

"What does this mean? Do they have the wrong man?" Lee asked.

"I don't know, but I need to let Sam know what she said."

Her ankle was throbbing as she stumbled back to her chair and quickly sent Sam a reply.

Trina is waking up. When Lee told her Marcus Silver was in jail for shooting her, she said no.

Sam was just getting ready to leave the police station when he got Lainey's text. Even as he read it, he couldn't believe what it said. He turned around and yelled at Trey, who was on his way back to the jail.

"Trey! You need to see this!"

Trey stopped as Sam came running.

"What's wrong?" Trey asked.

Sam handed him the phone.

Trey read the text twice, and then groaned.

"What the hell does this mean? You and I both know Marcus Silver killed Donny Collins."

"I don't know what it means. Maybe Trina was just reliving the shooting when she said no. You know... like she was telling the shooter 'no, don't shoot,' or something like that, but suddenly I don't feel as relieved as I did before," Sam said.

Trey sighed. "Nothing is ever easy, is it? So for now we leave the guards in place and continue limiting visitors until she explains what she meant."

Sam stood there for a moment, and then pointed toward the cells. "I want to ask Silver a question."

Trey shrugged. "Let's go."

Marcus Silver was in the first cell, sporting an orange jumpsuit and a horrified expression to go with it. When he saw the Jakes brothers come in, he stood up.

"I need to call my son," Marcus said.

"Oh, he's already been and gone," Trey said.

Marcus paled. "But I have to explain... I need to talk to him." He reeled as if he was going to faint, and grabbed on to the bars to steady himself. "Please. I have to make him understand I—"

That was the opening Sam needed. "What's so hard to understand about murdering four people in cold blood?"

Marcus groaned. "No, no, you don't understand. I didn't shoot your mother. I didn't kill Paul Jackson and Dick Phillips. I swear to God, I didn't do it."

The skin crawled on the back of Trey's neck. "So you're admitting you *did* kill Donny Collins, then?"

Marcus sank to his knees. "It was an accident."

"How did you two wind up in your car together?" Sam asked.

"He needed to get to the bus station and asked me for a ride. I had a car, so I did it. As soon as he got in he accused me of cheating. I denied it, but he kept saying he knew the truth. I thought Beth must have told him. He got out at the back lot of the bus station. I followed him. He was still mouthing off at me, and when he turned his back on me, I hit him in the head with a rock. I didn't mean to kill him. I was afraid, and it was just a knee-jerk reaction. I tried to rouse him, but he didn't have a pulse, so I panicked. I threw him in the back of my car and just took off out of town, and the first place I thought of where I could get rid of the body was the old mine. I didn't know anyone was there when I drove up. I got him out of my trunk and dragged him into the mine. I dumped him down that hole, and when I turned around the four of them were standing there staring at me in disbelief. They told me they were going to tell and started to leave. I screamed that I would kill them, too, so Paul turned around and knocked me down, and then they ran. You know the rest of it. Get my lawyer. I'll give a statement about Donny. But I didn't kill the others. I'll take a lie-detector test or any other kind of test you want."

Sam walked away.

Trey caught up with him in the hall. "What do you make of this shit?" he asked.

"I don't know what to think," Sam said. "But my gut feeling is he's telling the truth."

Trey groaned. "Then, who the hell killed the others?"

Sam turned on his heel and went back into the jail. "Marcus!"

Marcus was sitting on the bed staring down at the floor. He jerked at the sound of Sam's voice. "What?"

"Who else knew what went down between you and Donny?"

"No one," Marcus said. "I never told anyone. I never said the words aloud, not even to myself."

"Not even your father?"

"No! He would have turned me in himself."

Sam let the door to the cells swing shut as he headed for Trey's office to get his coat.

"Where are you going?" Trey asked.

"To the hospital."

Trey shoved a hand through his hair. "I'll stay here. I'm going to call that lawyer and tell him Marcus is ready to give a statement admitting guilt. Don't want to give him time to back away from what he said. I want it in writing."

T. J. Silver hadn't cried since the day his mother left them, but he was crying now. He'd gone home and locked himself in his bedroom, then lost it.

He cried because of the shame his father had brought to the family. He cried because of the hopes and dreams he'd had of going into public service with his father were over. There would be no announcement party. No need for the campaign manager he'd just hired. No need to hire the caterers he'd picked out.

He cried because the one thing he'd had to be proud of—the Silver name—was now tainted. Now everyone knew what his father had done. He couldn't decide whether to leave Mystic and settle somewhere else, where no one knew of his disgrace, or stand his ground and try to find a way out of this unholy mess. He wanted to talk to his father, but he wasn't sure what to say.

It took a long while before he got himself together, and then he washed his face and changed clothes. There were so many things left to do, he felt like throwing up.

One of his grandfathers had been fond of saying "Onward and upward," but he would be damned if he could remember which one.

Greg Standish learned of Marcus's arrest while he was having a burger at Charlie's. He'd made it through church with a surprising number of people commiserating with him about his wife's abandonment. They even had a special prayer service just for him during Sunday school, and when the preacher ended his service, it was with a prayer about faithfulness—something at which Gloria had obviously failed.

He was actually feeling pretty good about himself when he heard them talking about Marcus, at which point he went into shock. He couldn't wrap his head around the fact that Marcus had killed Donny. And then it occurred to him that meant Marcus would undoubtedly be arrested for killing Dick, Paul and Betsy, too.

Will Porter was standing at Rita's bedside when she took her last breath. Her family had been with him since sometime yesterday, and he was already as sick and tired of them as he had been of her. Thinking about what was still hanging over his head made him anxious. He'd been through so much, but it would be over soon.

He stayed until the funeral director picked up Rita's body, and then he got in his car and drove away. For the time being his in-laws were on their own.

Eighteen

It was midafternoon. The day was cool and clear on the mountain. Squirrels were scolding, and the birds that stayed through winter were strengthening their nests, preparing for the bitter days ahead.

The killer was sitting at the prearranged meeting place with the money on the seat beside him and a handgun in his pocket. He had no doubt about the Ledbetter grandson showing up with the package, because the family obviously needed the money, but he needed what was in the package more. He had no appreciation for the way fall had colored the mountain or the clear blue sky. His eye was on the dashboard clock.

When the time came and went, and fifteen minutes passed with no grandson in sight, his confidence began to fade. He was on the verge of true panic when he heard the sound of a vehicle coming down the mountain. At that point his heart started to pound. He felt his pocket to reassure himself that the pistol was still there as he watched an old green pickup emerging around the curve.

At first he thought there was a rider with the driver and groaned. He was sick of having to keep getting rid of extra witnesses, but as the truck came closer, he realized he was wrong. It must have been a trick of the light or the reflection of a tree.

The truck stopped within feet of where he'd parked. The driver got out carrying a package about the size of a large shoebox. He was a small, skinny man with long blond hair and a worn-out leather coat.

The killer grabbed the sack of money as he got out and went to meet the man.

"Well, I never thought I'd be seein' *you*. Right, here's your package," the man said.

The killer took the package and held out the sack. "Here's your money."

The grandson took it with a smile, and when he did, the killer pulled the gun and shot him point-blank in the middle of his forehead.

The sound echoed on the trail as the sack dropped at the dead man's feet. Moses Ledbetter wasn't going to heaven alone.

The killer picked up the sack, now splattered with blood, and ran back to his car. The tires spun, spewing gravel as he drove away.

Lila Ledbetter clapped her hands over her ears when she heard the gunshot. It took everything she had not to scream, because she knew something was wrong. She got to her knees on the floor of the car, where her daddy had told her to hide, and poked her head up above the dashboard of her daddy's truck. She was just able to see a man carrying away the package. She watched until he got in his car and drove away, then she jumped out of the truck. When she saw her daddy lying on the ground, she screamed.

"Daddy! Daddy!" she cried, and then saw the hole in his forehead and the red blood staining his white-blond hair. In shock, she turned toward the mountain and started running.

She ran and ran until her side was hurting and she'd cried out all her tears, then stopped, gasping for breath. There was still another mile before she reached the mailbox marking the road that led to home, so she started running again, screaming as she went.

It was the barking dogs that brought Bonnie Ledbetter out onto the porch. She thought they were barking because Jacob and Lila were coming home. But when she didn't hear the engine straining up the slope, she stood with her hand in her apron pocket, trying to figure out what had sent the hounds into such a frenzy. In the midst of their howling she heard her daughter screaming and started running down the road to meet her.

"Lila! Lila! What's wrong? Where's your daddy?"

"He's dead, he's dead! The man shot him and drove away."

Bonnie Ledbetter gasped, and then pulled her daughter to her breasts.

"Lord, Lord, I told him nothing good would come from that much money," she moaned, and then grabbed the little girl's hand and ran with her back to the house. "Go wash your face and dry your tears, girl. I'm gonna call the sheriff, and I need you to be ready to tell him everything you saw and heard. I won't let your daddy die without justice for his soul."

Sheriff Osmond was sharing the news with his deputy Wesley Rand, toasting the fact that the killer they'd been looking for was finally in jail, when the phone rang. He was in such a good mood that he answered it himself.

"Hello, this is Sheriff Osmond."

"Sheriff, Sheriff! This is Bonnie Ledbetter. You gotta come quick. Someone murdered my husband, Jacob, where Pike Trail meets Lassiter's Corner."

"Did anyone see who did it? Was anyone else hurt?" he asked as he was writing down information.

"My daughter was there, but she hid and then ran home to get me. I'm about to go down there now to be with Jacob until y'all come to carry him away. Lord, Lord, I told him no good would come from delivering that package."

"What package?" the sheriff asked.

"Something his grandpa Moses made before he accidentally blew himself up," she said.

"Blew himself up?"

"Yes, Moses used to blast coal seams for Colquitt Mines up in Georgia. When he retired he came home to the mountains but never quit messing with explosives. After he passed, the family found a package on his kitchen table all wrapped up with a note that said there was one thousand dollars due on delivery, but there was no name on it, and no phone number to call. Then a man called about it yesterday, and Jacob took it down the mountain this afternoon to get the

money. Now Jacob's dead, the package is gone and
Lila said the man took the money with him."

"Lila's your daughter?"

"Yes. She's ten, and she's all broke up about seeing her daddy die."

"Did she see the killer?"

"Sort of."

"Okay, I'm contacting the coroner, and me and
my deputies will be there as soon as we can. In the
meantime, don't touch anything, and don't walk near
the body, or disturb any footprints and tire tracks,
understand?"

"Yes, sir," Bonnie said, and then started to wail.
"We buried Moses this morning. Now I'm gonna have
to bury my Jacob, too. Why, Lord, why?"

That was a question Sheriff Osmond couldn't answer. As soon as he disconnected, he contacted dispatch.

"Send a message to the coroner that I have a murder scene at Lassiter's Corner on the Pike Trail above
Mystic. We're heading out there now. Oh, and dispatch any of my deputies who are free to the same
location."

"Yes, sir," the dispatcher said.

The sheriff turned around. "Wesley, you're riding
with me. We have ourselves a murder, and I'm feeling uneasy about the whole mess."

"What do you mean?" Wesley said as they headed
out the back to the parking lot.

"A man skilled in bomb making blew himself up,
and before he did that, he left a package in his house
with a thousand dollars due on delivery. When the

package was delivered, the deliveryman was killed. What does that say to you?"

"That whatever was in that package was illegal and the buyer didn't want to leave a witness," Wesley said.

Sheriff Osmond nodded. "And the man used to blast for Colquitt Mines in Georgia. So what are the odds that it was a bomb in that package?"

"I wouldn't bet against it," the deputy said.

"Now we have to worry about what that package is intended for," the sheriff muttered. "Let's go. We need to get up to the scene ASAP."

They were on the way to the cruiser when the sheriff's phone rang. He tossed the keys to Wesley and got in on the passenger side so he could talk while they rode. "Hello?"

"Sheriff Osmond, this is Trey Jakes."

The deputy took off out of town with the lights and siren blasting.

Trey heard the noise but didn't think anything of it. "We may have a problem, and I wanted you to be aware," he said.

"A problem with what? What's going on?"

"The main thing is, Marcus Silver admitted to killing Donny Collins, but he swears he had nothing to do with the other murders and offered to take a lie detector test to prove it. His lawyer just left. I have the whole statement filmed, signed and filed."

"What the hell do you make of that?" Osmond asked. "Do you believe him?"

"Sort of."

"Damn it. Who else knows about the 1980 incident? Who could have used that to put the blame on Marcus and completely mask their own agenda?"

"He swears no one knew about it. He said he never even talked about it aloud to himself. Beth Powell is the one who came forward and turned him in for the cheating scandal. She had her own reasons for not mentioning it at first. I'll get a full report on all the updates and email it to you."

"Okay, but I still don't understand why those three people were killed."

"Neither do I, but I just wanted you to know where we're at right now. Don't quit looking for answers. If anyone else happens to get murdered in the county, let me know."

"Like the guy I just got the call on, you mean?" Osmond said.

Trey had been pacing as he talked, but that stopped him in his tracks. "Are you serious? You just got a call on another murder?"

"Yes."

"Can you tell me about it?"

"An old man who used to blast for Colquitt Mines in Georgia accidentally blew himself up a few days ago."

"What does Georgia have to do with here? And how is that a murder?"

"He didn't die in Georgia. He died here, on the mountain above Mystic." Then Osmond went on to explain about the note, the phone call and the delivery, and that the victim's little girl had been there when it happened and might have seen the killer.

"What did they say was in the package?" Trey asked.

"They didn't."

The hair suddenly stood up on the back of Trey's neck. "Oh, shit. He built someone a bomb, didn't he?"

"As my deputy just said, I wouldn't bet against it, and if Marcus Silver isn't the person who committed the recent murders, then I would lay odds that your sister is still in danger."

"And she's waking up, which is only increasing his need to silence her," Trey said.

"Has she said anything?" Osmond asked.

Trey told him about the text they'd gotten from Lainey.

"What are you going to do?" Osmond asked.

"Since you just told me someone may be running around with an undetonated bomb, I'm about to put guards at every entrance to the hospital, and make sure they check everyone and everything going in and coming out."

"If I get any details from my witness, I'll let you know," the sheriff said.

"And if Trina wakes up enough to tell us who she really saw, I'll let you know, too."

"This is a true clusterfuck," Sheriff Osmond said.

"I have to agree," Trey said, and disconnected on the run.

Sam reached Trina's room and stopped to talk to Cain Embry, who was on guard today.

"Hey, Sam, did you guys really get the killer?" Cain asked.

"We have the guy who left the body in the mine, but it's beginning to look like we may have more than one killer running around."

"What? You've got to be kidding," Cain said.

"I wish. Just to make sure, we want to keep a guard on Trina until we're certain."

"Absolutely," Cain said.

Sam went into the room and saw Lee dozing in a chair next to Trina and Lainey asleep in a recliner. Trina was his baby sister, and Lainey was the love of his life. The fact that the two women who mattered most in his world were both injured and still healing gave him an unsettled feeling. He knew only too well how fleeting life could be, and he needed them healthy and well.

He laid a hand gently on Lainey's soft baby curls, then moved to his sister's bedside and took her hand. When she stirred slightly, his hopes lifted. She *was* waking up. He so wanted this nightmare to be over for all of them, but for that to happen, she needed to wake up and talk to them.

He stood for a few moments holding her hand, feeling the steady pulse at her wrist, and thought of what she was still facing. Even after she healed she was going to have to live with the memory of witnessing her own mother's murder. Lee seemed like a good man, devoted to Trina. He hoped they made it as a couple, because she was going to need someone.

He heard Lainey moan and then sigh. He turned and knelt down beside her.

When she opened her eyes and saw him, she smiled.

"Are you okay?" he whispered.

She nodded. "Just tired, and I left my pain pills in my car. Would you run out and get them for me? They're in the console, I think. Here are the keys."

Sam palmed the key ring and kissed the side of her cheek. "I'll be back soon."

She nodded and closed her eyes again.

Sam stood up and was on his way out of the room when he felt his phone vibrate. He saw he had a text and went out into the hall to read it.

There's been another murder. Osmond is working it. On the way to hospital. Wait for me there.

Sam stopped in midstep and then groaned.

Cain heard him and stood up. "Something wrong?"

Sam wouldn't even say it out loud. He turned the phone toward Cain.

"It's not over, is it?" Cain asked.

Sam shook his head and headed for the elevator. He was going to get those pain meds and get right back to Lainey.

Sheriff Osmond arrived on scene to find one of his deputies already roping off the area, and a grieving woman and child standing off to one side surrounded by a half-dozen armed men.

"Who are all those people?" Osmond asked.

"Mrs. Ledbetter, her daughter and her father and brothers. They don't trust us to keep her safe."

Sheriff Osmond sighed. "What's the crime scene look like?" he asked as the deputy tied off the yellow crime scene tape to a tree.

"Shooter's car parked there, waiting," the deputy said, and pointed. "Victim stopped here to deliver the package. You can see footprints where the two men met to make the exchange. There's one shot in the head. No scuffle. I'd say it was a surprise. Small footprints here. I don't know where those are from."

"Probably his kid's," Osmond said.

The deputy looked surprised.

"She was with him. She hid and came out after the shooter left. He doesn't know it, but he's left a witness alive. We have to make damn sure he doesn't find out about this one. Understand?"

"Yes, sir," the deputy said.

"Have you searched Ledbetter's truck?"

"No, sir. The door was open like that when I drove up. I just started securing the scene."

"Good job. The coroner has been notified. The crime scene crew will come with him. I'm going to talk to my witness," he said and walked over to the group. "Mrs. Ledbetter?"

Bonnie Ledbetter's eyes were swollen from crying, and the little girl standing beside her looked scared to death, but the men with them were hard-eyed, stone-faced mountain men who looked ready to go to war.

"Yes, I'm Bonnie Ledbetter. This is my daddy and my brothers, and this here is Lila. She saw her daddy get killed."

"I am so sorry for your loss," Osmond said, and then turned to Bonnie's father. "Gentlemen, I understand your concern, but I would feel better if you put your weapons up."

"No, sir. We'll just wait here while you do your talkin' to Lila and Bonnie, and then we'll be escortin' her home. And nothing personal, but just so y'all know, there will be full-time guards on her home until you get Jacob's killer behind bars."

Sheriff Osmond saw the grief and anger in their

eyes and understood. "Then, may we use the bed of your truck for them to sit in while we talk? You're welcome to stand with her. All I'm going to do is take their statements."

The man nodded.

Sheriff Osmond walked under the crime scene tape and took Bonnie's elbow, then escorted her to a seat in the truck bed. One of the men lifted Lila up beside her mother, and the sheriff pulled out a recorder.

"For the record, this is an interview with Bonnie Ledbetter, wife of the victim, Jacob Ledbetter, and their daughter, Lila. Lila was present at her father's murder." He held the recorder close to Lila. "Please state your name and age for the record, child."

The little girl's blue eyes teared up again as she looked fearfully at her mother. Bonnie nodded.

"My name is Lila Ledbetter. I am ten years old."

"Thank you, Lila. Now, in your own words, tell me what you saw when your father was shot."

Bonnie put her arm around her daughter for comfort.

Lila began to talk.

"I begged to come with Daddy. He said it might be serious business and I had to stay in the truck when we got to Lassiter's Corner. We talked about Thanksgiving with Granny on the way here."

Her features crumpled as she looked up at her mother. "We won't have any Thanksgiving at Granny's now, will we, Mama?"

"We'll talk about that later," Bonnie whispered. "Just finish your tale."

Lila nodded, wiped her eyes with the hem of her T-shirt and looked back up at the sheriff.

"When we came up on the corner, I saw the car. It looked like a car you drive to church. It was kind of a silver-gray color, and as soon as we saw it, Daddy started acting funny, like he recognized the man. He told me to get down on the floor and don't get up, no matter what I heard, so I did. He got out of the truck with the package. I heard him say to the man, 'I never thought I'd be seein' *you*. I brought the package.' I heard the other man say, 'I brought the money.' Then I heard one shot. It scared me, but I peeked over the dash and saw a man running back to the car. He got in, turned around and drove away really fast. I got out and saw my daddy and cried, and then I ran home to get Mama. The end."

"That's very good. You remembered a lot. This will help us catch the man who killed your daddy."

Lila nodded.

"Do you remember what the man was wearing? The one who shot your daddy?"

"Brown pants and a jacket the color of my daddy's best suit."

"That would be beige," Bonnie offered.

"Do you remember the color of his skin?"

"White like mine," Lila said, holding up one bony white arm.

"What about his hair? What color was it? Was it short or long? Was it straight or curly?"

Lila closed her eyes, and the sheriff knew she was picturing the events again in her mind.

"His hair was short like the preacher's hair. It was just brown, and it was straight."

"Could you tell how old he was? Was he skinny or

was he fat? Did he run with a limp or anything else noticeable?"

"He was average. I don't know how old. Just way older than me."

"Thank you, Lila. Do you remember anything else? You said you saw the man turn the car around. Did you get a look at his face when he turned the car?"

Lila shook her head. "The windows were dark."

"Anything else?" the sheriff asked. "Anything at all? Was there a bumper sticker or something else on the car that would help us identify it?"

"A shiny piece of paper on the bumper."

"Was anything written on the paper?" Osmond asked.

Lila frowned a moment, and then shrugged. "I didn't see anything. It was just shiny paper, like aluminum foil."

"Thank you, Lila." Osmond lifted the recorder toward his mouth and spoke into it. "The next person I'm speaking to is Bonnie Ledbetter, the victim's widow."

Bonnie lifted her chin. Her daddy was standing beside her, and when the sheriff said her name, he put a hand on her shoulder to remind her she wasn't alone.

Bonnie waited.

"Bonnie, what do you know about the package that Jacob was delivering?"

"What I know is that it was about the size of a shoebox and we found it on Moses' table. That was Jacob's grandfather. There was writing on the package that said 'one thousand dollars due,' but there was no name or phone number to contact. Yesterday evening a man called Moses' house while we were there. It was about the package. Jacob agreed to bring it down today. And now he's dead. That's what I know."

"You have no idea what was in the package?" Osmond asked.

"No, sir. No one unwrapped it. Moses didn't have anything valuable to sell, but he had a valuable skill. He blasted coal for the Colquitt Mines up in Georgia before he retired and came home. He knew how to make bombs. Jacob thought that might be what was in the package, but we didn't *know*."

"Can you tell me anything else that might help?" the sheriff asked.

Bonnie shook her head.

"Are you done with my girls?" the big man asked.

"Yes, we're done, and again, I am so sorry for your loss."

"What about their truck and Jacob's body?" Ledbetter asked.

"They're part of the crime scene. We'll tow the truck, and the victim's body needs to be autopsied first," Osmond said.

Bonnie let out a soft wail. "Why do you have to cut up my Jacob's body? You can see how he died. There's a hole in his head."

"I am sorry, but it's the law. We'll be able to find out more about the bullet and the gun that shot it, and that will help us catch the killer," Osmond said and offered her a card. "This is my card. You can call me anytime you want. Okay?"

Bonnie took the card as her father picked up Lila and put her in the cab of the pickup. Once Bonnie was in the truck, they drove away.

Sheriff Osmond was about to call Trey Jakes when

the coroner arrived. He pocketed his phone for the moment and went to help get everything set up.

Trey parked near the front of the hospital and headed in on a run. There was a panicked feeling in the pit of his stomach, a certainty that this was likely to get worse before it got better. He ran into Sam in the lobby, heading for the elevator.

"Walk with me," Trey said.

Sam thought about the pain meds in his pocket, then hoped Lainey could wait a few minutes more.

"Where are we going?" Sam asked.

"To talk to hospital security," Trey said. When they reached the hospital director's office, he knocked once and walked in.

The secretary looked up, clearly startled to see the chief of police standing in front of her desk.

"I already called the director. I'm supposed to meet your head of security here."

The director stepped out of his office. "Chief Jakes, come in," he said.

Sam and Trey followed him into his office.

"Chief Jakes, this is Aaron Peters, our security chief."

Trey nodded. "I know Aaron. This is my brother, Sam. He owns Ranger Investigations in Atlanta. He came home to help after our mother was killed."

"My sympathies to both of you," Aaron said.

"Thank you," Trey said. "Now, as to why we're here, we have reason to believe the person who committed the recent murders is still at large. We also suspect he's going to make an attempt to silence the only witness against him, who happens to be our sister, Trina, currently a patient here in the hospital. We've had private security on her room since she got here, first in ICU and now in a private room on another floor. She's beginning to wake up. Once she does, she can put a name to the man we're after, and he knows it."

"What do you need from us?" Aaron asked.

"You need to put immediate security at every entrance. We have reason to believe that since he can't get to his witness inside the hospital, he may try to take her out with a bomb, which would endanger everyone here."

"Oh, hell," Aaron muttered.

The director looked horrified. "How do we protect our staff and patients from something like that? Who do we watch for?"

"We don't know," Trey said.

"Just monitor everyone coming in and out, check everything they're carrying. Our sister is waking up. As soon as she does, we'll have a name and can make an arrest. Just help us buy time."

The director nodded. "Yes, of course. Aaron, get this in place immediately. Hire extra security if you need it."

"Yes, sir," Aaron said, and left the office.

"Is there anything else we can do for you?" the director asked.

"No, but we'll be in touch," Trey said.

They were back out in the hall before Sam spoke.

"You do know this is crazy. Can't we move Trina? Just get her away from this hospital?"

"No. For all we know the killer's got this place staked out, and she'd be too vulnerable in transit.

She's still safest here, where we can control the site and keep him from getting in."

"We're trapped," Sam said. "As trapped as if he had us pinned down and under fire. I don't like it. I don't like it at all."

"I know, but we're doing all we can right now."

"If we're right and our killer has a bomb, that's a whole other story," Sam said. "The collateral damage could be catastrophic, Trey. He could destroy this entire hospital with nothing more than a handful of the right kind of explosives."

"A bomb that small? How?" Trey asked.

"Because there are so many explosive elements already within these walls. All it takes is one good explosion to detonate the rest, understand?"

Trey paled. "The oxygen!"

"And dozens of other combustibles," Sam said. "One properly placed load can detonate everything here. The casualties would be seventy-five percent or higher, and the survivors would most likely be severely injured."

"Would it take someone with experience in explosives?" Trey asked.

"Not necessarily. If the bomb was built with a simple activator switch on a timer, then anyone could plant it."

"Can anyone just turn off the switch?" Trey asked.

Sam shook his head. "That's not how they're wired. It would have to be defused. I guess it's a good thing I came home, huh?"

Nineteen

Sam had gone upstairs long enough to give Lainey's medicine to the guard and update him, and then he'd hurried back down. He was walking the building's perimeter, looking for easy access from outside.

Trey was in the hospital parking lot waiting on his officers to arrive when his phone rang. "Hello?"

"Hey, Trey, I have some more info about the killing at Lassiter's Corner."

Trey recognized the sheriff's voice and pulled out a notepad. "Go ahead, I'm listening."

"My witness said the killer's car was silver-gray. She said it was the kind of car you drive to church, whatever that means to a kid. Oh, and it had dark windows. She only saw the killer from the back. She said he was way older than her. That his hair was cut short, like her preacher's hair. That it was brown. And she said there was shiny paper, like aluminum foil, on the rear bumper when he drove away."

"Ironic that her points of reference all have to do with church and preachers, and she was describing a killer. No wonder we can't figure out who he is. Being able to move about in the community with that kind of persona is flying under heavy radar."

"Huh. I didn't think of it like that," the sheriff said.

"So how long ago do you think the killing happened?" Trey asked.

Osmond checked his notes. "She called it in close to four, but the killing would have been earlier, because it would have taken Ledbetter a while to get down the mountain to his meeting, then add the time lapse for the little girl to run home up the mountain. I think it's about four or five miles up to their place. The killer has probably been on the move for at least two hours with his package now."

"Okay, thanks," Trey said and disconnected.

Before he could call Sam with the descriptions of the killer and his car, Trey's officers began arriving, and he let the thought slide.

The killer walked in with a beautifully wrapped gift box, smiled at the woman at the information desk, spoke to a doctor in the hall and moved on through the hospital to the chapel without notice. He wasn't expecting anyone to be there, so when he walked in and saw a couple on their knees in prayer, he paused and frowned. He couldn't just set the box down behind the little pulpit, as he'd planned, without being seen, so he sat down on the far side in the shadows, bowed his head and pretended to pray while waiting for them to leave.

Lee woke stiff and hungry. He stretched as he stood, then felt Trina's forehead for signs of fever. As he did, he noticed Lainey had fallen asleep in the recliner on the far side of Trina's bed. He checked his watch, then decided to run down to the cafeteria and get some food to bring up to the room.

He slipped out quietly, and then stopped at the door.

"Hey, Cain, I'm going down to the cafeteria. Can I bring you back some coffee, or something to eat?"

"No, I'm good, but thanks," Cain said.

"Lainey's still with Trina, but they're both asleep," Lee said.

"Okay. No problem," Cain said.

Lainey was dreaming that she was being chased by the panther when she suddenly woke. It took her a few seconds to realize someone was moaning.

Trina! She was trying to wake up.

Lainey jumped up from the recliner and hobbled over to the bed.

Trina was grabbing at the sheet as if trying to hold on to something. Her heart rate was climbing, making the monitor beep faster, and her eyelashes were fluttering against her cheeks.

Lainey reached for Trina's hand, thinking if she felt human contact she might calm down.

"Trina, honey. It's Lainey. I'm right here beside you. You're okay."

Trina's fingers curled around Lainey's hand.

"I'm here," Lainey went on. "Your brothers are close by. You're safe."

Trina's eyelids fluttered again.

Lainey could see how desperately Trina was trying to wake up. She remembered that feeling from her own surgery, that sense of trying to wade through a muddy morass just to get to a place where she could open her eyes.

But Lainey also knew how crucial it was to get the answer they were all waiting for and decided to see if Trina was able to communicate yet.

"Trina, honey, do you remember what happened to you?" she asked.

A tear rolled out from under Trina's eyelid.

"I'm so sorry, Tink. We're trying to find the man who shot you. Can you tell me who it is? Can you say his name?"

Lainey watched Trina's lips. They were barely moving, and she was moaning again.

"Was it Marcus Silver?" Lainey asked.

Trina tightened her grasp on Lainey's hand and shook her head in denial.

"Not Marcus, okay."

Trina eased her grip.

"Then, who was it, honey? We have to know so we can keep you safe."

Trina inhaled, her nostrils flaring slightly. When she exhaled, Lainey heard the word *son*.

She frowned. "Son? Did you say *son*?"

Trina squeezed her hand again.

All of a sudden Lainey gasped.

"Oh, my God! Are you trying to tell me it was T. J. Silver who shot you?"

Trina sighed. Tears rolled out from beneath both eyelids as she squeezed Lainey's hand again.

"T.J. shot you and Betsy?"

Trina sighed. It was so soft Lainey almost didn't hear it, and then she heard the word *yes*. Then the moment was gone and Trina was back inside her own head.

Lainey grabbed her phone and took off toward the door, got the guard and pulled him into the room.

"What's wrong?" Cain asked.

"Trina just woke up and told me who shot her. It wasn't Marcus Silver! It was his son, T.J. Do you know what he looks like?"

"No," Cain said. "But nobody is going to get to Trina, I swear."

"I'm calling Sam and Trey. Tell Lee when he comes back. He'll know who he is."

"Will do," Cain said, then followed Lainey out and took a stance at the door as she disappeared down the hall.

The couple in the chapel was still praying when someone came into the room looking for them. After a whispered conversation, the three of them left together. It was the opening T.J. had been waiting for.

He grabbed the gift box, hurried down the aisle to the small podium and knelt down behind it to remove the lid of the box. He looked down at the clock face with no small amount of trepidation, then flipped the switch to start the timer.

Fifteen minutes.

Time enough for him to be far, far away when the bomb went off. He put the lid back on the box, shoved it into the hollow space below the podium and took off up the aisle in haste. He slipped out of the chapel and started toward the hall leading to the lobby just as Lainey Pickett got off the elevator right in front of him.

Lainey's hands were trembling as she put in a call to Sam, and she was moving toward the elevator as it rang. Just when she thought it was going to go to voice mail she heard his voice.

"Hello?"

"Sam! Sam! It's T. J. Silver."

Sam actually stumbled. "What? What are you saying?"

"Trina woke up. I asked her again if Marcus Silver shot her. She could barely communicate, but she finally said the word *son*. I wasn't sure I understood, so I asked her point-blank if T. J. Silver shot her. She was crying as she said yes."

"Oh, my God, oh, Lainey! Thank you. Where are you?"

"I'm in the elevator on the way down to the lobby."

"I'll meet you just outside the front door," he said. "Are you okay?"

She was just about to answer when the elevator doors opened and she found herself face-to-face with T. J. Silver.

"Oh, hello, T.J.," she said.

Sam heard every word.

"Is he there?" he whispered.

"Why, yes, that's right," she said, frantically trying to hide the panic she was feeling.

"Oh, shit! Keep moving. I'm on the way."

"I will, love you, too," she said, and then fell into step just behind T.J., despite his obvious attempt to ignore her.

He was moving quickly, and Lainey had no excuse to slow him down.

Sam called Trey on the run.

When Trey answered, Sam started right in. "Trina

woke up. It's T. J. Silver, and Lainey has eyes on him in the lobby of the hospital. He's heading for the exit, which probably means he's already planted the bomb. Come in from the back. I'm going in the front."

"Got it," Trey said, and began directing his men as he put in a call to hospital security.

Lainey was almost running to keep up with T.J., and her ankle was throbbing because of it. The moment she saw Sam appear on the other side of the revolving door she stopped. He would take it from here.

T.J. was mentally counting steps to the exit when he saw Sam Jakes coming toward him, and the moment he saw Sam's face his heart dropped. He knew. He didn't know how, but he knew.

T.J. turned to run back the other way and saw two Mystic police officers coming his way through the lobby. When he turned to head the opposite way toward the gift shop, hospital security was already there and walking toward him.

T.J. shouted, enraged that he'd been caught. Then he saw Lainey Pickett backing toward the wall and knew what he had to do. He practically leaped in her direction. She was Sam Jakes' woman. He would make Sam back off or make him sorry.

Before Lainey knew what was happening, T.J. had her around the neck.

"If anyone comes a step closer, she's dead!" he shouted.

Sam stopped just inside the lobby. "Don't hurt her, T.J. You've hurt enough people. Don't hurt her, too."

Lainey was struggling, trying to get free, when T.J. tightened his grip and put his mouth against her ear.

"Be still or I'll break your damn neck like a tooth-pick," he said softly.

Lainey froze.

T.J. was trembling, trying to figure out how to get out before the building blew.

And then he heard a voice behind him and felt the cold end of a gun muzzle up against the back of his neck.

"Where's the bomb, T.J.?"

Lainey's heart skipped. It was Trey! "I saw him coming down the hall from the chapel," she said.

T.J. screamed, "You bitch!" and hit her in the back of the head with his fist.

Sam rushed forward, catching Lainey just before she hit the ground. A few feet away Trey had T.J. facedown on the floor and was in the process of putting him in handcuffs.

T.J. kept screaming, "Okay, okay, you got me. Drag me out of here and lock me up. I give. I won't fight."

Sam had Lainey in his arms, scared to death that she'd been hurt, but the minute T.J. started begging to be taken to jail, he knew time must be running down on the bomb.

Lainey groaned.

Sam held her close. "Thank God," he said, and carried her to a nearby bench. "Honey. Can you hear me?"

She reached for the back of her head. "What happened?"

"Look at me," he said.

She opened her eyes.

"How many fingers am I holding up?"

She frowned.

"Either I've gone blind or you forgot how the trick works. I don't see any fingers."

He cupped her face and then kissed her. "I love you more than you will ever know. Stay here a second."

He ran toward Trey, who now had T.J. on his feet.

Sam grabbed T.J. by the handcuffs. "Trade you," he said to his brother. "Get Lainey out of here and start evacuating the hospital. This little son of a bitch is going to show me where he hid the bomb, and if he doesn't do it in time for me to defuse it, I'll cuff him to the nearest piece of furniture and run."

Trey turned and ran toward Lainey, then picked her up in his arms as he headed for the exit, shouting orders to his men and hospital security as he went.

Visitors were running out the door, while the staff ran back toward the patients. They'd heard the words *bomb* and *evacuate*, and didn't need orders. They knew what to do. Moments later the fire alarms began to sound on every floor.

T.J. was screaming and begging as Sam grabbed the handcuffs and started dragging him backward toward the chapel.

"Stop! You're breaking my arms! You can't do this! I don't want to die!"

Sam yanked T.J. onto his feet and slammed him against the wall. "Did my mother beg when you stuck the gun in her face?"

T.J. moaned.

Sam grabbed him by the neck with one hand and grabbed his handcuffs with the other, and started pushing him toward the chapel.

"Walk faster!" Sam yelled, pushing T.J. so hard he

began to stumble. "Keep walking or I'll break your damn neck and find the bomb by myself!"

T.J. shrieked and then began to cry. "I don't want to die. Please. We need to leave."

"Is the bomb in the chapel?" Sam shouted. "I swear to God if you don't tell me now, I'll shoot you where you stand."

T.J. was too scared to move and would have dropped to his knees but Sam yanked him back up.

"Yes, yes, it's in the chapel!" T.J. shrieked.

Sam took off down the hall, dragging T.J. with him. Once they were inside the chapel Sam yelled at him again. "Don't make me look for it!"

"Behind the podium," T.J. cried.

Sam dragged him down the aisle, and then slammed him facedown beside the podium. When Sam pulled the beautifully wrapped box out in front of his face, T.J. shrieked again.

Sam slapped the back of his head. "Shut up. I need to concentrate."

T.J. sucked up the curse on the tip of his tongue.

"And don't fucking move," Sam added.

T.J. closed his eyes.

Sam felt along the bottom of the package for wires, and when it felt clean, he slowly lifted up the lid. He saw the clock face, the load of dynamite and the time left.

Less than six minutes.

Help me, God.

He opened his pocketknife, slowly eased a finger beneath a wire and, as he began eyeing its path, lost sight of the red carpet beneath his feet and the walls around him.

All of a sudden he was in Afghanistan, listening to the chatter of automatic weapons, hearing someone shouting in Farsi and someone else screaming in Dari, and feeling the heat on the back of his neck from the ever-present blast of the sun.

Lainey was crying and begging all the way out the door.

"Please, don't let Sam die! Somebody make him come out! Don't let him die."

Trey put her in his cruiser, and then waved at one of his officers, who quickly came running. For a moment Trey was face-to-face with Lainey.

"Everyone in the hospital is going to die if Sam can't defuse that bomb. Everyone. He's doing what he has to do, not what he wants to do, because that's what Sam does. Stay in the cruiser. Please. I need to help. One of my officers is going to take you a safe distance away."

Her heart was hammering. She was so scared she couldn't breathe, and yet she knew every word Trey said was the truth. "Yes. I'll stay. I promise. You go. I'll pray."

"Good girl," Trey said, and then he was gone.

Lainey was so afraid for Sam that she was shaking.

"Please, God, You saved Sam Jakes once for his mama. This time won't You please save him for me?"

And then she sat with her hands folded, reciting the Lord's Prayer beneath her breath as the officer drove the cruiser to the far end of the parking lot.

"Stay here. You should be safe this far away, but if it blows, just hit the floor."

She nodded, then watched as he ran back to the

building. It was almost two city blocks away, and she could barely make out what was happening beyond the chaos and hysteria. Because it had gotten her through many months of chemo, she had faith it would get her through this, as well.

Lee emerged from the cafeteria into chaos. Realizing they were beginning to evacuate the hospital, he took the stairs and raced to Trina's room.

A nurse came running in seconds later, unhooked the heart and blood-pressure monitors, hung the IV bag on a hook at the head of the bed and then they headed out the door with Lee pushing and Cain Embry running beside the bed on high alert.

Other patients were already in the halls, some in beds like Trina, others in wheelchairs. Lee was third in line for the freight elevator, and the moment they hit the ground floor, Cain grabbed the bed rail and guided her toward the exit while Lee pushed.

But being outside wasn't safe enough. Not if the building blew. Staff and visitors began pushing patients toward the far end of the huge parking lot, getting them as far away from the hospital as they could.

Avery was on day dispatch, following the unfolding chaos on the radios of both local and county police. It didn't take him long to figure out they had the killer cornered, and when he caught the name he nearly fell out of his chair. He couldn't get over the fact that a father and son had committed murder an entire generation apart.

He walked back to Marcus's cell and just stood and stared.

Marcus glared. "What? Why are you staring at me like that?" he demanded.

"I just never knew a whole family who was willing to kill to get what they wanted."

Marcus stood up so fast it looked as if he'd been ejected from his seat. He ran to the front of the cell, his voice shaking when he asked, "What are you talking about?"

"You had T.J. kill your witnesses, didn't you?" he said.

Marcus grabbed hold of the bars. "Are you crazy? What do you mean?"

"Whatever you were planning didn't work. They cornered your son in the hospital right after he planted a bomb there. He already killed three people you went to school with, and was willing to kill God knows how many others just to silence Trina Jakes. You people are freaks. I can't wrap my head around that much evil."

"You're wrong! I don't know anything about that!" Marcus shouted, but Avery was already gone, his footsteps fading, and Marcus was left with a god-awful truth. He didn't know how T.J. had found out about Donny Collins, but now he knew why the three survivors from that night's wreck had been murdered. It was all about running for office on a clean slate. Somewhere along the way his son had turned into a monster. Maybe the blood of the Silvers who'd grown their vast fortune had become too thin. Maybe part of it had to do with being abandoned by his mother when he was young. And maybe, just maybe, T. J. Silver had always been a narcissistic psychopath and he'd been too blind to see it.

Whatever the reason, this was their end.

* * *

Sam was intent on the task at hand. He could hear Carlos talking to him, asking him what kind of bomb he was working on and if it was one he could defuse.

Every time T. J. Silver made a sound, Sam would growl beneath his breath and T.J. would freeze. He was so scared of Sam Jakes that if he could have quit breathing to make him happy, he would have.

Sweat was running down Sam's forehead and into his eyes, making them burn. Every time he cut another wire he would pause to wipe it away with the back of one arm.

He heard people running out in the hall and thought the enemy was coming. He knew he needed to defuse the bomb before they got there, or he and Carlos would die.

He paused one last time to wipe the sweat from his hands onto his pants, and then slid a finger beneath the two remaining wires. Was it the red wire or the yellow wire? He glanced at the clock.

Fifteen seconds left.

Suddenly Lainey's face flashed before his eyes, and reality surfaced.

Ten seconds left.

He slid the knife between the wires.

Five seconds left.

He folded the red wire down the sharp side of the knife and made the last cut.

The clock clicked over.

The silence in the chapel was deafening.

Sam shuddered as T.J. began to sob.

His cell phone rang. When he heard the notes of "Amazing Grace," he started to shake. It was all he could do to answer it, and then he heard his brother's voice.

"Sam?"

"It's done. You need to call someone to come get it."

Trey sighed. "Thank you, Sam. Oh, my God, thank you. The county bomb squad just passed the city limits. They'll be here shortly."

"Good. Now come get this little pissant before I kill him," Sam said softly.

"Where are you?"

"In the chapel. Come on in. You can't miss us."

"We're on the way."

Sam wiped a shaky hand over his face. "Is Lainey okay?"

"Yes, but she's scared out of her mind for you."

Without saying another word, Sam dropped the phone into his pocket, then stood up, grabbed T.J. by the handcuffs and hauled him to his feet.

The pain that shot through T.J.'s shoulders was excruciating, but he'd learned the hard way that physical pain was far less frightening than Sam Jakes.

Sam wouldn't look at him. Couldn't look at him without wanting to put his hands around the bastard's neck and choke the life out of him where he stood.

It was only moments before Trey entered the room with two officers and the bomb squad behind him.

Trey read T.J. his rights and took him into custody while the bomb squad secured the disabled bomb in a special container and carried it out of the room.

Sam felt his brother's hand on his shoulder, but he couldn't look at him for fear he would lose it.

"Sam?"

"I'm okay," he said softly and walked out of the room, then down the hall and out of the hospital.

The slap of cold air on his face brought him fully back to reality, and he looked up and saw the morass of vehicles and patients all over the parking lot.

He didn't know where to go. He didn't know what he was supposed to do next. He needed Lainey, but he didn't know where to start looking for her, so he stood where he was and scanned the area.

Lainey was a long distance away, but she recognized Sam when he walked out of the hospital. All she could think was *Thank You, God.* She could tell he was looking for her. She climbed out of the police car and started walking, dodging people in beds, circling others in wheelchairs, moving past nurses and doctors, as well as an array of officers from the West Virginia Highway Patrol directing traffic in the lot.

She saw Sam searching the crowd and didn't even try to get his attention in all the noise. He was her homing signal, and she was locked on and moving.

She knew when he finally saw her because his expression shifted from frozen to broken so fast it scared her. Even though her foot was killing her, she lengthened her stride.

He was coming toward her now, moving faster, oblivious to all the people around him. And then all of a sudden she was in his arms.

He swung her off her feet and buried his face in the curve of her neck.

"Oh, Sam, Sam, I was so scared," she whispered.

He heard the tremble in her voice. "I know, baby, I know. So was I."

"Is it over?" she asked.

"All over but the shouting," he said, and started walking with her through the crowd.

"Where are we going?" she asked.

He paused long enough to give her one brief kiss. "We're going home."

Twenty

Seven days later Trina came home from the hospital weak and shaky, but glad to be alive. Her heart was broken at the loss of her mother, and going back to the farmhouse without her in it seemed next to impossible.

She had learned from her brothers of Lee's constant devotion to her and her care, and how he'd been the first to stand guard at her door when she'd come out of surgery. After all the tragedy and all they'd lost, holding on to their old grudge seemed ridiculous. She'd cried in his arms and he'd cried with her, and she wanted him back as much as he wanted her.

They were driving to the farmhouse, and she was trying so hard not to weep. She didn't want to live anywhere else, but she didn't want to live there alone. She glanced over at Lee, studying his profile as he drove, and knew it was a sight she wanted to wake up to for the rest of her life.

She fidgeted a little, not knowing how to even broach the subject of sharing a home, when he happened to glance over and saw her staring.

"What's wrong, honey? Are you in pain? Are you cold?"

She shook her head. "No, I'm fine. I think I'm just dreading going home without her," she said softly.

Lee reached for her hand. She clasped his gratefully, feeling his warmth and strength.

"I can't pretend to understand what you're feeling, but I can tell you what's going through my mind. I am so grateful you're alive and that I have the privilege of taking you home. If it makes you too sad to think of going home without her, could you think of it as going home with me? I love you, Trina. I want to spend the rest of my life with you."

Breath caught in the back of her throat.

"Oh, Lee, there's nothing I want more," she said.

He tapped the brakes and pulled over to the side of the road.

"I was going to save this for a more romantic moment, but right now I'm going to take being grateful to God over romance."

He pulled a small box from the inside pocket of his coat and laid it in her lap.

"Open it, honey. I've had it for months. That's how much I love you. That's how sorry I was for what I said that hurt you. And it's how happy I am that you're here to open it."

Trina opened the small box with trembling fingers, and then leaned back with a gasp at the sight of the solitaire diamond glittering in the beam of sunlight coming through the windshield.

"Oh, Lee, it's beautiful!"

He took it out of the box.

"Will you marry me, Trina? I promise to love and protect you for the rest of my life."

"Yes, Lee, yes," she said, and was laughing and crying as he slipped it on her finger. "It fits."

"Like I said, I had it for months. Betsy helped me with the size, and then told me to hold you forever in my heart."

He leaned across the seat, cupped the back of her head and kissed her. One long, slow kiss that eased Trina's fears and settled the uncertainty of her life. By the time they reached the farmhouse, she was ready to face the future.

But when they drove up and she saw cars already there, she frowned.

"That's Trey's police cruiser. And that's Dallas's car. I don't recognize the other one. What's going on?" she asked.

Lee smiled. "Why don't we get out and see?"

By the time she had her seat belt unlocked, Lee was opening her door. He helped her out of the car and steadied her steps as they walked up onto the porch and then into the house.

The scent of chicken frying met her at the door. The undertone of voices came from the kitchen, and when she heard someone speak, followed by a shout of laughter, the rest of her anxiety settled. She was home.

"Hey! You better not be eating without us!" Lee shouted.

There was the sound of hurried steps and giggles, and then her family surrounded her, hugging and kissing and welcoming her home. When she saw Sam standing in this house again after so many years, she started crying.

"I thought I'd been dreaming that you came to see me, but you finally came home, didn't you?" she said as he wrapped her up in a hug.

"Don't you think it was about time?" he said and kissed the top of her head.

Then she saw Lainey and started to cry.

"Welcome home, Tink," Lainey said as she took Trina's hands and kissed her cheek.

Trina laughed, and then glanced at Sam again.

"Please tell me Lainey's presence in this house means you've regained what was left of your senses."

Sam grinned.

Lainey slid an arm around Sam's waist as she leaned against his chest. "He has."

Dallas gave Trina a quick hug and a kiss, and then whispered in her ear, "Welcome home, sweetheart."

"This is the best welcome home ever," Trina said. "I was dreading this moment…coming into a solitary house, and then Lee puts a ring on my finger to remind me I'm not alone, and then my family is here, reminding me that life goes on. Mama would be so proud of all of us, I think."

The words *ring on my finger* elicited another round of congratulations and giggling excitement that made the moment that much more special.

Lee was watching, making sure she wasn't over-taxing herself too soon, and finally he slid an arm around her waist. "Come sit," he said.

"I want to sit in the kitchen," Trina said. "That's where we always sat when Mama was cooking. And when I get well, I will cook dinner for all of you to prove there'll be no dust settling on the appliances. Just because tragedy struck all of us in one way or another, we're better than that. We're stronger than that. We are not going to let love die in this house. Do you hear me?"

There was a brief moment of silence, and then Sam reached out and ruffled her hair, just like he used to do when she was little.

"Mom might be gone, but her spirit lives on," Sam said. "I do believe Trina has inherited her bossy streak. God help you, Lee. You're gonna need Him."

The laughter that ensued was loud and long as they traipsed back into the kitchen to finish cooking the first meal in a new phase of all their lives.

Long after the food was gone and the kitchen cleaned, long after everyone finally went home, the peace that settled over the old home place was complete.

Dallas and Trey had a date set for a Christmas wedding.

Lee and Trina were aiming for next Easter.

But it was Lainey and Sam who made the first move.

Three days later Sam was still at Lainey's, helping her set up the sale of her farm, patching up the little things that she'd had to let go over the past year.

Betsy's body had finally been released to the family two days earlier. Tomorrow was the funeral service, and while it felt as if there was a lot left to do, it was the final letting go that was really weighing on them.

Sam was inside the barn cleaning out the granary when he found the sack of treats Lainey bought for Dandy. With no horse to enjoy them, he was trying to decide what to do with them when Lainey entered the barn.

"Hey! Where are you?" she yelled.

Sam leaned out through the door. "In here."

She stepped up into the granary and saw him holding the package.

"Poor Dandy. He never did get any of those treats," she said.

"What do you want me to do with them?" he asked.

"Just leave them here," she said. "Maybe the people who buy the farm will have a horse, and if they don't, maybe these treats will serve as a seed of suggestion."

Sam set them in the corner, and then took her in his arms. "I have a question," he said.

"Then, ask," she said as she brushed dust from his cheek.

"Marry me?"

Tears welled. "Yes."

"Today?"

She sighed. "Yes."

He kissed her there in the granary, with dust motes floating in the air like flecks of gold, and felt the last knot of regret from his past slip away.

"You need a bath first," Lainey said.

He laughed.

She looked a little startled, and then she grinned. "Well, I didn't mean it quite like that," she said, but he was still laughing, and then he picked her up in his arms and carried her back to the house.

Sam took the much-required shower after she'd gone first, then he helped her rewrap her ankle and wrist.

As she stood in front of her closet, searching

through the new clothes she'd purchased, he couldn't help but notice the dark circles beneath her eyes, and he thought about how valiantly she must have fought to stay alive all through the chemo treatments. He wanted to take her home to Atlanta and start a new life with her there. He already knew that she would never be able to bear a child. Instead of sadness, he felt a sense of relief. He wasn't fit father material anymore, but there was enough of him left to be the best damn husband ever. She'd taught him that.

He watched her sorting through the new outfits, trying to choose something to get married in, and wondered if his spontaneous proposal was cheating her out of a storybook wedding.

"Are you going to be sorry you're missing all of the pageantry of a wedding?" he asked.

She immediately stopped and shook her head.

"Not at all! Mom and Dad are gone. Your parents are gone. And after everything that's happened, I don't feel like celebrating. I just want to be yours and you to be mine. It's all I've ever wanted, Sam."

He sighed.

"I don't know that I deserve you, but I have no words for how grateful I am that you still want me." He pointed. "If it matters, I like that one," he said, pointing to the jade-colored wool dress hanging on the back of the door.

Lainey looked. "You don't think it's too dark?" she asked.

"I think you will shine like the redhead you are in that dress. You're beautiful, Lainey, just as you are."

"Then, the green it is," she said. "Give me about fifteen minutes and I'll be ready."

"Then, I guess I better finish dressing, too."

He headed down the hall to get his leather jacket from the closet, and then went into the living room to call Trey. His brother answered quickly and seemed in a hurry, so Sam was hoping he wasn't on his way to an emergency of some kind.

"Hey, Trey, what's up? You sound rushed."

"I was, but it's all good. I just got rid of Public Enemies One and Two."

"Ah…Marcus and T.J. are no longer in your jail."

"They both had their day in court. Judge denied bail on both of them and bound them over for trial. They are, as we speak, on their way to county lock-up."

"Can't get them far enough away to suit me," Sam said.

"Oh, guess what came out during their depositions? Marcus kept saying he didn't know what T.J. was doing, and it appears he was telling the truth. T.J. stated, under oath, that he found out about the 1980 incident when his father got drunk a couple of years back. He said he didn't think anything of it until his dad decided to run for office, and then he felt like it would be in their best interests if he got rid of the witnesses, just in case."

"I can't wrap my head around how evil that little bastard really is," Sam said.

"He's a piece of work, for sure," Trey said. "So how's it going out there? Are you getting everything ready to put the farm up for sale?"

"We were, but at the moment we're getting ready to go get married."

Trey gasped. "Married? As in today?"

"Yes."

"Well, hell, Sam. What if we might like to be there?"

Sam grinned. "That's why I called. If you're not throwing someone in jail and Dallas isn't busy this afternoon, it would be good to have you guys, and Trina and Lee, too, as our witnesses."

"Absolutely. How long before you head to Mystic?"

"Probably fifteen or twenty minutes, and then we still have to get the license."

"Who's going to marry you?"

"Haven't thought that far," Sam said.

"Oh, my Lord! Well, don't worry about it. I have a few connections. Meet me in Judge Franklin's chambers. It's on the second floor."

"Okay, and thanks, Trey."

Trey laughed and hung up. He called Dallas first, gave her a timeline, and then called Judge Franklin. Within a few minutes he had the judge lined up, and Dallas was on the way to pick up Lee and Trina.

He was on his way to his office to change into a clean uniform when he thought of Lainey. Obviously she was on board with this hurry-up ceremony, but he didn't know a woman who would turn down flowers. Maybe he could talk the florist into making a quick wedding bouquet.

Sam and Lainey left the clerk's office in the courthouse hand in hand with a marriage license and met Trey, Dallas, Trina and Lee waiting for them in the hall.

Lainey looked at Sam. "You called them, didn't you?"

He nodded. "I felt a little guilty about asking you to marry me so fast."

Lainey hugged Dallas and Trina, Lee was grinning and Trey kissed her cheek and handed her a bouquet of white roses with white satin streamers.

"Follow me," he said, and led them to Judge Franklin's chambers.

Lainey kept trying to wrap her head around the fact that she would go to sleep tonight as a married woman. After so many years, she'd almost given up on the love of her life.

She heard the judge talking to Sam, and she glanced at Dallas, who gave her a quick thumbs-up. After that everything seemed to move in slow motion.

She repeated the vows word for word while hanging on to Sam with both hands. He hadn't taken his eyes from her for one second since the ceremony began, but as touched as she was, she had no idea what was going through his head.

Then Judge Franklin turned to Sam.

"Do you, Samuel Jakes, take Lainey Pickett for your lawful wedded wife? Do you—"

Sam knew what came next, but he had his own vow to make.

"I will never dishonor or abuse her. I will love her forever, and keep her safe in my arms and close to my heart, so help me God."

Lainey could barely see his face for the tears. In these few seconds his words, said with so much love, let her know their future would be as solid as the ground they stood on.

"Do you have a ring?" Judge Franklin asked.

"Yes, I do," Sam said. "It belonged to my grandmother and was given to me, the eldest son, to give to my wife." He turned to Lainey. "It is my honor to give it to you."

Sam's hands were steady, his demeanor steadfast. He meant every word that he'd said and was feeling pretty damn lucky that he was still alive to say them.

The old-fashioned ring was beautiful on Lainey's hand, but a little loose, so she curled her fingers into a fist, holding on to the symbol of their love as tightly as she held on to Sam's love.

Judge Franklin paused to make sure there was no second ring, and then smiled.

"By the power vested in me by the state of West Virginia, I now pronounce you man and wife."

"Thank You, God," Sam said. He wiped the tears from Lainey's cheeks, and then he kissed her.

Trey and Dallas were elated as Sam turned to shake the judge's hand. "Much appreciated, sir," he said.

"Totally my pleasure," Judge Franklin said. "Now let's get this license signed so you can celebrate something happy for a change."

Sam couldn't help thinking about his mother as they walked out of the courthouse. She would have been so happy for them, and then he let go of the sadness. This was the best day of his life.

As soon as they stepped out of the courthouse and started down the steps, Trey, Dallas, Lee and Trina tossed rice into the air, and then laughed out loud as it showered down on Sam and Lainey's heads.

Lainey was grinning as she turned around, then pointed straight at Dallas and threw the bouquet up the steps.

It was pure reflex that made Dallas react in time to

catch it, and then she sat down on the steps in tears. Despite their ages, they were all orphans. The only family they had left in their lives was each other.

"Happy life to both of you," Trey said.

"Happy life to all of us," Sam countered. "Thank you, brother. We'll see you guys tomorrow. Eleven o'clock, right?"

And just like that, the reminder that tomorrow they buried their mother ended the moment.

Sam took Lainey's hand. "So, my beautiful wife, are you up for a little wedding lunch at Charlie's Burgers before we go home?"

"Yes, thank you, and I'm warning you now...I'll have mine with onions."

Sam grinned as he glanced at his brother. "The wedding party is invited to join us."

"I wouldn't miss it for the world," Dallas said.

"Meet you there," Trey said.

Sam took Lainey's hand as they started toward his car. "We'll get your ring sized in Atlanta."

She nodded. "I'm going to take it off once we get home. I don't want to lose it."

"That's okay. It will just give me another reason to put it back on you and have two wedding nights instead of one."

She sighed. "I am so happy."

Sam put a hand over his heart. "And I am so blessed."

Lainey reached for his hand.

"Then, let's go do this, Sam Jakes. It's time to start living this life."

Epilogue

The sky was gray, the wind brisk and cold, as they laid Betsy Jakes' body in the ground next to her husband. Seeing their names together on the headstone left a hollow feeling in all of them, but Sam took heart from the message in Betsy's letter. This was just a ceremony to put away what was left of her. As she had reminded them, she was already in her beloved Justin's arms.

Despite the cold weather, the cemetery was crowded with people from town. Once the preacher finished speaking, the people swarmed them in an endless line of condolences. To Sam, it felt like salt being rubbed on an open wound. He wanted this day over with. He kept thinking of Trina. The service had been especially hard for her. When it came time to head to the cemetery, Sam had made the decision for her and told Lee to take her home, that she'd suffered enough for one day. Trina was in tears all over again, but so grateful to have been given respite.

Trey had heard little of the church service and was barely aware of the preacher's words there at the cemetery. As hard as he had tried, the only thing with him today was the last sight he'd had of his mother.

Sam had seen far too much death in his life and would forever regret that he'd denied her the only thing she'd ever asked of him: to come home. So here he was, and there she was, in the ground beneath his feet. It wasn't what she'd meant.

Trey looked above the barren trees lining the cemetery fence, closed his eyes and let her go while Sam stood at her grave with a heavy heart. He had come to accept that it had taken her death to get him back to Lainey. He didn't understand how great joy could come from so much loss, but he wouldn't question fate.

Time dragged until finally the people were almost gone.

Trey and Sam were about to take Dallas and Lainey to their cars when a woman tapped Trey on the shoulder.

He turned, ready to put his game face on again, and then saw it was Beth Powell, with Randy and Clarice.

"I know you're likely worn-out," Beth said, "but if you have another five minutes left in you, we'd like to share something with you and your family. It's just over here a bit."

Trey glanced at Sam.

"Yes, ma'am, we would be honored," Sam said. "Just let me get Lainey in out of the cold," he said, when she stopped him.

"No, Sam. I want to go," she said and clasped his hand.

Beth led the way up a small hill, then stopped.

The new graves were obvious.

"Yesterday morning I laid my Donny to rest here beside his grandson. This has been a heartbreaking time for our family, but because of Dick and Paul and Connie and Betsy, it has also been a time of great release. We're broken in ways from which we may never fully heal, but I need to thank you for giving Donny back to me. Randy has a father to be proud of, and Jack isn't resting alone. It was a horrible price to pay, but I wanted you to know that as long as I live, your parents will never be forgotten."

"I have no words," Trey said, and then he hugged her.

Dallas and Lainey did the same.

But Sam kept staring at the grave.

Donny Collins had waited a long time for justice, but in the end, things had ended the way they had begun. The four friends had seen Donny die and tried to tell. And it was the discovery of Donny's body by the children of those friends that had ultimately brought justice for their deaths all these years later.

"Thank you for sharing this," Sam said. "I learned a long time ago that it isn't so much about the tragedies that happen to us in life as what we take from them when they're over. I wish grace and peace to all of you."

Then he put an arm around Lainey's shoulders. She was shivering. He knew she was getting too cold.

"Come with me, sweetheart. I need to get you warm."

They parted there on the hillside, families forever bound by tragedy and fate.

* * * * *

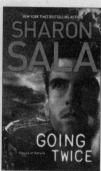

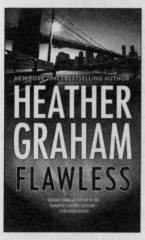

Lock the doors, draw the shades, pull up the covers and be prepared for *Thriller* to keep you up all night.

Edited by #1 *New York Times* Bestselling Author

JAMES PATTERSON

TED BELL
STEVE BERRY
GRANT BLACKWOOD
LEE CHILD
LINCOLN CHILD
DAVID DUN
HEATHER GRAHAM
JAMES GRIPPANDO
DENISE HAMILTON
RAELYNN HILLHOUSE
GREGG HURWITZ

10TH ANNIVERSARY EDITION

ALEX KAVA
J. A. KONRATH
JOHN LESCROART
ROBERT LIPARULO
DAVID LISS
ERIC VAN LUSTBADER
DENNIS LYNDS
GAYLE LYNDS
CHRIS MOONEY
DAVID MORRELL
KATHERINE NEVILLE
MICHAEL PALMER
DOUGLAS PRESTON
CHRISTOPHER REICH
CHRISTOPHER RICE
JAMES ROLLINS
M. J. ROSE
JAMES SIEGEL
BRAD THOR
M. DIANE VOGT
F. PAUL WILSON

THRILLER

"Breathless, explosive, exhilarating."
—SANDRA BROWN

EDITED BY
JAMES PATTERSON

Revisit these heart-pumping tales of suspense, including thirty-two of the most critically acclaimed and award-winning names in the business. From the signature characters that made such authors as David Morrell and John Lescroart famous to some of the hottest new voices in the genre, this blockbuster will tantalize and terrify.

Available April 26, wherever books are sold!

REQUEST YOUR FREE BOOKS!

2 FREE NOVELS
FROM THE SUSPENSE COLLECTION
PLUS 2 FREE GIFTS!

YES! Please send me 2 FREE novels from the Suspense Collection and my 2 FREE gifts (gifts are worth about $10). After receiving them, if I don't wish to receive any more books, I can return the shipping statement marked "cancel." If I don't cancel, I will receive 4 brand-new novels every month and be billed just $6.49 per book in the U.S. or $6.99 per book in Canada. That's a savings of at least 19% off the cover price. It's quite a bargain! Shipping and handling is just 50¢ per book in the U.S. and 75¢ per book in Canada.* I understand that accepting the 2 free books and gifts places me under no obligation to buy anything. I can always return a shipment and cancel at any time. Even if I never buy another book, the two free books and gifts are mine to keep forever.

191/391 MDN GH4Z

Name	(PLEASE PRINT)

Address	Apt. #

City	State/Prov.	Zip/Postal Code

Signature (if under 18, a parent or guardian must sign)

Mail to the **Reader Service:**
IN U.S.A.: P.O. Box 1867, Buffalo, NY 14240-1867
IN CANADA: P.O. Box 609, Fort Erie, Ontario L2A 5X3

Want to try two free books from another line?
Call 1-800-873-8635 or visit www.ReaderService.com.

* Terms and prices subject to change without notice. Prices do not include applicable taxes. Sales tax applicable in N.Y. Canadian residents will be charged applicable taxes. Offer not valid in Quebec. This offer is limited to one order per household. Not valid for current subscribers to the Suspense Collection or the Romance/Suspense Collection. All orders subject to credit approval. Credit or debit balances in a customer's account(s) may be offset by any other outstanding balance owed by or to the customer. Please allow 4 to 6 weeks for delivery. Offer available while quantities last.

Your Privacy—The Reader Service is committed to protecting your privacy. Our Privacy Policy is available online at www.ReaderService.com or upon request from the Reader Service.

We make a portion of our mailing list available to reputable third parties that offer products we believe may interest you. If you prefer that we not exchange your name with third parties, or if you wish to clarify or modify your communication preferences, please visit us at www.ReaderService.com/consumerchoice or write to us at Reader Service Preference Service, P.O. Box 9062, Buffalo, NY 14240-9062. Include your complete name and address.

SUS15

SHARON SALA

32792	TORN APART	___ $7.99 U.S.	___ $9.99 CAN.
32785	BLOWN AWAY	___ $7.99 U.S.	___ $9.99 CAN.
32677	THE RETURN	___ $7.99 U.S.	___ $8.99 CAN.
31830	COLD HEARTS	___ $7.99 U.S.	___ $8.99 CAN.
31816	WILD HEARTS	___ $7.99 U.S.	___ $8.99 CAN.
31659	GOING GONE	___ $7.99 U.S.	___ $8.99 CAN.
31592	GOING TWICE	___ $7.99 U.S.	___ $8.99 CAN.
31548	GOING ONCE	___ $7.99 U.S.	___ $8.99 CAN.
31342	DON'T CRY FOR ME	___ $7.99 U.S.	___ $9.99 CAN.
31312	NEXT OF KIN	___ $7.99 U.S.	___ $9.99 CAN.

(limited quantities available)

TOTAL AMOUNT	$ _____
POSTAGE & HANDLING	$ _____
($1.00 for 1 book, 50¢ for each additional)	
APPLICABLE TAXES*	$ _____
TOTAL PAYABLE	$ _____

(check or money order—please do not send cash)

To order, complete this form and send it, along with a check or money order for the total above, payable to MIRA Books, to: **In the U.S.:** 3010 Walden Avenue, P.O. Box 9077, Buffalo, NY 14269-9077; **In Canada:** P.O. Box 636, Fort Erie, Ontario, L2A 5X3.

Name: _____

Address: _____ City: _____

State/Prov.: _____ Zip/Postal Code: _____

Account Number (if applicable): _____

075 CSAS

*New York residents remit applicable sales taxes.
*Canadian residents remit applicable GST and provincial taxes.

MIRA®

www.MIRABooks.com

MSS0416BL